SHOOTING DOWN HEAVEN

Jorge Franco

SHOOTING DOWN HEAVEN

*Translated from the Spanish
by Andrea Rosenberg*

Europa
editions

Europa Editions
214 West 29th Street
New York, N.Y. 10001
www.europaeditions.com
info@europaeditions.com

Translation by Andrea Rosenberg
Original title: *El cielo a tiros*
Translation copyright © 2020 by Europa Editions

Library of Congress Cataloging in Publication Data is available
ISBN 978-1-60945-589-7

Franco, Jorge
Shooting Down Heaven

Book design by Emanuele Ragnisco
www.mekkanografici.com

Original cover design:
Penguin Random House Grupo Editorial / Patricia Martínez Linares
Cover image: collage with *City of Medellín* (Getty), *Firework Display at Night*
(Beasely/EyeEm/Getty), *Firework Display at Night* (Raedel/EyeEm/Getty)

Prepress by Grafica Punto Print – Rome

Printed and bound in Great Britain by Clays Ltd, Elcograf S.p.A.

In memoriam.
For Humberto, because of whom I am what I am.

SHOOTING DOWN HEAVEN

1

Nelson doesn't need to read the lyrics as he sings karaoke. He knows them by heart and is crooning with his eyes closed. *Loneliness is fear that silence locks in, and silence is fear we kill by talking.* The tune's going one way and Nelson another, but he doesn't care. He's told me, I'm going to sing you your daddy's favorite song, so I listen intently. *And fear is the courage to begin thinking about life's final journey without moaning or shrinking!*

"Libardo would be crying by now," one of his friends from way back whispers in my ear.

"He had a song for every woman," says another.

Either he didn't understand who I was when we were introduced, or since I'm a grown man now, he doesn't feel any compunction about mentioning Libardo's lovers to me. Or maybe mobsters are always loose-lipped.

They pour me more whiskey without asking if I want any, even though I've drunk only half my glass. The guy to my right says, "But this was his song, just for him, and it was a real nightmare because musicians never knew how to play it. I warned him the song gave him away: a guy can't go around admitting he's afraid of fear."

He breaks off as the crowd starts clapping for Nelson. I'm anxious about my friends outside, hoping they don't leave. My suitcase is still in Pedro's SUV. And I don't have Fernanda's address.

Nelson comes over and says, "Your dad would be doubled up bawling his eyes out right now."

"Yeah, so he said." I gesture to the guy next to me.

"So what did you think?" Nelson asks me.

"Great, you guys sing great," I say.

"Nah," he says. "It's just a hobby—we get together every couple of weeks to let off some steam." He laughs, then looks at me and says, "Your dad would have loved to come sing karaoke. He was a real music lover."

It's true. Libardo was obsessed with stereo systems; he always had the latest model, not just at home but also out at the farms and in his car. If he was in a good mood, he'd listen to music with the volume way up, cheesy popular stuff that Julio and I used to mock relentlessly.

"You don't invite any women?" I ask Nelson.

"Would you believe it," he says. "The one time we brought women, they took over the microphone and didn't let us sing."

Another man comes up, fat and grinning, holding a sheet of paper, and asks, "Did you already choose your songs for the second round?"

"I'm doing '¿Y cómo es él?'" says the guy to my left.

"Come on, Baldomero," says Nelson. "Again?"

"I didn't sing it last time."

"Yeah, because you didn't come. But the time before, and the time before that, and the time before the time before that . . ."

"Well, whaddaya know," Baldomero complains. "Now he's deciding what we can and can't sing."

"Let's go and ask for the song list so you can look at what else they've got," the fat guy suggests, and the two head off.

"I'm leaving too," I tell Nelson.

"It's still really early!" he says. "We go up to five rounds around here. One of these days we'll get you in front of the mike too."

"Me?"

They're like little kids. They can't sit still, roaming around from chair to chair, table to table, talking loudly, laughing raucously. I can't pick out any of the ones who used to come visit Libardo, but it's been twelve years—maybe it's the same guys but they've gotten old. I wonder what they're up to these days. Are they still on the wrong side of the law? Did they do their time? Are they still packing heat—not that that means anything in Medellín. Will they actually end up dying of old age?

"How'd your mom get on?" Nelson says, and the question perplexes me.

"Get on with what?"

Nelson stammers something into his drink, claps for the fat guy, who's started singing. This guy's good, he tells me, he knows what he's doing. With what?, I say again. This guy's amazing, a kick-ass bolero singer. Nelson, when did you last see my mom? It's been a while, kid, I haven't seen her for two years, she's as gorgeous as ever, I bet, he says. I bet, I say. Huh? What do you mean?, Nelson says. I haven't been back for twelve years, I just arrived today, I explain. Oh, shit, Nelson says, everything must seem so different to you.

"What's up with my mom, Nelson?"

"The world's most gorgeous tits," he says, letting out a boozy guffaw. "Sorry, kid, we used to say that to your dad to needle him."

The others are singing along with the fat guy for the chorus. *And I'm dying to have you next to me, so close, so very close to me.* Nelson raises his glass and joins in. Then he says, "Libardo had a good ear but a terrible voice," and he repeats, "It's a shame he isn't around for this, he'd have loved it."

I down what's left of my whiskey, picturing Fernanda the last time I saw her on Skype. There's nothing wrong, she's fine, she seemed the same as always. But what if she was hiding something? Just imagining the worst makes me give in to the urge to pour myself another.

"Yeah, let your hair down," Nelson says, smiling. "Today is La Alborada."

Suddenly we hear pounding on the door and then shouting and a scuffle. Some of the men get up, and others keep singing. What's going on?, one of them asks, and picks up one of the pistols lying on the table in the middle of the room. Another does the same and barks, turn off the music! Outside, the shouts and blows are getting louder. Everyone around me's pulling their guns out of their waistbands, jackets, or leather holsters. The only one who hasn't noticed what's happening is the guy singing. Turn off the music! Who's standing guard outside?, another guy asks. The music cuts off, and the fat guy keeps singing at the top of his lungs, *you're my moon, you're my sun*. John Jairo's out there, somebody says. And Diego too, says Nelson, probably referring to the beefy bouncer who almost didn't let me in.

I fear the worst: two gangs settling scores, or a visit from the police looking to make these guys pay, twelve years later. A short, stocky guy known as Carlos Chiquito moves toward the door, hiding his gun behind his back. Everybody else stays put, as Libardo used to say when things got hairy, on top-shelf reserve.

Carlos Chiquito opens the door to reveal several men arguing. There are some women too. The first one I see, his face flushed and distorted with rage, is Pedro the Dictator. Behind him, La Murciélaga is waving her hands, also furious. Carlos Chiquito raises his gun, and I raise my voice to say, "Hold up, I know them! They're friends of mine."

Everybody backs off, relieved. I head to the door as Carlos Chiquito tries to get things under control.

"Calm the fuck down, dipshits!" he says.

Pedro spots me and shouts, "Let him go! Let him through!"

"Who?" Carlos Chiquito asks, perplexed.

I squeeze between the bodyguards and ask Pedro, "What's going on? What's all the fuss?"

"Are you O.K.?" Pedro asks.

"What did they do to you, Larry?" La Murciélaga asks.

Standing next to them is Julieth and some other people I hadn't seen earlier. Nelson pokes his head out the door.

"What's going on, kid?"

"Nothing, Nelson, just my friends looking for me."

Carlos Chiquito orders his men to shut the door. I want to say goodbye to Nelson, but two bodyguards have formed an impenetrable wall. Pedro hugs me. "We assumed the worst, man," he tells me. Who are those guys?, Julieth asks. Pedro got us all freaked out, says La Murciélaga, and with this business about your father showing up, we thought . . . Swear to God, Pedro breaks in, I thought you'd been kidnapped. How did you know I was there?, I ask. I saw you, says Julieth, and I told these guys I'd seen you go in with a couple of dodgy-looking dudes. They turned out to be friends of my dad's, I explain. We should go somewhere else, La Murciélaga suggests. Yeah, Pedro says, let's get the check and go. I feel like everybody's looking at me, like they're thinking, great, this bullshit again. Libardo's son getting into trouble again.

In the car, I gradually piece back together all the muscles and bones that came loose from my skeleton in the chaos. Exhausted, I try asking again: "I want to go home, Pedro. I want to say hello to my mom."

"It's no big deal, man," he says. "It was just a misunder-standing."

"No, it's not that," I tell him.

I'm too tired to repeat what I've already told him so many times. It's not that, it's everything.

"You sure you're O.K.?" asks Julieth, who's sitting next to me with her hand on my thigh.

I'm not O.K., but I'm not about to tell her that. Maybe

later I'll tell Fernanda and confess how sad it's made me to discover that Libardo opened up to these guys more than he did with us, that they know more about my dad than she, Julio, and I do.

2

Libardo steeled himself to keep from falling apart when he saw Escobar's body lying on the roof of the run-of-the-mill house where the world's most wanted man had been hiding out. The rumor reached him before he saw the announcement on TV; like everybody else, he thought it was another made-up death, just like the numerous other times Escobar had died over the course of his life. But within half an hour they'd started reporting developments on the radio. On a hunch, he'd called Fernanda to go pick us up from school.

Though I'm younger than Julio, the two of us were in the same grade—eleventh—but we'd been put in different classes. My brother had failed ninth grade, but I was a good student. Our driver usually came to get us, so that afternoon we were surprised to see two SUVs drive up; Fernanda was in one, and the boys were in the other. She was distracted, smoking a cigarette and drumming her fingers on the steering wheel as if she were playing along to a song. Confused, Julio and I walked over. Fernanda wasn't very clear; she said she'd come to get us because there were going to be demonstrations later that afternoon. Julio asked her who was going to be protesting, and she said the students. The students again, she said indifferently. But I already knew. The school secretary had interrupted biology class and whispered something to the teacher. After she left, he told us what was being reported on the news. It felt like everybody in the class was turning to stare at me.

"Pablo's dead," I said to Fernanda once we were in the car.

She looked at me in the rearview mirror, and Julio, who was riding up front with her, said in surprise, "What?"

"That's just a rumor," said Fernanda.

"That's why you came to get us," I said.

"Is it true, Ma?" Julio asked.

"It's hearsay—nothing's been confirmed yet," she insisted.

Julio turned on the radio, Fernanda switched it off, Julio turned it on again, and she told him, turn that off, I've got a headache. She doesn't want us to find out, I piped up from the back. Julio rotated the dial, searching for a news station. Fernanda looked at me again in the rearview mirror and said, "I don't want to hear anything about it."

She pressed the cigarette lighter on the dashboard and pulled a pack out of her purse, but she couldn't shake a cigarette out. Julio stopped the dial on one of the many stations discussing the news. The announcer, very worked up, said that the area had been cordoned off, taken over by the military; the corpse of the individual presumed to be Escobar was still lying on the rooftop, and some soldiers were raising their arms with their fingers held in a V for victory. Fernanda smacked the cigarette pack harder against her leg and cursed. The lighter popped out, and she told Julio, turn that off and get me a cigarette out. Julio said, this is going to blow up, referring to the news.

Fernanda didn't speak again, and Julio kept switching from station to station. All of them were full of excitement and speculation; every report was heralded as breaking news. Fernanda was on the verge of crashing the car. I was looking out the window, which was shut despite the stifling afternoon, and I seemed to detect in people, in everything I saw, the upheaval described on the radio. If what was already being reported as fact was true, that Thursday in December was going to split our recent history in two. All of us felt it: Fernanda as she stomped on the brake and jerked the steering wheel, urgently smoking a cigarette, and Julio, his eyes glued to the radio, as if it were transmitting the images being described. And me, still staring out the window and sensing reproach on every face, as if everything that was being set in motion were my fault.

Fernanda entered the house through the kitchen door, went upstairs, and shut herself in her room. From outside we could hear the TV in the living room. We found Libardo intent on the news, muttering and as pale as a sheet. As soon as he saw us, he scrambled for the remote and shut the TV off. He smiled as if we'd caught him up to something.

"We were listening to the news in the car," Julio said.

"Everything's going to be O.K., boys," Libardo said, but his voice sounded nervous.

"It's going to be a shitshow, Pa," Julio said.

"It's been a shitshow for a while," Libardo pointed out, and then asked, "Where's your mom?"

"She's upstairs," I said.

I went over to the coffee table, picked up the remote, and turned the TV back on. Now they were unsteadily trying to lower him from the roof on a stretcher. There he was, stretched out, bearded, bloody, his belly exposed—in other words, dead. Waiting for him below were more arms outstretched to receive him, touch him, make sure it wasn't some sort of trick. The bullet that had penetrated his ear had made his face swell up and distorted his features. It was impossible to be certain it was him.

"Turn that off, Larry," Libardo ordered.

"Why doesn't anybody want us to know anything?" I whined, clutching the remote control.

"Because people are saying things that aren't true."

"Is he not dead or what?" I said defiantly.

Libardo hesitated. The image on the screen trembled as the stretcher disappeared into the fray. The reporters tried to follow it, panting and bumping into each other or getting tangled in the camera cords. The chaos transmitted live made Libardo anxious.

"Turn that off, dammit," he said, his teeth clenched, and shouted, "Fernanda, Fernanda!"

"She's got a headache, Pa," Julio told him.

The telephone started ringing.

"Why are you still watching?" Libardo said. "They're taking him away now."

"Well?" I asked. "Is he alive or is he dead?"

The telephone kept ringing.

"Answer that!" Libardo yelled toward the kitchen. "He's dead," he said at last, and his voice shook again. He wiped his face and turned off the TV. We could still hear the telephone ringing, until somebody finally answered it.

"It's all going to be O.K.," Libardo said.

I tossed the remote on the sofa and Julio ran upstairs to his room.

"December's fucked now," I told Libardo, but he shook his head. He sat down in his leather armchair and said, "The only one who's fucked is the dead guy."

Libardo spent the rest of that day making phone calls. He didn't leave the house and shut himself in the garage several times to talk on the car phone. His booming voice had been reduced to a murmur of curt replies, threats, and inquiries about what other people thought, or where so-and-so was, or why somebody wasn't answering his calls. He paced back and forth, keeping a constant eye on the street corners through the window.

He'd turned the TV back on, but the volume was at a murmur. They were still showing the house in Los Olivos, the roof with the broken tiles, the bloodstains, the crowd being held back by a flurry of police officers and soldiers. The defense minister spoke, then the government minister, the mayor, the governor, the chief of police, the head of the army, and finally the president. Libardo listened closely to all of them, clutching a glass of rum that he filled up repeatedly as soon he'd drained it.

Fernanda didn't come out of her room for the rest of the day or all night. One of the domestic staff carried a pitcher of water up to her, and later a bowl of soup. Julio and I went down when they called us for dinner. We continued to watch the news on the TV in the kitchen. We were by ourselves when Libardo came in to get more ice.

"Juan Pablo has spoken," he told us.

"And?" Julio said.

"He said he was going to get revenge and kill everybody."

"Them or us?" I asked.

"Them," Libardo said, "or at least that was how I heard it."

"Is there school tomorrow?" my brother asked.

"Of course there's school."

"Are we going?" Julio asked again.

"Yes, of course. Everything's going to be exactly the same."

When he turned around, we noticed he had his gun shoved into the waistband of his pants, in the back, above his hip. Then I looked at the screen and my eyes widened in horror.

"Look," I said.

"What is it?" Libardo asked.

I jutted my chin toward the TV. There was Escobar again, laid out on what seemed to be an autopsy table, though the scale hanging from the ceiling made it look like they'd put him on a butcher's table. He had his pants pulled down around the middle of his thighs, his white underwear and his belly still exposed; his beard was thick like a prophet's, and his unruly hair was damp with sweat and blood. The image was just a photo snapped by some cold-blooded person, but it was enough to make Libardo collapse into a chair and, for the first time since he'd heard the news, weep disconsolately. I fled to my room, not because of what they were showing on the TV but because I'd never seen my dad cry like that. I caught a glimpse of Julio, clumsy and inexperienced with other people's grief, placing a hand on his shoulder, but Libardo kept rubbing savagely at his face, gulping and cursing through clenched teeth.

By then, elsewhere in Medellín, people were already setting off fireworks to celebrate the death of the villain.

The British Airways employee was initially thrown off by the four first names on María Carlota Teresa Valentina Rivero Lesseps's passport, but she managed to identify the passenger's last name and started calling her Miss Rivero. The employee checked her in and handed her the baggage receipts for her suitcases, the passport and boarding pass, and the courtesy pass for the VIP lounge. Her family always called her María Carlota, or just Carlota, and it was later, in school, when people had started calling her Charlie. Her long name was a whim of her parents, since they hadn't been able to agree on just one name.

Once she was through passport control, Charlie pulled her carry-on through the displays in the duty-free shop. There was nothing she didn't own already. She spritzed on perfume from a tester to refresh the dose she'd applied that morning. In her head she reviewed her list of Christmas gifts, nagged by the feeling that she was forgetting somebody. In another store she bought two gossip magazines and a pack of gum. On her way to the VIP lounge she got a text message from Flynn asking how everything was going and whether she was through passport control. Charlie gave him a thumbs-up, and Flynn sent back a heart.

In the lounge, she helped herself to some nuts and requested sparkling water with a slice of lemon. She sank into an armchair that looked out on the runway and, watching the airplanes land and take off, pondered what it was about Flynn that didn't quite satisfy her. What it was he was missing. Part of her decision to spend Christmas in Colombia was to see whether distance had any effect on her feelings for him.

She leafed through the magazines for a while, occasionally glancing up at the screen with the list of flights that were about to take off. As soon as the one for Bogotá started flashing, she gathered her things and went to the bathroom. A final inspection in the mirror was deemed satisfactory. She liked the combination of the Burberry trench coat and ripped jeans. She headed for the gate, filled with anxiety about returning. She pulled out her phone to text Flynn the message she'd promised him: I'm about to board. An incoming call from an unknown number interrupted her. She was hesitating anyway about whether to add an I love you. She started walking faster—gate 27 was far away and the terminal was crowded. I love you, she finally wrote. Her phone rang again, with a long number and the international code for Colombia. She also got another message from Flynn. Me too, have a good flight, call me when you get in. Several images of the previous night flitted through her mind. Flynn performing oral sex on her, Flynn's cock, the way he'd smacked her buttocks when she came, the emptiness she'd felt afterward. In another message, Flynn told her he missed her already, and in another he asked if she was on the plane yet. At a third phone call, she started to get irritated; she still had ten gates to go. As she hurried down the terminal, another request from Flynn came in. Send me a photo now, right this moment, I want to see what you look like. Then another call from the unknown number, and just as she reached her gate, when there were very few passengers left to board, she got another text message that wasn't from Flynn but from Cristina, her sister, that said, please pick up, Dad's dead.

La Murciélaga flaps in the passenger seat to the beat of a song that's completely out of step with the moment and the situation. It's way too early to be wiggling around like that. A female singer with a robotic voice demands, *Papi, give it to me hard, give it to me hard against the wall, hard, hard against the wall, papi.* As he drives, Pedro the Dictator tells us the story of a friend of his who fell through a manhole and spent the whole night down there because nobody heard his cries for help. He breaks off every now and then to laugh loudly. In reality, he's only telling the story for himself: La Murciélaga is lost in her music, Julieth is texting, and I don't really give a shit.

Splayed out on the backseat, I close my eyes and cross my fingers that we'll be driving a while so I can try to sleep a little despite the loud radio, Pedro's laughter, and the alien sounds that La Murciélaga is making.

Rush hour hasn't ended yet, and we're creeping along toward a place that sells hydroponic marijuana, which she claims is more potent and less harmful.

"They grow it in pure water from the very beginning and fertilize it with volcanic stone," she'd explained.

"Wow," Pedro had said.

So that's where we're headed, even though I told them to count me out, I couldn't hang out with them all night. At any moment, I said, Fernanda was going to call me to tell me I could leave. But what if she isn't home, getting ready for my arrival, and instead is at the casino, glued to a betting table? I ask Pedro which casinos Fernanda's been going to.

"None," he tells me. "She quit doing that stuff a while ago."

"No way," I say. "She'd have told me if she'd stopped gambling."

"Who's Fernanda?" La Murciélaga asks.

"My mom," I tell her.

"I know her!" Julieth says, almost proudly.

"So why are you asking him?" La Murciélaga says, pointing at Pedro.

"Because I don't live here and he does."

"I don't get it," she says, moving her arm to the beat like a charmed snake.

"Believe it or not, Larry may look like a moron, but he's an economist from the London School of Economics," Pedro says.

La Murciélaga turns and asks, "Really?"

"No," I tell her. "I started a degree at City University of London, but I didn't finish."

"Well, your mom says it was at the London School," Pedro says.

"She doesn't know the difference," I say. "Besides, I was studying banking and international finance, not economics."

"That sounds cool," says Julieth.

"Anyway, we ran out of money and I had to drop out."

"What do you mean, you ran out of money?" Julieth asks in surprise. "I remember the cars you had and the clothes you used to wear."

"He's got money, Juli," says Pedro. "Don't listen to him, he's just pretending to be poor."

"Really?" La Murciélaga asks again.

We live off of what Julio is able to make on the farm. There are good months and bad ones. I scrape by in London working at a real estate agency, and when the farm has a good month

they wire me some extra cash. It's not that I'm pretending to
be poor, it's that we used to be really rich.

"Listen to this." La Murciélaga turns up the volume on the
radio and bops in her seat. Pedro keeps the beat with his palms
on the steering wheel, Julieth goes back to texting, and all I can
think of is taking a shower and then sleeping.

"Call Fernanda, would you?" I ask Pedro.

"You call her," he says.

"My cell phone doesn't work here in Colombia."

"She said she'd call."

"She's flaky. Please call her."

Pedro dials reluctantly. I grab his cell phone and just hear it
ringing.

"So much for proper English manners!" Pedro teases.

Fernanda doesn't pick up. I leave her a voicemail: Ma, it's
me. Give me a call on Pedro's cell. I got in ages ago and I just
want to get to your house and rest.

Pedro turns off the wide avenue and onto steep, narrow
streets. We drive through some residential buildings and then
enter a business district.

"Where are we?" I ask.

"Solar system, planet Earth, third rock on the right," says
La Murciélaga, and Pedro eggs her on by giving her a high five.

On the radio, a man is begging to the music, *touch it, mami,
touch it, mami, touchittouchittouchit, touch my heart, mami*. La
Murciélaga lets out a euphoric whoop and keeps wriggling to
the reggaeton beat.

Suddenly, Pedro brakes hard and throws the SUV into
reverse.

"What's up?" asks La Murciélaga.

"Check out these jackasses," says Pedro. He parks in front
of a contemporary furniture store, pokes his head out the window, and yells, "You all are real screw-ups, drinking this early
in the day!"

There's a group sitting around behind the store window, and one of them stands up and comes outside, his arms spread wide. La Murciélaga, recognizing him, lets out an excited shriek as if she hadn't seen him for years.

"Ro!" She starts chanting: "Ro, Ro, Ro!"

"Hey, old man," Pedro greets him, while Ro grabs his head roughly and says, "Fucking dictator, where've you been, dude?"

I think back, but I can't place Ro. When I left we were all just coming out of puberty, and now we're approaching thirty. When I left we hadn't finished growing; our bodies weren't done yet, our beards were scraggly, and our voices cracked when we talked. Now everything seems to have settled into place, even if just for a little while. And we act like we're going to be young forever.

La Murciélaga stretches over Pedro to kiss Ro on the cheek. Julieth rolls down the window and pokes her head out to give him another kiss. Seeing me next to her, Ro narrows his eyes, trying to figure out who I am.

"It's Larry," Pedro tells him.

"Larry?"

"Larry has no idea where he is," La Murciélaga says, and giggles.

"Larry," Pedro says again. "The one who was in London."

Ro looks at me closely and thinks a moment. "I don't remember you either," I tell him.

"Larry," he says, and then asks, "Libardo's son?"

"Yes," Pedro answers for me.

Ro's expression goes cold, though he holds out his hand to shake. Pedro reminds me who Ro is. Rodrigo Álvaro Ospina, son of a former governor, former senator, former ambassador, one of our neighbors way back when. Though we didn't go to the same school, we were sort of friends because we used to see each other outside, back when we played in the street.

"Larry got in today from London," Pedro tells him. "He's

an economist from the London School of Economics," he says, and La Murciélaga chimes in with a servile giggle.

"That's great," Ro remarks, without much enthusiasm.

"What are you guys up to?" Pedro asks.

Ro looks back at the group inside, and a woman raises her glass of aguardiente in greeting.

"Tere brought a bag of green mangoes, so we had no choice but to open a bottle of liquor to go with them," Ro says plaintively.

"Mangoes, yum," says Julieth.

"More like aguardiente, yum," says Pedro.

Ro laughs so he can buy time to study me again. Then there's a short but piercing silence, throughout which my heart's only desire is that Ro will keep his mouth shut and not invite us in. But that doesn't happen, and he finally makes up his mind:

"Come on, come inside for a bit and then we'll go see La Alborada. There's still some booze left. And time."

I let out a dissident snort. Pedro turns and tells me, "Chill, man, let's stay here for a bit—I've got everything all worked out. With me, happiness is guaranteed."

He gets out, opens my door, and gives an exaggerated salute. And he asks, "By the way, man, did I welcome you to hell yet?"

What sounded like shattering glass, at gate 27, turned out to be Charlie's scream. The few passengers still waiting to board froze. She dragged out the scream into a mad, maddening lament. It sounded like a mentally ill person was trying to force her way onto the plane, or somebody having a panic attack. A couple of airline workers hurried toward her as she sat doubled over on the floor next to a row of seats, her face red and distended from the scream. They helped her up and led her over to a seat. Charlie kept moaning, her cell phone clutched to her chest. They asked her what was wrong, what was happening, and she just shook her head.

At the counter, they made the final boarding call. One of the employees asked if she was on that flight. Charlie nodded. They asked if she was sure she still wanted to travel, and she said yes and begged, please don't leave me, I've got to be on that plane. The employee signaled to his colleague at the counter to wait and asked Charlie for her passport and boarding pass. Shaking, she rummaged for them in her purse. The employee rushed over to the counter with the documents, and the one who stayed behind said, I'm sorry, but you have to board now, they've announced the final call. And he asked her again, Are you sure you want to go?, we can book you for another day. At this, Charlie jumped up. No, she said, I'm going, I have to go. Have you been drinking?, the employee asked. She looked at him in confusion. What? I asked if you've been drinking, he repeated. Alcohol?, Charlie asked. Yes, alcohol. She stopped sobbing and let out a laugh and shook her head. Let's go then, he said.

On the jet bridge, a small group was still waiting to enter the plane. Just four or five passengers. Charlie was pulling a small suitcase, though it looked like the suitcase was actually pushing her. Larry was the last one in line, and he turned to look at her. She grabbed the handrail as her knees buckled. She landed on her butt on the floor, alone, in the middle of the passageway, beneath a glaring fluorescent light. The people waiting to board turned to stare at her. Charlie's agonized sobbing peeled the skin from their bones. Nobody appeared behind her to help, nobody went over. Two more people from the line moved forward into the plane, and Larry was the only one left outside. He peeked inside the plane to see if a crew member had noticed what was going on, but they seemed to be busy helping the passengers settle in. So he walked halfway up the jet bridge, to where Charlie was, and asked in English, "Are you O.K.?"

She shook her head.

"Can I help you?"

She nodded and replied in Spanish, "Help me into the plane."

Larry helped her up. A flight attendant appeared in the airplane doorway and urged them to hurry. Larry held Charlie's arm and with his other hand pulled her suitcase behind him.

"What's wrong?" he asked.

"My father just died."

"I'm really sorry."

The two of them boarded the plane. The flight attendant pointed her to her seat. Larry followed behind. Charlie stopped at the fourth row in first class and dropped into the seat. He asked if that was where she was sitting, and she nodded. He opened the overhead compartment and stashed her suitcase inside.

"If you need anything, I'm in the back, row 35," he told her, but she was crying again, her face in her hands.

He headed further back toward his row, threading his way between people who were still organizing their things. Suitcases, hats, stuffed animals, Selfridges bags full of crap. Larry tried to turn around and go back to tell Charlie that he was on his way to a funeral too. Maybe that would give her a little consolation. She wouldn't feel so alone, he thought, as if grief could be shared. But it was different too—he was going to a funeral that was twelve years late. Another flight attendant asked him to take his seat, saying that the flight had been delayed already and was being held up even further by the boarding process. Larry obeyed and found his spot, between two strangers. He'd be there for the next eleven hours. He closed his eyes, thinking.

There's no flight in the world worse than one that's taking somebody to say a last goodbye . . .

Three days after Escobar's death, we gathered around the table again. Before, everybody used to do their own thing—Julio and I off to school, or the two of us with Fernanda, or her with Libardo—but it took just three nights for the four of us to end up at the dining room table again and discuss the subject as a family for the first time. During that period, Libardo was constantly in and out of the house; one night he didn't even come home to sleep, but Fernanda wasn't worried. I was. The country was in turmoil—whether for good or for ill, something transformational had happened, something so significant that nobody was talking about anything else. Even today everybody remembers what they were doing when they heard about Escobar's death. So I kept a close eye on Libardo. I read his facial expressions, his mood, to guess what was going on. Relax, son, he kept saying, without my even asking anything. But the more he said it, the more I worried. I tried to keep close to him so I could eavesdrop on his phone conversations, but he'd shut himself up in his study, talk in a low voice, or persuade the other person to meet face to face. When he talked to Fernanda, they'd go off by themselves and speak in monosyllables. She didn't share much with us. She asked to us to let Libardo do his thing, saying he'd always taken care of us and that wasn't going to change.

Through the news programs and the press, I learned the important bits. Or at least the bits I sensed were important for us. In all the chaos, everything was a jumble, and I even became infected with the country's jubilant mood. I believed—I'd always believed—that without Escobar around, our lives were going to change for the better. I hoped Libardo would rethink his path, would have no choice but to go back to normal, by which I meant the way other people lived. But that was never in his plans, as he made clear that night when we finally came together, sitting around the dining room table.

"We're going to go on vacation like we do every December," he said, not meeting our eyes. He was staring at his plate of food, which was a sad affair that night.

"To the farm?" asked Julio, who loved spending vacations there.

"No," Libardo said. "We're traveling a little farther this time. I'm arranging for us to go to the Dominican Republic, to one of those all-inclusive resorts."

"We're coming back here, though?" I asked.

He raised his head and looked at us in silence, his accustomed vigor and swiftness now gone. Libardo was forty-eight and kept himself in good shape, muscular and active, but over those three days he seemed to have aged twenty years. Fernanda was endlessly stirring her coffee with a little spoon, her eyes fixed on her plate too, as if she already knew what Libardo was hiding.

"Of course we're coming back," he said.

"I don't believe you," I said.

"Why would you say that, Larry?" he asked with studied calm.

"I think you're trying to hide us."

Fernanda kept staring at the table; Libardo gripped his knife and fork and pushed his food around pensively. Then he spoke, but not the way he usually did—it was like he was reciting a speech.

"I don't deny they're trying to scare us. It's not enough for them to have taken Pablo down. They want to grind the ruins to dust and make sure there's absolutely nothing left. Nothing that would support us and help us rise up."

Fernanda lifted her head and looked at him. Maybe she thought his tone sounded pathetic, inappropriate for explaining the situation to a couple of teenagers. He returned her gaze and blinked nervously, sweat beading on his upper lip.

"Who's 'they'?" I asked.

"In these situations," he said, "nobody stands tough. They turn tail, they roll over to save themselves or to profit from it. Everybody else is shitting themselves, but you know me"—he looked at Julio and me and pointed at his chest—"you know I'm not one to run, much less roll over. I'm no rat."

Fernanda and Libardo started talking over each other. The dining table was big for the four of us. I was surveying them, even Julio, from an unbridgeable distance. It felt like they weren't going to hear me unless I shouted. Even though my breath was catching in my throat, I stood up and drowned them all out, shouting at my father, "They're going to kill us, and it's all your fault! You don't care about us! All you're interested in is money—you don't give a crap what happens to us!"

Fernanda leaned her elbows on the table and covered her face with her hands. Libardo looked at me in bewilderment, his lip quivering. Julio interrupted me.

"Shut up, Larry."

"Even if we never come back, even if we hide, they're going to kill us," I kept saying. "They managed to kill him, so killing us will be a cakewalk."

"We're going to beef up our security and fight back," Libardo said. "We've worked hard for years. We're not going to let everything be wiped out just like that."

"That's your war," I told him, "not mine."

"Oh, sure, you little brat," he said. "You'll keep your mouth shut when it comes to your motorcycles, your nice clothes, your trips, your fancy watches, but when they come after us, you run."

"Libardo. Larry," Fernanda said. "Don't make things worse."

"Of course I'm going to run," I said. "I'm not going to let myself be killed because of you."

A fist in my face knocked me to the floor. Fernanda screamed. When I opened my eyes, I expected to find myself face to face with Libardo, but it was Julio who'd punched me. On the floor I gasped for breath, and so did he, straddling me and hitting me every time I tried to lash out. Libardo lifted him up by the arms, and Julio kicked in the air, still trying to get at me. Libardo carried him off and ordered him to his room.

I got up slowly, aching and dazed. I leaned against the chair and saw that Fernanda still had her elbows on the table and her head in her hands. I thought she was crying, but she was motionless and silent. Libardo was pacing around the dining room. He was agitated and snorting like an irritated animal. He wouldn't look at me. I went to my room too. I heard them arguing for a good while. I couldn't hear what they were saying, but it was easy to imagine. Maybe the people who were after Libardo weren't going to kill us. They already knew we would destroy one another without their help.

The explosions are going off more and more frequently and the sky is lit up with sparkle on a night full of low, swift-moving clouds. Pedro the Dictator sticks his head out the window, looks up, and says ecstatically, "God bless La Alborada."

"Where are we going?" Nobody answers me. I'm starting to believe they're all tuning me out when I ask that question. La Murciélaga and Julieth are singing at the top of their lungs while Pedro is looking at text messages on his phone. A firework goes off close by, and La Murciélaga lets out a yelp of terror.

"No," she complains, "I'm never going to get used to this. Tonight's going to give me a heart attack."

Julieth laughs and says, "I love fireworks. Let's get some bottle rockets, Peter."

"They're illegal around here," says Pedro. "You have to go to Envigado or who-knows-where."

"What?" I ask. "So where did everybody get the ones they're setting off right now?"

There's another boom very close by, La Murciélaga shrieks again, and nobody answers me. Fireworks are going off around us, and according to Pedro, the tempo will increase as midnight approaches. Medellín is going to explode again, just like it did when Escobar and his thugs, Libardo among them, blew it off its foundations and left it turned ass over teakettle.

"Do you like setting off bottle rockets, Larry?" Julieth asks.

"I've never set one off in my life," I tell her.

What I don't mention is that I've fired plenty of guns: Colts, long Colts, Smith & Wessons, and even assault rifles, all before my fifteenth birthday. Not because I wanted to, but because from the time I was born, Libardo insisted we needed to learn to defend ourselves, and set up a shooting range on the farm. Whenever we went there on vacation, he made us practice. Fernanda never said anything either way, but she always started at every shot, resigned, knowing deep down that we really were going to need to defend ourselves, but tormented because we shouldn't have been shooting real weapons at that age. I could load a nine-millimeter with my eyes closed before my voice even changed.

Afterward I forgot everything, all of Libardo's instructions, every recommendation about how to aim, inhaling and then holding your breath as you fire. I even forgot the applause when I hit the target and the twinkle of pride in his eyes when he bragged about his sons' bravery, marksmanship, and spunk. I forgot it from the day when, in the middle of a party, Libardo decided to show off our shooting skills and ordered his men to untie a two-month-old calf, one that didn't even have any meat on it yet, and release it real far away, more than a hundred yards off, and then had them bring him his arsenal and announced that the night's meal was going to be on us—on me and Julio, I mean—because we, he declared, were going to shoot the calf dead with a single bullet in the head.

He handed Julio a semiautomatic shotgun; I was better with handguns, so he gave me a Glock. He'd never asked us to shoot an animal before, or a bird, or even a tree—nothing that was alive. We'd always shot at people-shaped targets, sure, with a black bull's-eye on the head, but never an animal.

I started shaking from the minute they released the calf. Julio would shoot first because he was the oldest. Lucky for me. I prayed he'd hit it so I wouldn't have to go next, but he was shaking too; his smile was nervous, and he was sweating. He liked animals more than I did, especially livestock; it was like he was made for the farm ever since he was a kid, built for barns and corrals. Libardo was putting him to a test that he was bound to fail. Even so, he adjusted his stance and took aim at the calf, which was fidgeting restlessly, anxious to return to the pen and be with its mother.

"Right in the head, son," said Libardo, belching rum, and then, to top it off, "Blow its head off—the body's going on the grill."

Julio couldn't hold still, not because the calf was moving, but because he was thinking the same thing I was, and wishing, like me, for that calf to take off for the horizon, run into the brush, and disappear amid the vegetation, saving itself and saving us from doing what we didn't want to do.

"What are you waiting for?" Libardo asked, exasperated, because Julio kept aiming the gun but couldn't make up his mind to shoot, and the guests were starting to jeer and laugh.

He looked at me very seriously, as if to say, get ready, if this kid can't pull it off, you're my other card, the ace up my sleeve. But he said again, "Go on and shoot, dammit—we're all getting bored."

Fernanda was watching quietly, but when she saw how Julio was shaking, she slowly walked over. She must have been planning to intervene, to face Libardo down, and she knocked back the rest of her drink in one go. But before she could confront him, the shotgun went off and she jumped, as usual, at the bang. Libardo, for his part, hopped up and down excitedly, though his delight faded when he realized that though the calf was dead, the shot had torn one side of its body apart. Despite the mistake, the guests applauded, and to restore the festive mood, Libardo said, "It'll be chicken after all, ladies and gentlemen—the kid's wrecked our beef."

Anyway, that was the last day I ever held a gun.

"I like shooting bobble rockets," says Julieth. "You never know what they're going to do."

"This one night," Pedro breaks in, "she set off two bottle rockets in two different apartments. They had to take one poor old lady to the emergency room with heart palpitations." He chortles and continues: "She was watching TV, and the bottle rocket came in the window and went off on her bed."

Julieth and La Murciélaga crack up. Julieth tries to say something, but she's laughing too much to catch her breath.

"We had to run so hard," La Murciélaga says, "our legs almost gave out." She points to Pedro. "This asshole ditched us—he got in the car and took off."

"I wasn't about to get myself caught," says Pedro.

Julieth, finally able to speak, says, "It was in the papers."

"Did they catch you?" I ask.

"No, the two of us got out of there." She gestures at La Murciélaga. "We jumped down a gully and got away, but it was on Teleantioquia and in *El Colombiano* and they said the old lady almost died of fright."

"Is it always like this, or just today?" I ask.

"What?"

"Huh?"

"La Alborada?"

"Medellín," I say. "Is it always like this or just today?"

The three of them exchange puzzled glances. There's no need for them to reply. It's hard to say what I mean by "like this." Looking back, I recall that it's always been like this; Medellín has always bobbed on the waves of a restless sea.

"Let's go buy the hydroponic weed," says La Murciélaga. Julieth hops excitedly and Pedro says, "In my dictatorship, ladies, drugs will be a staple good."

The other two clap and burst with pleasure, like the fireworks booming outside.

8

T he flight map on the screens showed the plane leaving Europe behind, poised over Portugal, about to enter the Atlantic. But to them the large blue blotch was much more than an ocean. It was a zone of oblivion into which Charlie and Larry had each tossed their histories when they left Medellín years earlier. The pasts they dropped are still lying there on the seafloor, and there they'll remain until the ocean dries up.

Charlie found him with his eyes closed, as if he were sleeping, though he denied it afterward. Standing in the aisle, she asked, "Did I wake you?"

"No," he said.

"You had your mouth open," she said.

"How long have you been there?" Larry asked her.

"A little while. I wanted to thank you."

The passengers on either side of Larry grumbled in irritation.

"I didn't do anything," he said.

"Of course you did," said Charlie, and fell quiet, as if she was still in shock from the news, or waiting for him to say something else. They looked at each other in silence, and then she said, "Come with me."

"Where to?"

"Up there. Come on."

Larry lifted his legs to climb over the woman dozing beside him. Charlie led him to the first-class galley and wordlessly poured two glasses of gin at the bar the flight attendants had set up. He asked about the flight attendants, more to say something than to find out where they were. "They're probably napping," Charlie said.

"As long as the pilot's awake," he said.

"Yeah, right. The only people awake on this thing are the two of us."

Charlie smiled for the first time, though the smile was shot through with sadness. He took the opportunity to ask her name, and she looked at him in silence, thinking, or hesitating, and finally said, "María Carlota Teresa Valentina. But don't worry," she added, seeing Larry's expression. "You can call me Charlie."

He told her his name while she downed her drink. Larry wasn't even halfway through his. She poured herself another and asked, "Why are you going to Colombia?"

"I'm going to my dad's funeral."

Charlie opened her eyes wide, very surprised, as if she couldn't believe the coincidence. Larry explained: "He didn't just die now. It was years ago, but they found his remains a few days back."

Charlie cleared her throat awkwardly. She didn't understand. A flight attendant suddenly appeared and asked to get by them so she could open a door and pull out a folder full of papers. Still smiling, she told them they were welcome to anything they wanted, but they needed to take their drinks to their seats. Larry knocked back the rest of his gin to prepare to return to coach, but when the flight attendant left, Charlie told him, "The seat next to me's empty—come and sit with me."

"But . . ."

"Come on, man," Charlie insisted. "Everybody's passed out."

Larry couldn't help smiling when he dropped into the puffy chair and felt the cool leather against his skin.

There are some things you don't forget . . .

Charlie's eyes were glittering from all her crying, or from

the two gins she'd downed. She tucked the blanket around her legs, reclined her seat a little, grabbed the full glass she'd brought with her, and said to Larry, "All right, tell me the story."

9

Libardo watched Escobar's funeral on TV. He'd made up his mind to go to the cemetery, but when he learned that other close associates wouldn't be going, he was overcome with fears and doubts, and on the day of the funeral he stayed away.

"If anybody was going to be there, it should have been me," Libardo sobbed.

"In the coffin?" I asked, distraught.

"No," he said, tenderly ruffling my hair. "No, son, I mean the funeral—I should have been with him till the very end."

He was tormented by that guilt day and night. He cried in front of the TV when he saw the casket and the crowds chanting Pablo's name and waving hundreds of white hand-kerchiefs. When he saw the mother, the musicians playing the dead man's favorite songs, and when the casket sank into the earth.

That weeping was also a symptom, a warning about the fragility of the moment. I felt vulnerable even in my own home, as if the walls were gradually disappearing or the doors no longer closed, as if the roof had suddenly blown off and every-one was an enemy. I didn't say anything; I swallowed my fear in silence, though I was sure it was obvious. I could see it in Libardo, in Fernanda, in Julio, in the staff and bodyguards, in everybody who came to visit us, so why wouldn't they notice it in me? But it was better to keep quiet; anything I said could be misinterpreted and lead to an accusation or an argument. After the dining table incident, I kept my opinions to myself and let them make the decisions. I'd said what I had to say that night: because of Libardo, we were going to be killed.

As he'd planned, we spent Christmas in the Dominican Republic. It was the four of us plus our grandparents—Libardo's parents. Julio and I got more gifts than we had in years past. It was Libardo's way of assuaging his guilt and trying to convince us not to return to Medellín. Julio wanted to spend the rest of our vacation on the farm, and Fernanda already wanted to go back, even though she'd been enjoying herself at all of Santo Domingo's biggest casinos.

The thirty-first saw the arrival of Libardo's two sisters, who lived in Tampa, with their husbands and children, and Benito, a distant cousin of Libardo's, whom he always claimed to love like a brother. Benito also brought his whole family. Nobody from Fernanda's side came. She only had one brother left, Juan David; he was thirteen years younger than her and studying music in New York—financed by Libardo, of course.

On the final night of 1993, thirty members of the family celebrated together in a restaurant with a band, party hats, whistles, and confetti, everybody trying to make Libardo believe that nothing serious was happening and life was going on as usual. Everybody except Fernanda, who could never fake anything. Even I joined in the jubilation, since my grandmother had asked that, for Libardo's sake and everybody else's, we all surround him with happiness. But at the stroke of midnight, when the Happy-New-Year hugs began, Libardo started crying again. And one by one, the rest of the family ended up crying too. Everybody except Fernanda and me. While they all sniffled into one another's shoulders, she called me over to sit next to her.

"Want a little champagne?" she asked.

"I don't like it," I said.

I didn't like alcohol yet. I didn't smoke either. Once, before all of this started, Libardo had offered me a drink at a party, and when I turned it down, he said, don't tell me you're going to turn out queer. As if queers don't drink.

"Toast with me, Larry," Fernanda insisted. "Just a sip."

Without waiting for my response, she poured champagne into two glasses, passed one to me, and raised hers.

"Here's to you and me, and to not drowning when the boat goes under." She said it without dramatics, smiling, her eyes glittering from the many glasses she'd already drunk.

That toast gave me a different awareness of her beauty, but I couldn't translate it into words just then. I knew she was beautiful: everybody said so—my friends, my classmates, her friends who confirmed it every time they saw her, Libardo's buddies who stared at her avidly, the people on the street who recognized the former Miss Medellín 1973 and told her she was as gorgeous as ever, if not more so.

But right before trying the champagne, I looked at her and saw something new in her beauty, something almost supernatural, a sort of magnetism sparkling in the depths of her eyes.

In time, when I met other women and fell in love, I realized that what I'd seen in Fernanda that night was her own demons.

10

I t isn't raining, but hundreds of people are marching along with black umbrellas and blocking traffic. There are more groups in different places around the city. In silence, they walk slowly toward a meeting point in downtown Medellín, protesting La Alborada. They hate the noise and love the animals that could die of fright from the exploding fireworks. Their open umbrellas symbolize a call for rain. Only a party-pooping downpour can save them.

"Turn off the music," I ask La Murciélaga.

"For fuck's sake," says Pedro.

"Just for a minute, please."

The only sound is the demonstrators' footsteps on the pavement. Not a cheer, not a murmur. The silence is more powerful than any protest chant, though the fireworks shatter it with increasing frequency.

"You good?" La Murciélaga asks me. Without waiting for a response, she turns the music all the way back up. She doesn't even hear when I thank her. Pedro sticks his head out the window and yells at the marchers: "In my dictatorship, the only rain you'll see will be bullets, asswipes."

La Murciélaga shimmies in her seat, and I remark to Julieth, "I'll bet she dances when she's on the toilet too."

Pedro manages to find a shortcut out of the jam of cars, and we drive toward Las Palmas. The plan is to head up into the hills, taking our time, and get to the top around midnight, when the fireworks reach their crescendo. Beforehand, I called

Pedro aside and said, you know what I'm going to say. Yeah, he said, but relax, when she calls I'll drive you back down or find somebody else to do it, it'll be packed up there.

If Fernanda doesn't call me in the next hour, come hell or high water I'm going to go find her, and then I'll get some sleep. I dream of sleeping twelve hours straight.

"Pit stop," says Pedro, and we stop at a bar-restaurant-dance club that's hopping. He calls the guys in the other car so they'll stop too.

"Don't you have a friend named Charlie?" I ask La Murciélaga when we settle at a table.

"Male or female?"

"Female."

"Charlie? I have two guy friends with that name, but no women."

"She studies in London."

"What about her?"

"Her dad died yesterday."

"Oh, Larry, I really don't get you. What are you talking about? The only dead person I've been hearing about is your dad."

"Who told you? Pedro?"

La Murciélaga shakes her head.

"Did you read it in the paper?" I ask.

"I don't read the papers," she says.

It had appeared on the front page and been reported on TV. They showed the grave where he'd been found but, supposedly out of respect, not the corpse. The bones. La Murciélaga hadn't seen it on the news. She didn't watch the news either. It was Ro who told me, she said when I insisted, nodding her head in his direction.

"What else did he say?" I ask.

"Nothing," she says.

Tonight I'm the newcomer, and Ro, by contrast, is the long-time friend. She's not going to drop him in it for my sake, but it's obvious Ro's bothered by me; he keeps eyeing me from the other end of the table.

"So who's Charlie?" La Murciélaga asks.

"Someone I met on the plane."

"And you like her," she says.

I smile and take a drink.

"Men are such dumbasses."

"About what?"

"Everything," she says, and drinks some aguardiente. "You're so impractical," she adds. "Let's dance, Larry."

"I don't know how to dance to this stuff."

A robotic voice is endlessly repeating *grind it, grind it, grind it, mami*, and the dancers are trying to look sexy but they actually make me want to laugh. Or cry.

"You just dance," says La Murciélaga.

"Like a coffee grinder," I say, and she isn't amused. "That's what the song says, right?"

"You're such a drag," she says, gets up, and wiggles her way onto the dancefloor.

As the night crawls on, La Murciélaga becomes increasingly vampire-like. Weirder and more alluring. But all of that mystery evaporates in an instant whenever she hops up and down and squeals about the fireworks. Then afterward she goes strange again.

In the distance Medellín is visible, half splendid and half destitute. I still find this landscape deeply moving: because of everything that's changed, everything that's been lost, and because this hole amid the mountains, this cauldron where so many have died, which exiled so many and marked us all, is still standing, tougher than ever, as if it had never been the city from which I had to flee or where my father was killed.

Pedro sits down next to me to pour himself a drink. Seeing an opportunity, I ask, "Have you been to my house?"

"Which one? In London?"

"No, Fernanda's place, where she lives now. I've never seen it."

"Not even in photos?"

"No. All I've seen is her headboard," I say.

When we Skype, she's always in bed. She's refused to show me anything else. Maybe she's ashamed to show me how tiny it is.

"Well, you'll be going there later," Pedro says.

"I can take a taxi."

"Don't be melodramatic," he says. "Let's wait for her to call."

"I don't get why she didn't pick me up at the airport, or why she won't let me just go there now. I don't get it at all, Pedro."

He studies me for a moment and says, "What's up with you, Larry? You've changed."

"Everybody's changed," I tell him. Even him, I think, though he looks the same as ever.

"There's always something left," he says, "but with you it's like there's nothing."

"You've only been with me two hours."

He checks his watch and corrects me. "Three."

"Fine, three, but I'm tired. I haven't slept since I boarded the plane."

I get up, and Pedro looks confused. "Hey, man, it's no big deal," he says.

"I'm just going to pee," I tell him.

Fireworks are booming near and far. I look for the lights in the sky, but only the noise floats in the air. As I urinate, I think about my house. A huge house, way too big for four people, a mansion for two kids. We're probably going to talk about the house again now, about the years we lived there without the blessing—or tragedy—of having it all. We'll talk about Libardo again as if it were yesterday, now when there are some days I don't think of him at all. Libardo has returned from a time that doesn't exist and become real time, a date, a number, a death certificate, and he will make a place for himself where he will stay. And I'll go back to being "Libardo's son" or "Larry, Libardo's kid" and nothing more.

11

L arry was drinking to process his trip home too. Charlie got up to fetch two more glasses of gin, and when she stood she noticed she was already feeling the effects of the drinks. She'd become more limber again, as if the alcohol had lightened her pain.

The rumpled blanket and the cushion dented with her weight remained in the seat. She left her shoes on the floor, next to her purse, and Larry spotted the little packet of Kleenex he'd given her in one corner.

She reappeared with two brimming glasses and said, "The first memory I thought of when I heard the news was this one time when I got lost at Disney World. I was five years old, and I was lost for half an hour, terrified with all those people milling around me. But I kept looking for my parents, positive they'd appear at some point. I feel the same way now, except one of them I'm never going to see again."

She started crying again and tried to console herself with a couple of sips from her glass. Larry shifted in his seat.

"The 'never' part is what kills me," Charlie sobbed.

"Do you have any other siblings?" he asked.

"A sister. Two years younger than me," she said quietly, with the volume of sadness, of nighttime, her eyes glassy. Then she added, "This is where everything ends. I can't see anything beyond this moment."

"Parents leave us so much, but they take something too," Larry said.

Charlie shook her head, took a long swig, and said, "I feel like he took everything."

Two fat tears welled up in her eyes, and she swiftly wiped them away with her hand and let out a wail that disarmed Larry.

"Your father's death," he said, "obeys the laws of life. My father's obeys a natural law in Colombia—the law of the jungle."

"Was he murdered?" Charlie asked, worried she might be prying.

"He was kidnapped," Larry said.

Charlie raised her eyebrows, opened her swollen eyes wider, and sighed.

"He disappeared one day, and I never saw him again," Larry said, then fell silent. She didn't ask anything else.

The airplane shuddered with a couple of powerful jolts. Instinctively, she grabbed Larry's hand, and he was caught off guard more by the squeeze of her fingers than by the turbulence. Though the flight smoothed out again after a few seconds, Charlie downed the rest of her drink.

"Death gets a kick out of scaring us," Larry said.

12

D espite the sense of unease provoked by Escobar's death, that December, free of his shadow, felt different. Getting out of Colombia on that vacation made us believe things were going to get better. Libardo allowed Fernanda to convince him we should go back so Julio and I could finish high school at our old school. They've only got one year left, she said, and then they'll go do college somewhere else.

We returned at the end of January. There was a strange feeling in the air that nobody could identify. A mix of uncertainty, fear, and calm. People talked about how there might be some attempt to seek vengeance, retaliation, but there was also talk of opportunities and rebuilding, starting over. I deluded myself that people would stop looking at us like they had before, that Libardo's sins had died along with Escobar's, even though lots of people were still scared, waiting for him to lash out one last time from beyond the grave.

Rumor had it that his hand was out there somewhere, that when they'd opened his casket at the cemetery so the crowd could get a look before he was buried, somebody who loved him had removed his hand and swore to use it to seek vengeance.

"But how did they manage that?" I asked. "It's not like the casket would have been left open that long."

"Somebody cut it off," said Julio.

"Nobody cut anything off," said Libardo.

"How do you know?" I asked. "You weren't at the funeral."

Libardo gave me a reproachful look. He hated to be reminded he'd let fear keep him away. As a precaution, he claimed, though I didn't see the distinction.

"It's a symbol," said Libardo. "The hand business is a legend to show that Pablo's still got the power—his hand is still active, he lives among us."

"Who has it?" Julio asked.

"Nobody," Libardo replied. "I told you it's like a symbol. He's still here, people loved him a lot, they respected him."

"So everything's going to stay the same?" I asked.

"Yes . . . no," Libardo said. "I mean, Pablo's legacy means we can live in peace, and like I said, with him gone, the government won't be fucking with us anymore."

"What's a legacy?" Julio asked.

But Libardo failed to tell us—maybe didn't want to mention—that Escobar's enemies weren't going to be satisfied with his death. And Escobar's enemies were also Libardo's enemies, my family's enemies—which means they were my enemies, even though I had no idea who they were.

We started to suspect it, though, as Libardo shed the optimistic tone he'd had at the start of the new year and became irritable and paranoid. He wouldn't let us leave the house without his men, and even Fernanda had to have bodyguards when she went to the casinos.

"I might as well not go," she said. "Those guys bring bad luck."

Julio and I started our final year of high school, which would also be our final year in Medellín. Libardo already planned to send us to France so we could improve our French, and then we'd go on to college, also abroad. He was sure he'd be able to handle the pressure without our noticing. But the noose swiftly tightened on him. Pablo's inner circle shrank as members were killed or kidnapped, or fled, or turned themselves in. There were a lot of rumors about who had actually killed Escobar, and the more theories that emerged, the more enemies we had: the gringos, the government, Los Pepes, the Cali cartel, the Norte del Valle cartel, the victims, and on and on. But the only ones who publicly claimed responsibility for all those deaths were Los Pepes, and they were the ones Libardo feared most. The group, whose full name was Persecuted by Pablo Escobar, went from victims to victimizers. They celebrated their acts of vengeance by leaving triumphant messages with each corpse.

"I know who those bastards are," Libardo told somebody over the telephone. "I know their names and their faces. I know where they live and how they work, but there's nobody left to wage war against them, man—everybody's turned chicken."

It was a matter of surrendering or holding firm. The country was in the grip of a moralistic fervor, and overnight we became the target of the same people who used to cheer us on. Even at school, where we were supposedly beyond the reach of society's prejudices. And then, to top it all off, Fernanda threw gas on the flames.

"Your dad has a mistress," she told us.

That day, she'd been clutching a glass of white wine ever since we got home from school. She walked through the backyard and paced around the pool, staring into its depths as if she were searching for something under the water. She saw us watching her from the living room and didn't even lift her hand to wave, didn't even smile. She took a long swig and then lay back on a deck chair to stare up at the sky. She stayed like that till it grew dark and then came into the study, where Julio and I were doing our homework. She'd refilled her wineglass, and that was when, leaning against the doorjamb, she told us about Libardo's mistress.

"How did you find out?" Julio asked.

"You already knew?" she asked him.

"I don't know shit."

"Don't talk to me like that."

"I just want to know how you found out, who told you, to see if it's true."

"Of course it's true," Fernanda said. "I've seen her. I know who she is."

"Who is she?" I asked.

"A tramp," she said, and her voice splintered.

I looked down, and I think Julio did too. Fernanda dropped into an armchair, let her body sag, and wailed, "She's a twenty-two-year-old little twerp, and he's already given her an apartment and a car."

Her sentences tangled together, her eyeliner was smeared, and she was sniffling.

"He's twenty-five years older than her—she could be his daughter," she continued. "I can't believe he's not embarrassed to go out with her."

"They've been seen out together?" Julio asked.

Fernanda nodded, then said, "At least with the others he didn't take them out—he just wanted to sleep with them."

"Others?" I broke in.

Fernanda straightened up and stared at us as she took another sip of wine. "Oh, sweeties." She slid forward and fell to her knees on the rug, and shuffled toward us with her arms held wide, still gripping the wineglass. I wanted to get up and run, to flee the pathetic sight of an intoxicated mother seeking her children's compassion. But I was paralyzed, and she hauled us into her embrace, squeezed us tight, and burst out sobbing. I looked at Julio out of the corner of my eye, pressed against her other shoulder, while Fernanda, unawares, spilled cold wine down my back.

13

A bald guy with a long beard, wearing flip-flops and a loose shirt, a prophet of the new era, gives La Murciélaga a long hug. She comes back to the car giving jubilant little skips. She's finally got that hydroponic weed she was after. We've had to come all the way from Las Palmas to Belén to make this woman happy.

"All right, kids, let's blow this place," she says as she clambers into the front seat next to Pedro the Dictator. And she adds: "The world can end now."

The noise of the fireworks is relentless. Some of the explosions are sharp and booming, like a slamming door, like a set of cookpots clattering from a cupboard to the floor. Others announce themselves with a whistle before they detonate, an exhalation in the night before bursting out in lights. There are high ones and low ones, near ones and far ones. No matter what they look like, they're all money that burns up in seconds, giving boundless pleasure to the person setting them off. The same euphoria that people feel from firing their guns in the air.

I often saw Libardo and his friends riddle the sky with bullets in celebration of something. A successful shipment, a lucrative business deal, a law passed in Congress for their benefit, or the death of somebody who'd been in their way.

"Where to now?" Julieth asks.

"Let's go back to Las Palmas," says La Murciélaga.

"It's nine fifteen p.m.," says Pedro, as if he were an announcer on Radio Reloj.

"Can you drop me off at my place?" I ask, but they all look at me as if they didn't understand a word.

"Your mom hasn't called yet," Pedro tells me.

"I don't care. If she's not there, I'll wait for her in the foyer. If she isn't ready to see me, I'll stay downstairs till she opens the door."

"All right, whatever you say," Pedro tells me.

For the first time all night, I feel relief. And also a chill in my abdomen and eddies in my guts. A freefalling void. Fear? Fear, anxiety, joy, respite. Though I know there won't be silence tonight, at least I won't be in this SUV anymore with the music blasting, in a smoky haze that smells of fireworks. Pedro's cell phone rings again, and I try to catch a glimpse of the screen.

"Inga!" yells Pedro.

He's no longer talking normally but shouting and laughing insults and mockery. He slaps the steering wheel in excitement.

"Can you turn the music down, Murci?" I ask, but she doesn't hear me, or doesn't want to.

We're gonna get down, get down, get down, we're gonna get down, oh, oh, oh. La Murciélaga sings, and Julieth sways haltingly to the beat. I stretch forward and lower the volume. La Murciélaga slaps my arm.

"What's your problem?" she scolds me. "Don't crush my groove."

"My head's going to explode," I tell her.

Julieth ruffles my hair. La Murciélaga turns the volume back up, Pedro keeps yelling like he's standing next to a waterfall.

"Hang on, I've got something for you," La Murciélaga tells me and rummages in her purse. "Pull over, man," she says to Pedro. "Let's stop a minute."

I thought she was looking for an aspirin, but she pulls out the bag of hydroponic marijuana and starts rolling a joint with impressive skill.

"No, Murci," I say. "I thought . . ."

But before I can think, the SUV has filled up with smoke and the smell of weed. And when Pedro tells the person he's talking to, we're coming to get you, my relief evaporates, and once again my prospects dim.

The joint passes from hand to hand and mouth to mouth.

"Inga needs us to rescue her," Pedro says.

"Where is she?" La Murciélaga asks.

"She says some aliens kidnapped her."

"Who's Inga?" Julieth asks.

"The Swedish chick," La Murciélaga replies.

"You don't know her?" Pedro asks. "The Swedish chick who came to Medellín to learn Spanish."

"So has she learned it?" Julieth asks.

"Not much, but she did learn to do coke."

Julieth expels the smoke with a laugh. Her laughter is still beautiful, like when we used to laugh together in bed.

"So let's rescue her," La Murciélaga says.

"What about me?" I ask.

"You? Smoke," says Julieth. She blows smoke in my face and sticks the joint between my lips. The three of them look at me like I'm about to perform an amazing somersault. I toke, and they keep watching me to see if I inhale. I expel the smoke, and Julieth smiles at me. She passes the joint up to the front.

Oh, oh, oh, we're gonna get down, get down, get down, we're gonna get down.

We drive past the old airport. People used to say that if you jumped real high there, you could touch the airplanes' wheels as they took off.

"Is it still in operation?" I ask.

"Yes."

"No."

"Yes or no?"

"Yes during the day, no at night," Pedro says.

"I've seen planes landing at night," La Murciélaga says.

"That must be when you're tripping," Julieth says.

"The runway doesn't have any lights," Pedro says.

"No plane could fly tonight with all this smoke," I tell them.

And I'm flying low, only a few inches off the ground. La Murciélaga starts another round. This time I snatch the joint and take a drag.

To my left is Nutibara Hill. As a boy I used to imagine that the restaurant at the top was a flying saucer. As soon as we found out that the restaurant rotated, we begged Libardo to take us. And it did rotate, but very slowly. Julio and I were disappointed. What did you expect, Libardo asked us, that we were going to be eating on a merry-go-round?

"Is there still a restaurant up there?" I ask.

"Where?" Julieth asks, looking up at the sky.

"On the hill."

"Yes."

"No."

"I think it closed," says Pedro. "I never went."

"I did," says Julieth. "It spun."

It doesn't look like a flying saucer now. It doesn't even look like a restaurant.

La Murciélaga laughs. I don't know why she's laughing. Well, I know why but I don't know at what. People are setting off fireworks on top of the hill too. It looks like a volcano spitting out its first sparks. I remember the other hill, farther north, the one people said was a dormant volcano. I don't remember what it was called, but I do remember you could see it from our high school, and we used to fantasize that it might wake up. I would imagine Medellín filling with lava and everybody fleeing toward the mountains. The lava catching up with us, lapping at our heels, in this city that looks like a mug of nasty soup.

"What's the name of that hill that was a dormant volcano?" The three of them look at me, Pedro in the rearview mirror. "What's up with you, Larry?" he asks.

"There's a volcano here in Medellín?" Julieth asks. "If there is, I'm going to go live somewhere else."

"No more of this stuff for now," La Murciélaga says and snuffs out the joint in the ashtray.

To my left I see the spiral of cars trying to climb Nutibara Hill. Everybody wants to watch La Alborada from a high place. We're all getting high too.

Get down, get down, the song says, and we're going up, up, up.

14

What is it about nighttime that focuses pain when a person is grieving, or uncertain, or in an airplane seat? What is this fear of opening our eyes and admitting to sleeplessness in the eternity of a nocturnal flight? Were Charlie and Larry sleeping? Or were they pretending to sleep, like pretty much everybody else? She'd laid her head on his shoulder, and he could feel her breath on his ear. He could just see her eyelashes and the tip of her nose out of the corner of his eye. His neck hurt from sitting in the same position for so long, motionless as a doll out of fear of waking her, if she was actually sleeping, since he didn't dare ask. Sometimes Charlie started the way you do when you dream you're falling, and her eyes moved restlessly under her eyelids as if she were looking for something in her dream. She must have been looking for her father among the living, who else, to refuse him his death.

A flight attendant emerged from the shadows and walked slowly down the aisle. She was smiling, perhaps out of habit or, why not, malice. She'd be looking for the passenger with a hand fondling their private parts. Two people groping each other under a single blanket, a couple attempting a bit of gymnastics to suck each other off, a man with a substantial erection as he slept. Smiling and stealthy, she slipped past them, and when she saw Larry her smile disappeared.

She's going to catch me sneaking into first class . . .

He stroked Charlie's hair, barely grazing it to avoid waking her. The flight attendant kept going, apparently buying Larry's pretense that he was traveling with his girlfriend. He felt the pain, rising from his big toe to his head, more strongly, but his soul was brimming over.

What is life playing at when it introduces a man to a sad, beautiful woman and, within an hour of his meeting her, has her snoozing on his shoulder like the sleeping beauty from a fairy tale?

15

The bank statements arrived, and Libardo discovered that Fernanda had been disobeying his order not to go to the casino by herself. She tried to cover her gambling with cash, but if she lost a bundle, she'd use the credit card. What Libardo didn't know was how she was getting out without the bodyguards noticing. One night she didn't come home at the usual time, and he decided to go ask the head bodyguard, a former police captain known as Dengue, where she was.

"We dropped her off at Margarita's house at 3:30 this afternoon, just like we do every day, and we wait for her there until she comes out," Dengue told Libardo.

"And she doesn't move from there? She doesn't leave?"

"No, boss," Dengue said. "The only one who leaves is Margarita, but she's always alone."

"What?" Libardo asked, perplexed.

Dengue repeated himself, and Libardo raised his hands to his head.

"You're a bunch of morons," Libardo said. "If Fernanda's going to visit Margarita, how come Margarita leaves on her own? So who's Fernanda visiting, then?"

Visibly upset, Libardo told Julio and me that he was going to look for Fernanda and asked us to go to bed. But when he left, we sat on the stairs to wait.

When Libardo and Dengue arrived at Margarita's house, they parked across the way, crossed the street, and rang the bell. A maid answered, and he asked for Margarita and was told she'd gone out. When he asked for Fernanda, the maid started crying.

Libardo and Dengue went back to the car.

"What do we do, boss?"

"Wait," Libardo snorted.

They sat for a long time in silence, Dengue fidgeting in his seat. Finally Libardo asked, "Have you worked out what's going on yet?"

"Yes, boss," Dengue replied. "We're waiting."

"Right, waiting," Libardo said.

The lights of another car shone on them. It was Margarita coming back home alone. Libardo leaped out of the car and got in front of her before she could put the car in the garage. She gripped the steering wheel as Libardo slowly approached.

"Oh, Libardo," said Margarita.

He stopped by the rear door. Through the window he saw a shape on the floor of the car, covered by a blanket. Libardo knocked on the window and Fernanda's head poked out from under the blanket. Her hair was tousled, and she was grinning from ear to ear.

At around eleven at night, Libardo burst through the front door of the house and dragged Fernanda inside. The living room was dark, and my brother and I were still sitting halfway up the stairs, just as we'd been when he left to look for her. She was barefoot, carrying her high heels. She tried to get free, but Libardo grabbed her forcefully and tossed her onto the sofa. Libardo hadn't seen us, though she caught our eyes before he pushed her.

"Don't you move," Libardo warned her, and as soon as he took two steps to leave, she sat forward. He grabbed her by the shoulders and threw her back on the sofa. "Don't move, damn it," he said again.

"I want a cigarette," Fernanda said.

She was drunk. She was slurring her words. Though she

seemed lost, she kept turning around to look at us whenever she could. I was afraid of Libardo's rage, afraid he might hit her, but he left her lying there and went to the study. Fernanda was breathless, and since she'd closed her eyes, I thought she'd passed out from the alcohol. Libardo came back to the living room. He was carrying something shiny in his hands. I was convinced it was a gun. Fernanda opened her eyes when she heard him return. He showed her what he was carrying, and she burst out laughing. It was a pair of handcuffs. Libardo grabbed her by one arm to lift her up, forced her to turn around, and cuffed her hands behind her. She kept laughing. He pushed her onto the sofa again, harder now, and she grimaced with pain.

"I don't like you sneaking around doing these things," Libardo hissed at her.

She sat up defiantly. "I'm not doing anything wrong."

"And how do I know that?" he asked.

"Oh," she said, "you think I'm like that skank you're seeing?"

He grabbed her face hard. With his other hand he started unbuckling his belt. Fernanda looked at us out of the corner of her eye.

"Are you going to hit me?" she demanded.

"No, better—or worse," he said, and unzipped his fly, still gripping her.

"No," Fernanda said, and turned to look at us. Then Libardo saw us.

"You little shits," he said, and Julio and I sprang up like we'd been hit by lightning and bolted for our rooms.

The strongest image of that night that's stayed with me is Fernanda in handcuffs. I still don't know whether it was part of a sexual game or the start of some sort of torture. Libardo was capable of anything. And it pained me to see Fernanda with her hands bound, as if she were the criminal.

16

T here aren't too many houses in El Poblado with people still living in them. Before I left they'd already demolished almost all the European-style ones; a few newer mansions remained, gringofied, with huge garages, pools, and lawns as tidy as golf courses. Even those had started being demolished too, to make way for apartment buildings. All signs indicated that El Poblado would become what it is now: a brick beehive. Pedro the Dictator took us to one of those remaining houses to rescue the Swedish chick.

He went in to get her, and we stayed in the car, the music blasting the whole time. *What can I say without you thinking I'm joking, you won't let me rock you but you're totally smoking.*

Five minutes later the Dictator comes back, confused. "I can't find her," he says. "Come help me look for her."

"I'll wait here," I say. "I don't know her."

"It's a cinch," says La Murciélaga. "She's Swedish and about five foot nine."

Julieth prods me to urge me out of the car, as if she didn't have a door on her side. I get out because I'm thirsty; maybe I can get a glass of water inside.

"What if those bastards did something to her?" Pedro says.

"Do what?" La Murciélaga asks. "If she's here, it's because she knows them."

"Whose house is this?" I ask. "Who lives here?"

"There are some really weird people in there," Pedro says, and pushes the door open.

"What's that noise?" Julieth asks.

"What's that smell?" I ask.

"Charred meat," Pedro says.

"They're not grilling Inga, are they?" says La Murciélaga.

We enter a large living room lined with glass doors that look out on the backyard. The lights are off, and there's a group of people sitting in a circle in front of a fireplace, the only source of illumination in the room. They're all singing along to a guitar with their eyes closed. They rock their heads back and forth while intoning something that goes, *thank you to life, which has given me so much, it's given me laughter and it's given me tears.* They sway slowly, shoulder to shoulder, and several couples are holding hands. A woman gestures to us to join the group. In response, Pedro signals for her to come to us. She gets up and approaches, still singing.

"We're here for Inga," Pedro tells her. "She called and said she was here."

"Inga?" the woman asks quietly.

"The Swedish chick," Pedro says.

"Oh, right," she says. "She's around."

"Where?"

"Somewhere. Come have a seat till she shows up."

"Can we take a look for her around the house?" Pedro asks. "We're in a hurry."

"*And your house, your streeeeeet, and your gaaaaarden,*" the woman intones, and goes back to the group.

Pedro suggests we split up and check the bedrooms and bathrooms.

"Or wherever you guys think they might have her," he says.

"I don't know her," I say again.

"How are you not going to spot a Swedish chick among all these natives?" says Pedro, irritated.

"Did you see the fireplace?" I ask. "They're roasting something wrapped in rags."

"What was Inga doing with these weirdos?" La Murciélaga asks.

Julieth tugs my hand and says, "You come with me."

Something about all this reminds me of Libardo right after he'd disappeared. Back then, too, somebody suggested splitting up to look for him, and I went up to his room, where I already knew he wasn't, but it was the only place in the world I thought he might be. Should be. I found him in the photos Fernanda had hung on the wall, and I reviewed his history with us in each one. Happy fragments of his crazy life, some of them now faded with the passage of time, others in black and white like old movies or like they say dreams are. Those walls held only smiles and hugs, the things people like to immortalize in photos. The perfect life of an imperfect family. The handsome, ambitious man with his beauty queen and one son who looks like him and another who looks like her. At any rate, that man wasn't the Libardo I'd gone looking for in his room, the one others were combing the hospitals and morgue for, searching high and low, scouring heaven and earth.

"Murci told me that Swedish chick's a huge slut," Julieth says in my ear.

Or that's what I hear as I let her lead me to the second floor. Pedro and La Murciélaga stay downstairs.

"But don't tell her I said that," Julieth says.

"Let's go to the kitchen—I'm dying of thirst," I say.

"In a minute," she says, and casually opens the door to a bedroom as if it were her own. There's an unmade bed, soda bottles on the floor, but nobody's there. "Inga?" Julieth asks, but Inga doesn't answer.

We go into a hall bathroom, two more bedrooms, and the master, where there's a naked couple screwing.

"Sorry," Julieth says, closes the door, and cracks up, leaning against the wall.

The people downstairs are still doing their thing: *thank you to life, which has given me so much, it's given me sound and the alphabet.*

I don't know why, but right from the start I knew Libardo wasn't coming back. Or, rather, when nobody could think of anywhere else to look for him, I said to myself, Dad's not coming back. I said it to Julio, and he freaked out, knocked me on the floor with a blow to the chest, and told me, don't you ever say that again. The people close to Libardo tried to give us hope—we were the littlest mourners, we were the sons. But I think we all knew he wasn't coming back. We wanted him to come back, but every one of us, deep down—my grandmother, Fernanda—we all knew why he'd been taken.

After that, Julio, Fernanda, and I would sleep together at night, all three of us in her and Libardo's bed. We slept in our regular clothes so if anybody called with news in the middle of the night, we'd be ready, just in case. Of course, it isn't really accurate to say we slept. We'd get only an hour or two of shut-eye. By four in the morning, we'd be in the kitchen drinking hot chocolate, not talking, afraid to look at one another and discover the truth in one another's eyes.

"Do you have a girlfriend, Larry?" Julieth asks, heading up to an attic.

"I don't know," I say. She stops and looks at me, puzzled.

"I don't think so," I add, in an attempt to be clearer.

Julieth scolds me. "I'm being serious, Larry."

"I really don't know," I tell her. "I met someone on the plane, but . . ."

"What?" She breaks in, surprised, almost worried. "Are you being serious? You're still hung up on her?"

Could be. I regret having told Julieth, especially given our history.

"Go on, keep going." I shoo her along so she'll stop quizzing me.

She turns around and climbs up a steep staircase. Her round

butt is right at my eye level. Immediately, I recall that butt without clothes.

"Inga, Inga!" Julieth yells into the dark maw of the attic. She climbs up a little higher and stops.

"What's up?"

"Where's the light switch?" she says.

"Let me get by."

I scooch to one side, but we end up jammed in the narrow stairwell. She grabs my face and plants a wet kiss on my mouth. Our tongues intertwine, we swap spit. I slide my hand to touch her.

"You should turn on the light," she says.

I tread gingerly, groping the walls—there's got to be a switch somewhere. Julieth sits down on the landing, staring into the darkness, and calls again, "Inga!"

All we hear is the muffled singing of the group downstairs.

"She isn't here either," says Julieth. "Let's go."

"I wouldn't be surprised if those guys killed her," I say.

"Grow up, Larry," she says, and moves past me, without giving me another kiss.

Actually, I don't want any more kissing, just a glass of water and to get out of here, go home, talk to Fernanda, and sleep for two days straight. This house is bringing back bad memories— it looks like the one we used to have, my friends' houses, my girlfriends' houses, places where I wasn't given a warm welcome. What's Libardo's kid doing here? Sometimes I didn't get past the gates, other times I'd manage to reach the front door, and only rarely was I allowed in. I never complained about it. I told Fernanda on the condition that she didn't say anything to Libardo, but she couldn't keep her mouth shut. And then he'd say something like this: when you go to Gabriel's place, tell his dad I said hi—the two of us set up a car dealership in Panama last year. Or, tell Valentina's dad we've got to get together again, we haven't seen each other since last January.

Like that, pretty smooth but with the information necessary to bust down the doors that were shutting in my face.

"Larry," says Julieth.

"What?"

"Why are you still standing there? What are you doing?"

"Thinking."

"Oh, Larry," she says. "What we had was a long time ago. It was great, but I'm seeing somebo—"

I cut her off. "Let's find the kitchen. I'm thirsty."

Downstairs we run into Pedro and La Murciélaga, who look upset. Did you find her?, Pedro asks. Not a trace. You're shitting me, La Murciélaga says. Where did that chick get off to? Maybe she left. Right, she got tired of waiting for us and left. *Thank you to life, which has given me so much, it's given steps to my weary feet* . . . Jesus, what's up with these people? How long are they going to keep singing the same damn thing? Let's jet, Pedro, the Swedish chick's massive, she can take care of herself. *With them I've walked cities and fields, beaches and deserts, mountains and plains* . . .

"Hey, guys." The woman who first greeted us appears out of nowhere. "Did you find your friend?"

The four of us shake our heads.

"Nobody saw her leave?" Pedro asks her.

"Actually I never even saw her come in," the woman says.

"Do you people realize the kind of diplomatic shitstorm that'll kick up if something happens to this Swedish chick?" Pedro asks, his tone menacing.

The woman shrugs and says, smiling, "The meat's ready. Come on, there's enough for everybody."

"The hell with your meat," Pedro says, furious. "Let's get out of here."

He takes off like a bat out of hell. Pedro, Pedro, La Murciélaga calls after him, trying to catch up. Did you call her cell? She doesn't have a cell phone, he says. O.K., so call the number she called you from, Julieth suggests. Pedro whirls around and says, do you think I'm an idiot, that's the first thing I did, and this dude answered who said he'd lent her the phone, full stop. That's super sketchy, says La Murciélaga. And Julieth says, don't get all worked up over it, she probably went off with some guy. Pedro stops again. Julieth says, don't look at me like that, you know what she's like.

Inside the house, the singers seem to have reached the song's climax. Pedro grabs his head and yells, "In my dictatorship, pansy-ass parties like this will be outlawed!"

La Murciélaga puts her arm around him and leads him to the car. Julieth and I follow behind as the people in the house keep intoning hoarsely, *thank you to life, thank you to life, thank you to liiiiiife.*

17

Death brought Charlie and Larry together. For her, it was her father's, a noble death, that of a prominent, well-respected man. Larry's father, on the other hand, was a criminal, disappeared, unseemly even in death. She would have a corpse she still remembered, elegant and done up for the funeral. She'd be able to hug it and weep over it. Whereas Larry would find a heap of bones, maybe with a bullet hole in its skull, a grin of false teeth, or a shattered femur.

Charlie slept, and Larry pondered why people attach so much importance to the dead body when the thing that really hurts is the absence.

Is it just so they can be certain the person's dead? . . .

"I fell asleep," Charlie said, and he started. "I'm thirsty," she added.

"I'll bring you some water," Larry told her, then realized he hadn't addressed her by the formal *usted*.

Before he could get up, she downed the last dregs of gin and melted ice in her glass, gulping as if it were water. Larry took the opportunity to shift in his seat and stretch a bit.

"Did you rest any?" he asked.

"I don't know," she said. "I don't really know how I feel. Everything hurts, and at the same time I don't feel anything. I don't know if this moment is real or if I'm making it up so I can get through the flight. I want it to be over already and at the same time I want it to never end, for us to keep flying till . . ."

She fell silent and closed her eyes again. Two fat tears rolled down her cheeks and disappeared somewhere on her neck.

"Rest here if you like," Larry said, gesturing to his shoulder.

"I'll get your shirt wet."

"I don't mind."

"Plus I feel guilty falling asleep," Charlie said.

"Guilty?"

"It feels unfair that he's dead and I'm sleeping."

"But . . ." Larry was going to say, but he's dead. He stopped and said, "You need to rest, you've got a hard day ahead of you."

"I've got a hard life ahead of me."

"It's tough at first," Larry murmured. "You think you're not going to be able to do it, but after a while . . ."

"How long?"

"I don't know, it depends. Maybe months, maybe years. When you least expect it, you feel like somebody's tugging on you."

"Who?"

"I don't know. Something or somebody. An invisible hand, an unknown force. Suddenly you feel yourself being pulled, and without realizing it, you're on the other side."

"Who helped you?" she asked without looking at him, lying on his shoulder, in a voice he wouldn't have even heard if they hadn't been so close together.

"Nobody."

"You?"

"Not even me."

Larry had to tell her the truth.

Reality itself opened my eyes and reached out its hand to lift me up. Libardo wasn't the solution—he was the problem. Without him, there wouldn't be any uncertainty or fear . . .

"The truth," said Larry. "The truth was what saved me."

He said it knowing that the truth was such a complicated

thing that, at that moment, Charlie wasn't going to find out more.

"What's going to save me?" she asked, more to herself than to him. Then she added, "Or who?"

They sat in silence a while, listening to the noise of the engines. They were midway across the ocean—they were a dot in the vastness, the everythingness and nothingness, an abyss between two worlds—a sort of limbo. The two of them up in the sky, traversing the night at an incredible speed inside a metal tube full of fuel. They both were leaving an old era and entering a new one.

"Thank you," Charlie said.

Something vibrated inside Larry, a shiver wrapping him from head to toe, something like a signal for his heart. Suddenly, a passenger let out a thunderous snore that drowned out the drone of the engines. Charlie laughed loudly, the first time the whole flight. Larry laughed too.

"I envy him," he said.

"Go to sleep, then."

"I'd rather talk to you."

"So let's talk about something else," Charlie suggested. Two more snores rang out, and they laughed again. "Where do you think we are?" she asked.

"In the middle of nowhere," he replied.

18

Where did we get the idea that after Escobar's death, we'd wake up in a city cradled by birdsong and morning rain, refreshed by the warm breeze on sunny afternoons? That wasn't the kind of city we were built for—we weren't made to live in paradise. Escobar's own son, his blood still hot, had sworn vengeance, and even though he spoke in the haste of a tantrum, the fury in his words had whipped up hate. The men who'd slain the monster weren't content with cutting off its head. They wanted to gobble up its corpse, right down to the entrails. The government, borne along by momentum like a lumbering tank, was looking to finish the job. Libardo started getting cabin fever, and Fernanda decided to go back to the casinos, even if it meant being escorted by a couple of the boys. It was the only place she felt relaxed.

In the enormous house, the bunker Libardo had built to protect us, my brother and I used to hang out every afternoon, staring at each other or watching TV to learn about all the things Libardo and Fernanda refused to tell us. We speculated about what would happen next and what we would do. I was set on fleeing, but Julio wanted to stay. His passion was the family's farms; he hadn't even considered going to college, wanted to start running them straight out of high school, overseeing the livestock and harvests.

"I'll die if I have to go live somewhere else," he used to tell me. "Move to another city and, even worse, speak another language."

"You might get killed if you stay," I said.

"I'd rather die of a bullet than of sadness," he said.

Looking at each other, what we saw was two pipsqueaks talking about life and death, surrounded by bodyguards and maids. The fragile calm we enjoyed was sheltered by Libardo's fortune. In a world where money determined everything, we believed that money would get us absolution too. But we hadn't figured that the money was going to run out sooner rather than later.

Escobar's family was urgently seeking asylum, though they were a hot potato that no country wished to take on. If even they were looking for a new life abroad, how could we not leave too? We weren't bound to them by any sort of affection, though in a way their life resembled ours.

Libardo never told me, but I overheard him saying it to someone else: the shipments will get taken care of—there's too much money and power involved for an empire to collapse overnight. He said with convincing frankness: our national hypocrisy will save us. But his optimism was belied by his irritable mood, the insults he hurled out left and right, the threats he issued whenever he talked on the phone, and especially the fear that showed on his face.

Things weren't any better at school. For starters, nobody had expected us back. They'd assumed we'd gone into hiding, so there was a huge commotion when we showed up under increased protection. Our bodyguards had instructions not to budge from the school all day. We weren't the only ones; I'm not sure how many other students like us there were.

That first day, Fernanda insisted on speaking to the headmaster. Her presence at the school always caused a stir. She knew it and encouraged it. She'd get herself dolled up like back when she was a beauty queen and wear tight blouses so her tits would bounce when she walked. At first it was nice knowing our mother was pretty, but as we got older, the tenor of our classmates' comments changed. They lusted after Fernanda, or at least that's what they wanted us to think. That day, she fixed herself up nicer than ever. She needed to show that nothing had changed and put space between all of us and the death of Libardo's boss.

"You deserve special treatment," she told us, though I didn't understand why she wanted them to favor us. Was she looking to turn the tables and have us switch to being victims instead of victimizers? It was a nice concept, but she'd have to persuade an entire nation, the whole world, everybody who was pointing zealous fingers at us.

We arrived in two SUVs, and four of the boys, four of Libardo's fighters, piled out and opened Fernanda's door, offering her a supportive hand so she could descend elegantly in her high heels. I felt as if the entire school, students, teachers, and staff, were all turning to stare at us. Some of the youngest kids came up to her thinking she was who knows who. Fernanda tousled the hair of a few of them. She smiled at all of them. Julio and I kept our eyes glued to the floor as we climbed the stairs to the headmaster's office. Fernanda's heels rapped like stone on the steps.

"I'm here to see Mr. Estrada," she announced herself.

They didn't ask who was making the request. They already knew her. Libardo's wife. Libardo's kids.

"If you don't mind waiting, Doña Fernanda," the assistant said. "The headmaster's on the phone just now, but he'll be with you momentarily."

She settled on a sofa in the waiting room and signaled for us to sit beside her. I shook my head no; Julio didn't even respond. I made one last attempt: "Let's go, Ma."

"No sir. I need to remind him of several things he has an obligation to understand."

The obligation she was referring to was a number of commitments the school had made to us in exchange for favors received. A new chemistry lab. Twenty-five computers. New sound equipment for the auditorium. Ten TVs, one of which ended up in the headmaster's office, to mention just a few of Libardo's donations in the past year alone.

"You can go in now," the assistant told Fernanda.

The headmaster couldn't mask his discomfort. He was so exaggeratedly kind that it was obvious he was faking. Who knows what doubts and feelings were gnawing at him as he watched Fernanda sit down in front of his desk, the two of us by her side, coquettish and serene as if nothing were happening.

"I thought you were still off on a long trip," Estrada said. "In one of those exotic countries Don Libardo's so fond of."

"Duty first, Enrique," Fernanda said.

"That's all well and good," the headmaster said. "But with the country in such chaos . . . A lot of our families have gone to live abroad, and I thought you had too . . ."

He was probing, groping, brazenly weighing us up, smiling, slavering.

"Not at all, Enrique," Fernanda declared. "Here we are, and here we're staying. This is the boys' last year, and it's better for them to finish their studies in the same place. This school is like home to us now."

Estrada offered thanks, bobbed his head, mentioned the positive outcomes they'd achieved thanks to Libardo's contributions. He blew sunshine, but through pointed teeth. He invoked morality, adherence to norms, principles, our generosity, and my talents, my math skills, my good grades in general. Of Julio he merely said, the boy takes after his father. He's a good boy, he added. And when he finally said, what can I do for you, Fernanda leaned forward slightly to make her case.

"Our family's going through a difficult time right now," she began.

"I imagine so," the headmaster said.

"Julio and Larry may be all grown up now, but they're sensitive, and this new situation is affecting them deeply. I haven't tried to hide anything from them: they know everything, and though Libardo and I avoid arguing in front of them, we're under a great deal of pressure and do sometimes make mistakes."

"I understand perfectly," Estrada said.

"I'm sure that in the coming year they're going to do their very best. That's why I've brought them with me today, so they can commit to being good students despite the unfortunate circumstances, to work hard and get good grades."

Estrada smiled at us. Fernanda kept going: "However, Enrique, in exchange I'd like to ask you to talk to the teachers and urge them to have a little extra patience with them, to take into account that my boys' home life has fallen apart."

"With luck all of this will pass," the headmaster broke in.

"No, Enrique, no," Fernanda said. By now there wasn't much left of the woman who'd walked in. Her expression was gloomy, and she was no longer flirting or speaking in the cheerful tone she'd started out with. "No," she repeated, and shook her head. Her voice cracking, she said, "Libardo isn't going to leave that woman, no matter what happens."

"What?" Julio interrupted her.

"It's the truth," said Fernanda. Sobbing, she added, "He's in love with her."

"That's why you came here?" I asked. "That's why you brought us?"

"Boys," the headmaster said, trying to placate us.

"This is ridiculous," Julio said, then got up and left.

Fernanda covered her face, still weeping.

"You're unbelievable, Ma," I told her. "We're all going to be killed, and the only thing you care about is Dad's mistresses."

"What do you mean, you're all going to be killed?" Estrada asked, confused.

Fernanda shook her head, but she couldn't speak. So I got up and left too.

"Julio, Larry," Estrada called out as I disappeared through the door. The whole school was in class now. I saw Julio walking rapidly toward his class. I went over to the railing of the bridge connecting the offices with the classrooms, and there, from the third floor, I saw Libardo's men leaning on the SUVs, smoking and laughing. One of them was even racing around the car after another one, the two of them chasing each other like children. And I saw Pedro the Dictator get out of another car and run toward the classrooms, all in a rush, already late on the first day of school.

19

It isn't love that makes the world go round, I tell them, it's economics. And then I ask, remember Clinton? The one who got the blow job?, Pedro the Dictator asks. That's the one, I say, though I'd meant the president, not the man. What are you talking about?, La Murciélaga asks, who got a blow job? And Julieth says, what does that have to do with the topic at hand? You were talking about love, princess, Pedro says. Sure, Julieth replies, but why's this dude bringing economics and that gringo into it? Because Larry's an economist, remember, Pedro says. I'm not an economist, I say again, I started but never finished. You may not have finished, Pedro says, but if they saved your credits you're still a work in progress. You guys are such dorks, says La Murciélaga. I was talking about those people, the ones singing at the house, says Julieth, they believe in love. Well, if love means I have to sit around singing with a guitar by a fireplace in a room that smells like burnt meat, I'd rather be alone for the rest of my life, La Murciélaga says. No, Murci, I'm not talking about romantic love, Julieth says, that's not what I mean, but I do think those guys have got a different kind of power. Who's got the hooch?, Pedro asks, and La Murciélaga pulls half a bottle of aguardiente out of her purse. You go first, the Dictator tells her.

The bottle passes from mouth to mouth; when it's his turn to drink, Pedro takes a swig without even slowing down. I, for one, believe in universal love, says Julieth. What kind's that?, Pedro asks. Where everybody loves everybody else, La

Murciélaga says. Then I believe in universal love too, says Pedro, and Julieth punches him in the shoulder. Dumbass, she says, I'm talking about the force that makes the world go round. Economics, I say. Oh, no, no, no, Julieth exclaims, and clutches her head. What a bunch of idiots, you know what I'm saying, stop screwing around.

We move up the Las Palmas highway at the snail's pace that the traffic permits, along with the rest of the crowd looking to watch the fireworks from a good vantage point. Thousands of lights explode in the sky above Medellín, from one end to the other, as if the entire valley were erupting. As if all of Medellín were a volcano. Roll another joint, Murci, we're going to be here a while, Pedro says. I've got one ready, she replies. Light it up, then. Nobody answered me about the volcano, I say. What? The name of the sleeping volcano in the middle of Medellín. Hahahaha, La Murciélaga cracks up. Nothing and nobody in the city is sleeping right now, Julieth says. Lowering the window, she adds, listen to that noise out there. Open all the windows to let the smoke out, Pedro orders. And the smell, says La Murciélaga, my hair ends up reeking of weed and tomorrow my mom's going to ask me what's that weird smell. Don't tell me your mom hasn't tried it, Murci, Julieth says. My mom?, oh man, you clearly haven't met her. No way, Julieth says, we always think our parents don't do anything, that they've never done anything, when in fact they've done all the same things we have and more. My dad doesn't know the difference between a line of coke and a joint, Pedro says. La Murciélaga laughs. Mine have tried it, Julieth says. What? Marijuana. What about coke? I don't think so, but marijuana they have, Julieth says. She turns to look at me and says, do you remember those nights out on the town with your mom, Larry?

La Murciélaga passes me the hydroponic joint, and in her dark eyes I see curiosity and compassion. Epic nights out,

Pedro says, just epic, Fernanda is unstoppable. Is?, I ask, is she still partying? I mean, she's got a lot of energy, Pedro says.

A car goes by, and they shoot a bottle rocket or a roman candle at us, I don't know, something glittery and deafening that whizzes past our windshield like a bolt of lightning. La Murciélaga screams and Pedro yells, fucking assholes! He stomps on the gas to go after them, but there isn't much he can do with all the traffic and the bendy road. Do you see her often?, I ask Pedro, who's still cursing: those bastards practically fired that fucking thing right through our window! He keeps speeding up and braking, trying to pass the cars ahead of us. At the karaoke bar, a friend of my dad's asked me how my mom was doing, do you know anything about that, Pedro? I want to see their face when I shove those fireworks up their ass, Pedro says. They're nuts, says La Murciélaga, who's only just now recovering from the fright. What's my mom up to, Pedro? Pedro, you're going to get us killed, Julieth yells. Let them go, you're never going to catch up, says La Murciélaga, and adds, it just scared us—we're over it. They did it deliberately, Pedro says, are you over that too, you chickenshits? He gives up, though he's still fuming, if I run into them up there, they'll see, they'll see. He looks at me furiously and says, we're in full-on combat mode here and you're asking me about your mom, give me a break, Larry.

We merge with the line of cars, like everybody else. The music on the radio and the fireworks fill the silence that descends after Pedro's fit of rage. Maybe Julieth and La Murciélaga are thinking the same thing I am, that those people deserve to get their asses kicked. Pedro's cell phone rings and we all jump. Our defenses are still low. I still don't understand why I can't go home yet. Why's Fernanda punishing me with exile my very first day back? The Dictator could turn down the music to talk more comfortably, but instead he's shouting at the top of his lungs. He curses, insults, roars with laughter, getting worked up, tells the person on the other end of the line what happened: a crappy little dark blue Mazda, he says, yeah, a 323 with three twats on board, if you see them let me know. Who are you talking to?, La Murciélaga asks, but he doesn't answer, instead telling the other person, just think, if that bottle rocket had come through the window it would have ruined this handsome mug. He laughs again and curses again. La Murciélaga stubs out the joint in the ashtray. Julieth looks at me, and I tell her, I don't know what I'm doing here. La Murciélaga turns around and says enthusiastically, it's La Alborada, sweetie.

Outside I see the orange sky and, down below us, the glow. The noise and euphoria summon Dylan Thomas once more to the tip of my tongue—"wise men at their end know dark is right"—and Thomas summons her once more to my memory. Are you sure you don't know a Charlie who lives in London?, I ask Julieth and La Murciélaga. Male or female?, Julieth asks. Oh, so tedious, La Murciélaga says. Female, I tell Julieth. Pedro ends his conversation, and La Murciélaga asks again, who were you talking to? That was Ro, he replies, they're already up there, at the overlook past El Peñasco. Who is she, what does she look like?, Julieth asks me. Some woman he met on the plane, La Murciélaga answers. She's got black hair down to like here, I tell Julieth, gesturing to just below my shoulder. Her dad died day before yesterday, I say. Hers too?, Julieth says. Mine died a long time ago, I point out. At this rate, Pedro says, the fireworks will be over by the time we get there. She's got a small nose and a pale complexion, I continue, but Julieth isn't listening, nor anybody else. They start belting out the reggaeton song that comes on the radio.

Boom boom, let it go boom, pump up the room, if things are feeling hot, make her zoom-zoom.

But I'm overcome with sleepiness. I rest my head on the back of the seat and once again look out and down, toward the smoking crater that's about to erupt.

20

Out of nowhere, as if they were old friends, Charlie asked him to tell her a secret.

"What kind of secret?" Larry asked, and she said, "One that no more than two people know."

"A secret . . ." said Larry, pretending to think, and she laughed. She had him trapped.

There was no way out, no possible excuse: everybody's got a secret, or lots of them. A sin, a hidden desire, a loathing that nobody else knows, an aberration.

"Tell you what," Charlie said. "Hand me your glass, and while you're thinking I'll go get us some more gin."

"On one condition: you tell me one too."

They shook on the deal, and she went to fetch the drinks. Larry still felt cornered. When she returned, he tried to throw her off: "I have several varieties of secrets. Which kind do you want? Level C is little secrets, level B is regular secrets, and level A is big secrets."

"Level A, of course."

"I need more time for that kind of secret," he said. "But I've got some real high-quality level C ones."

"I'm willing to negotiate. Tell me a level B secret."

They clinked their glasses and drank. Larry cleared his throat.

"A few years back, not long after I arrived in London, having decided it was where I was going to live, I did my first grocery run and spotted these bags of lentils and tossed one in my cart because I was craving a home-cooked meal. I called my mom for the recipe; she doesn't cook, but she asked around and found out for me. Since I didn't have a pressure cooker, it was going to be a slow process, but I wasn't in a hurry. I just left the lentils cooking and would occasionally go in and stir them with a wooden spoon. I started watching a movie on TV, and by the time I got back to the kitchen, the spoon wasn't there anymore."

Larry fell silent. Charlie prodded him. "And?"

"It disappeared. Maybe it dissolved in the soup."

Charlie looked at him mockingly. Crossing her arms, she asked, "So what's the secret?"

"Well, nobody else knows that story."

"No, that doesn't count."

"What about if I tell you that I once, in a fit of love-induced spite, drank two bottles of whiskey all by myself, sitting on a wall beside the Thames?"

"That doesn't either."

"Aha," Larry said. He leaned his head back and pondered. She watched him. Feeling awkward under the pressure, he said, "Once, when I left school, instead of going home I told the driver to take us to Éxito. I was with two friends, and we knew exactly why we were going: to shoplift."

"Hang on," Charlie broke in. "That doesn't count either."

"Let me finish," Larry said. "The secret isn't the shoplifting. So yeah, we were going to steal things, stupid crap we could stick in our pockets and down our pants. We'd done it once before. We each got our own stash and then bought something cheap to explain the alarm. We'd showed the guard our receipt and walked through. The alarm went off, and they let us through. That's how it worked the first time, and we thought it would be exactly the same."

"Did you get caught?"

"Hold your horses. We waited in line at different cash

registers, and before we'd paid, a man in a suit and tie came up to one of my friends. He took him off to get my other friend, and finally they came for me. The man asked us to go with him. He led us to this little room, like an office supply storeroom. He asked us to empty our pockets. We refused, and he threatened to call the police. At that, very slowly, we started putting the items we'd stolen on a table."

"What did you steal?"

"A bunch of crap, like I said. I'd nicked some dental floss, a lipstick . . ."

"A lipstick?"

"I wanted to give it to my mother." Larry took a sip and cleared his throat. Something changed in his voice. "The man ordered us to pull down our pants. We refused again, and again he threatened to turn us over to the police. Reluctantly, we unbuttoned our pants and pulled them halfway down our thighs. A few more small things fell out. He told us to put them on the table, next to the others. Then he felt around my friends' underwear, and when he got to me, he didn't just feel around outside."

"Jesus," Charlie said, and Larry nodded. "What did you do?"

Larry took another long sip and said, "Nothing. I think I closed my eyes . . ." He took a deep breath and added, "No. I didn't, because I clearly remember the look on my friends' faces. All three of us were shaking, and they were staring at me in horror. Maybe they thought the guy was going to do the same thing to them, but he fondled me for a while and then told us to leave, said if he ever saw us there again, the next search would be at the police station."

"That's outrageous."

"Yeah. When I got home, I heaved my guts out."

"You didn't tell your parents?"

Larry shook his head.

If I answer that question, I'll have to reveal another secret. If

I'd told Fernanda, she definitely would have told Libardo, and he'd have killed me for letting somebody touch me, he'd have killed the man who touched me, all of the employees, the owners, he'd have blown up the store, every single location, the delivery trucks, the billboards, everything, absolutely everything . . .

"No," Larry said, "it stayed between me and my friends, and we never talked about it again."

Charlie let out an indignant sigh. The noise of the engines was ricocheting inside their skulls. Larry shook his head and said, "All right, your turn."

21

Fernanda taught me how to dance. Before I even learned to walk, I was dancing with her. She'd lift me up in her arms—she listened to music constantly—and she'd rock in time to the songs, always love songs. When I was up to her waist, we used to dance at parties, and she'd tell me I was her favorite dance partner. I kept dancing with her when I was the same height, and later when I was taller too. Eventually I didn't enjoy it so much—I was ashamed to dance with my mom. These days, I'm too self-conscious to dance. It strikes me as a somewhat ludicrous activity; I don't see the point of it, whether it's about self-expression, celebration, emotions, or a million other things that have never really convinced me. But Fernanda insisted. She knew Julio was a lost cause. She said Libardo had no rhythm. You're the only one, sweetheart—and she'd ask me with so much love in her eyes that I'd end up relenting, the two of us always turning into the main attraction for anybody watching.

Fernanda was way out of Libardo's league. She wasn't from a wealthy or prominent family—she was a normal girl, middle class, but pretty and ambitious. He was from humbler stock—very, very humble. He dropped out of high school and joined the street gangs in the upper section of San Cristóbal. When I asked him what he used to do in the gangs, he told me, we did everything, we fucked shit up everywhere, we were always getting into trouble. He even sounded nostalgic about it. When I asked him how he met Escobar, he told me Benito had introduced them. And when I asked him why he did what he did, he told me, because that's how life is, kid, you'll understand that one day.

I never did understand, but I figured it was like being born black or white, tall or short. That was what we were, end of story. Though there was always something or some-body to remind me who I was. At first it used to piss me off— I would come to blows. Now I just brush it off.

Once, after a kiss, a girlfriend, my very first one, told me, you're not to blame for what you are. It was true, but that didn't clear me of the burden. Fernanda often told me the same thing when I was freaking out about being Libardo's son. And then she'd give me a hug because ultimately she, too, was "to blame" for what I was. Over the course of my life, I've heard it a million times: you're not to blame for what you are. I heard it over and over until the phrase wore out and lost all meaning.

Another girlfriend in London told me that too, the one I decided to tell my story to because I was convinced I'd found the love of my life. You're not to blame, Larry. And I said, shove your platitude up your ass, and she stormed out in a fury and I never saw her again. I later realized that when women said that, they weren't really saying it to me but to themselves instead, rationalizing being friends with me, kissing me, having sex with me. If you're not to blame, then neither is anybody else. Just like that, easy-peasy.

The only person I'd have wanted to hear the phrase from was Libardo himself, but he never said it. Even after the many times I told him he was to blame, he kept quiet. It took me a long time to realize he stayed quiet because he didn't feel any blame. He never felt guilty about his actions: the accusations never bothered him, he wasn't tormented by his crimes, and he hadn't decided to have children so he could be burdened with remorse. He must have understood it from birth, what he told me that time: that's how life is, Larry.

At any rate, you always had to interpret what was behind Libardo's words. When he told us, I want you to go to the best school, to speak English, French, whatever languages you can, to study at the best university, to start companies, it was his way of telling us he didn't want us to be like him, who never went to college or even finished high school and who spoke street Spanish. He didn't want us to follow in his footsteps.

He used to brag about his friendships with important politicians and businessmen, about the deals they made and the meetings they invited him to. And the thing he boasted about most was the parties. Him and his beauty queen, because they didn't invite him without Fernanda. Until one day she realized something.

"None of the other men take their wives," Fernanda said, connecting dots.

"Of course they do," he said.

"They bring their girlfriends, mistresses, whatever," Fernanda said, "but none of them are married to the women they take."

Libardo huffed. "What do you know?"

"I've seen photos of them in the society pages with very different women. They're lying to you, Libardo. They want to make you think you're one of them, but they only invite you to the parties they take their hussies to. And they're putting me on that same level."

Libardo grumbled, perturbed. "I'm not going to butt into their lives," he said. "They can sleep with whatever women they want. Those parties are where we do business."

"Well, you're going to have to go on your own from now on. I'm not going to be considered one of those tramps."

Fernanda wasn't looking at him as she spoke, emphasizing her irritation. He got up, walked to the window, and stared out.

"Did you know?" she asked.

"No," he said. "I don't pay attention to those things."

They were both quiet a while, and then it was Fernanda who stood up and said, "I'm going to have them serve dinner."

"Fernanda."

She stopped.

"Given what you've said," Libardo asked, "are you sure you want me going alone?"

"Is that a threat?"

Libardo didn't respond. He kept looking at her, leaning against the glass. She took a step forward and said, "I hope I'm wrong. I hope that when you need those guys, they'll have your back."

She left the room, leaving a trail of truth behind her.

That same night, after dinner, we were in their room watching TV when Libardo told Fernanda, "The deputy attorney general agreed to talk to us. But I'm not going. One of the Arangos, a Molina, and Benito are going in my place."

I looked at Fernanda, whose demeanor was like a thermometer for measuring her reaction. She was concentrating on a small hand mirror, plucking her eyebrows. She arched them, brought them together by scrunching her forehead, raised them again, brought the mirror close to her face, and skillfully kept tweezing.

"Didn't the Arangos turn themselves in?" she asked.

"Just Jonathan."

I looked at her again to see if her expression had changed, if she was looking at Libardo, but she was still focused on her eyebrows. Suddenly she moved the mirror, and her eyes met mine. I looked swiftly back at the television.

"So you're going to surrender too," Fernanda said.

"No fucking way," Libardo said. "The Diago meeting isn't official."

Fernanda got up from the bed and went into the bathroom. Libardo kept talking: "Pablo implicated him in the group. I think he's playing dumb and we're going to have to have a talk with him. If he helps us get the government off our backs, it'll give us some breathing room to fight the other bastards."

Fernanda peered out and said, "Larry, Julio, look at the time. It's going to be impossible to get you up in the morning."

As I left, I heard Fernanda say to Libardo, don't talk to them the way you talk to your people. He said, I wasn't talking to them, and anyway they're men now. Then don't talk to me like that, Fernanda said, and don't act like a thug in front of your sons. Libardo raised his voice, indignant: Thug? Thug? I couldn't make out anything after that; I didn't want to hear what came next.

A little while later, after I was in bed and had turned out the light, Fernanda came into the room.

"Larry."

My heart started beating faster. When she came in like that, it was because something had happened between them. I always used to wonder why she came to me and not Julio. Sure, I was more like her, I looked like her and had her features, shared her sensitivity and some of her tastes, but Julio was her son too, the older one, and it should have been his job to console her. But she chose me, her kindred spirit, as she told everybody we were—she used to say it proudly, like a peacock, and her eyes would shine, her words sparkle.

"You asleep, Larry?

She came over to the bed and groped for the edges of the mattress so she didn't bump into it. Sometimes, when she came to my room like that, it was because she'd been drinking and she'd trip over a shoe, over some clothes I hadn't picked up, or she'd get lost in the darkness and end up on the floor, laughing uncontrollably. I didn't find it at all amusing to see her sprawled on the floor, collapsed in laughter, crawling over to my bed, where she'd climb in, reeking of alcohol.

"Larry?"

She was sober now. She smelled like the creams she applied before bed.

"Larry."

I shifted a little. There wasn't much point in pretending to be asleep. It never put her off. I moved over to give her room. She lifted the sheets and slipped into bed. She spooned me from behind and murmured, "I don't want to sleep with him."

"What's wrong?"

"He's really worked up. It's best to leave him alone."

"What's going to happen to us, Ma?"

"Nothing, darling," she said, and ran her fingers through my hair, and then, as if time had ceased passing, as if I hadn't gotten older and she was still dandling me in her arms, she added, "Go to sleep now, sweetie."

22

At midnight the sky over Medellín turns to day. December has arrived amid the inebriation and fireworks.

"It's December, Pops!" Pedro the Dictator exclaims, and hugs me enthusiastically, as if December almost hadn't come.

The noise stuns and shakes the ground; the sky turns white, yellow, red, and silver. Medellín is a castle of pyrotechnic toys that's exploded. The people crowded along the overlooks chug aguardiente straight from the bottle, leap and shout, climb onto car roofs to shout louder, and some are even singing the Antioquian anthem. There's something touching about all this excitement. Maybe it's all that time I spent abroad, the years I had no homeland.

"*Oh, liberty that perfumes the mountains of my land,*" La Murciélaga sings, or rather shrieks, lifting her shirt and displaying her own ample, voluptuous mountains—bounteous, the poets might say. Around her the men whistle and holler; she covers herself again and lets out an extravagant laugh.

"*Let my children breathe in your fragrant essences.*" Pedro finishes the lyric from Antioquia's anthem.

There's so much excitement in the air that even Ro hugs me. He emerges from the crowd, we come face to face, and it's as if he has no other option but to hug me. He attempts sincerity: "I don't know what's up between me and you, but I forgive you," he says.

Would you believe that bastard. Am I supposed to thank him for his forgiveness? I know exactly what's up between him and me, but the distance and the years of absence have made me wary. Or simply a stranger.

"Relax, man," I tell him. "We're all good."

Later it's Julieth who goes honest on me. She pins me against one side of the SUV and, pressing close, whispers, "That kiss you gave me woke up some memories."

The look on her face suggests she's about to go for another one. But I feel like my mouth stinks, reeking of aguardiente, marijuana, airplane cabin, all these hours I've been awake. It feels dry with fatigue, sticky with lack of sleep.

"What do you say if later on . . . ?" Julieth says.

"I don't think so," I say. "I haven't been able to get home to say hi to my mom."

"Oh, right," Julieth says. "I'd forgotten about the funeral."

"No, that's not it."

"Anyway," she interrupts me, "don't go yet. That kiss got me thinking."

"Larry!" Pedro calls to me in the distance and lifts his arm, holding the cell phone in his hand. "It's Fernanda!"

I scurry away from Julieth and rush toward him. I snatch the phone and use my hand as a barrier between the noise and my mouth.

"Ma?"

"Hello?"

"Ma."

There's noise here and noise there; she can't hear me and I can't hear her.

"Ma, don't hang up."

I get in the car and try to close the windows, but the key isn't in the ignition.

"Larry, where are you? I can't hear you."

"I'm in Las Palmas, at a viewpoint."

"Larry?"

"Ma, you're not coming in clear, but I can hear you."

"There's a huge racket here," Fernanda says. "The fireworks woke me up."

"What, Ma?"

I look around to see if I can spot Pedro. I need the keys.

"Why aren't you here yet, Larry?"

"You said I shouldn't come."

"Speak up, I can't hear you."

"I'm heading there now. I'll find someone to take me."

"I can't sleep with these fireworks, honey."

"Don't go to sleep, wait for me."

"Come again?"

"Don't go to sleep."

"Larry, the connection's really bad."

"What's that, Ma?"

"This is so frustrating," Fernanda says.

I stick my head out the window and see Julieth dancing with a dozen strangers. "Julieth," I call to her, "where's Pedro? I need the keys."

"I don't know," she says. "He's around."

"Pedro's got keys," Fernanda tells me.

"No, Ma, I'm looking for Pedro so he can give me the car keys."

"He's got keys," Fernanda says again.

"The car keys, Ma."

"Larry," she says, "I don't know if you can hear me. Call me right back from somewhere else."

"Ma, don't hang up!"

I curse the phone and everything around me. Screw tonight, fuck La Alborada. I stick my head out the window and yell, why don't you all shut up, assholes? Nobody hears me; they all stare at me, laughing. Julieth dances up and sticks her tongue in my mouth.

"I couldn't wait," she says.

"I have to go."

"No, come on, lame-o."

"Help me find Pedro."

"Did you not like it?"

"I have to get my suitcase."

"Is it because of that girl you met on the plane? I'll tell you right now, I don't care—I've got a boyfriend too."

"Julieth, I haven't slept since yesterday and I haven't seen my mom in three years."

"And I love him," she says. "We've been together five months, and he's the man for me, but that doesn't mean what you and I had wasn't important to me, Larry."

Some moron tosses a string of firecrackers that goes off right between our feet, and Julieth and I are forced to hop around to the rhythm of the explosions. The man points and laughs and his friends egg him on. I grab him by the shirt, yank him toward me, and yell in his face, "What's your problem, motherfucker?"

His friends intervene. Careful, buddy, they warn me. Julieth butts in too: "Chill, everybody chill, he just arrived, he lives in England, and he's not used to this."

"Let go of me, asshole," says the guy who threw the firecrackers at us.

"Let him go, Larry," Julieth hisses at me, rolling her eyes as if warning me that something worse might happen.

"Leave me the fuck alone," I tell the guy.

"England's clearly rubbed off on you," he says.

Julieth digs her nails into my arm and says again, "Let him go, Larry. What he did is normal here."

"That's why you're all so fucked," I say, as if I weren't another fucked Colombian myself.

I let go of the guy, and he goes off with the others, all of them giving me dirty looks.

"I had no idea you were so violent," Julieth admonishes me.

"I'm not," I say. "He attacked us."

Julieth spreads her arms wide and gestures to the sky, to Medellín in front of us, exploding in a crackle of lights. "What's wrong with you?" she says. "It's La Alborada, don't you get it?"

Everything's justified here. Fireworks, violence, bullets, dead bodies . . . all our evils have an excuse. And from pretext we move on to resignation, and from there to complete acceptance, as if it were normal. But if I say all that, I'll look like a party pooper, and if I say the only thing I want right now, with all my heart, is to see my mother, I'll look like a dumbass.

"Help me look for Pedro," I say.

"He left the car unlocked, so he'll be back any minute. Also," she adds, "don't move from here or somebody'll steal the stereo."

The guy who threw the firecrackers at us comes up again. His friends are still with him and he's got a bottle of aguardiente.

"Hey, buddy, come here," he says, though he's the one approaching me. "Let's be friends, here, have a swig."

I take a long swallow to calm my fury. Everybody notices, and they laugh and try to smooth things over with another joke.

"Dude's a big drinker, huh."

"My name is Arthur," the guy joshes in English, doing a sad imitation of a British accent. He laughs wanly and says, "No, man, I'm kidding. The name's Arturo, but everybody calls me Artu."

I don't say anything. Julieth speaks instead.

"He's Larry."

"Larry what?" they ask.

Julieth eyes me carefully, the way people always look at me whenever I have to say who I am.

"Larry," I say, and then, after a pause, I add, "The son of God."

They celebrate my joke by passing the bottle around, from Artu to Julieth and around until it comes back to me and I drink again. The aguardiente kicks me in the gut, makes my insides shudder, sets my stomach and my face on fire, warns me that I've had enough.

"No more," I say, coughing alcohol.

A cloud of smoke drifts over us. It comes from down below, from Medellín, and it smells like sulfur. They'll say it's the smell of the fireworks, but to me the smell says that down there, nothing is O.K.

23

W here to even start?" Charlie said. "I'm nothing but secrets."

It sounded like she was confiding in him, as if that were her contribution to their game, which she was already showing signs of regretting. Now she was the victim of her own invention.

"We're all hiding something," Larry said. "We always take a secret with us when we die."

"When something overrides your willpower, it feels like you need to hide it," Charlie said, staring at the no-smoking sign. She moistened her lips with the glass and grabbed Larry's hand. She said, "Let me think."

"We can drop it if you want," Larry said, his eyes fixed on her hand holding his.

"What?"

"The secrets thing."

"No, no. It's my turn. Just give me a minute."

She let go of his hand and sat there quietly. Larry stealthily brought the hand she'd held up to his nose and then his mouth, grazing it against his lips just as she had with the glass.

Out of nowhere, Charlie laughed loudly. The other people in their row, who were sleeping, shifted in their seats. She covered her mouth, still laughing.

"I don't know if I should tell you this," she said.

"You don't have to," Larry said.

"I'd forgotten all about it. Seems like everything that has to do with my dad is coming back."

"That's natural."

"There's nothing natural about what I'm about to tell you," she said, and began: "Once, before putting on my school uniform, I went to pull out some underwear and the maid had accidentally put some of my dad's underwear in my drawer." She laughed again, though it seemed more like she was buying time. "I saw they weren't as big as I'd have guessed. I was as tall as him, since he was pretty short. And he was slim—he took care of himself. They smelled clean when I sniffed them so I put them on. They were too big, but they stayed up. They were those boxer-brief things."

Larry ran his hand through his hair. He glanced over at the window, but the shade was down.

"I left them on, put on my skirt and the rest of the uniform, and I went to school like that. I didn't tell anybody. All day I kept going to the bathroom to look at myself, and I twirled and jumped around hoping somebody would notice what I was wearing underneath."

Larry gave an obliging laugh. No matter how hard he tried, he just couldn't get comfortable in his seat. Charlie sighed again and asked, "Do you want to rest, or should we have another drink?"

"What do you want?" Larry asked.

"Another drink."

"I'll go."

When he got back with the little bottles, she stared at him. "Tell me something," she said. "Am I delusional, or did you kiss the hand I was holding?"

Larry turned red. Charlie grabbed that same hand and squeezed.

24

Were there twiddling our thumbs, staring at each other, when they came to tell Libardo that the meeting with Deputy Attorney General Diago had been a failure, and he went off like dynamite. All through the house you could hear him shouting, menacing, all his threats condemning the prosecutor who'd betrayed him. Benito and Dengue tried to calm him down and explain that it wasn't a betrayal, that Diago's hands were tied.

Libardo and the few capos who had stuck together were fighting on two fronts: against the government and against Los Pepes. They were fighting the government with money, and the others with bullets. But Libardo was trying to neutralize at least one of his enemies, and with the government he had the advantage of having been almost entirely overlooked by the law. Though there were rumors that Libardo was close to Escobar, most people thought he was just a "dog washer," the lowest rank in the hierarchy of the drug lords' henchmen, one of many who surrounded Escobar to feed his ego with praise, pats on the back, and vulgar jokes. The jesters that every king requires. The gringos had him in their sights too, but they hadn't been able to prove anything, and up to the last minute they were setting traps in the hope he'd stumble into them. Among his peers, though, his exploits were well known—all those stories I refused to believe.

"Diago assures me you can relax," Benito told him. "Your files vanished when the Palace of Justice was burned."

"What about the trial in Caucasia?" Libardo asked. "Diago himself warned me there was a witness who might drag me into it."

"That's all two-bit bullshit, Libardo. Don't waste your energy on it. You need to focus on how we're going to handle the people here and in Cali."

My grandmother called Libardo into the breakfast room, where we were sitting with her. "Don't worry, Ma," he said, "everything's fine." He said that every day, and contradicted himself every time he flew off the handle.

"Why don't you go talk to him?" my grandmother suggested.

"Who?"

"Pablo."

"But . . ."

"He'll hear you out, he'll help you straighten things out, son."

My grandmother noticed we were all gaping at her in astonishment.

"I always ask the dead for help," she said. "They give the best advice. They can see the whole picture from up there . . ." She pointed to the sky and crossed herself. I caught a glimpse of Julio's face and stifled the urge to laugh. Libardo was still bewildered.

"You're saying I should go to the cemetery?"

My grandmother nodded.

"Alone?"

She shrugged.

"I'll go with you," said Julio.

"No," said Libardo.

"Go alone, son. That way the two of you can talk more easily."

I told Fernanda what my grandmother had said, and as a punishment for my tattling, I got the usual harangue. "Doña Carmenza is in no mental state to be giving advice," she said.

"Can you imagine? He'd be completely exposed in the cemetery; it's probably still full of reporters and cameras, not to mention hitmen watching to see who comes to visit and leave flowers—then they can mark them, and you know what comes after that. She may be your grandmother, but if she's saying she talks to the dead, it's because she's nuts. Sorry, but who comes up with this crap? I hope Libardo doesn't listen to her."

He half listened. He did go to the cemetery despite the warnings and visited Escobar's grave site. He wasn't there long. He couldn't concentrate, felt uncomfortable talking to a dead man, so he prowled around the grave for about fifteen minutes and then left.

"There weren't any reporters anymore, or at least none that morning," he told us. "There wasn't anybody, not even gawkers. The grave is still covered with flowers, though, and some of the bouquets have the senders' names. It's a huge pile of flowers like you wouldn't believe—it's overwhelming. I got a knot here." He touched his throat. "But I couldn't do anything," he concluded.

"You didn't talk to him?" Julio asked.

Libardo made a tired gesture.

"I could hardly believe what I was seeing," he said. "Everything that's happened up till now has been like some awful movie, but being there, practically treading on his toes, I realized what a motherfucker death is."

Fernanda took his hand. "What were you feeling?" she asked.

Libardo looked down, took a big breath, and screwed up his mouth, like he was holding down whatever he wanted to say but couldn't so as not to involve us. He picked up a glass of water from the table; I thought he was going to drink to clear his throat, to swallow his bitter pill, but he raised it and dumped the water on his head. Fernanda immediately let go of his hand.

"What are you doing, Libardo?"

He looked at Julio and me, smiled at us like when he'd been drinking, but he was sober. The water ran down his face, down his neck, and wet his shirt. He was sober, booze-wise at least. Something else had him intoxicated—maybe fear, or doubt, or, worst of all, certainty. He ran his hands through his wet hair and said to us, "Keep a cool head, boys. Above all, a cool head."

All right, chill, man, Pedro the Dictator tells me, you're going to have plenty of time to see your mom. You're going to spend so much time with her you'll get sick of her, whereas this is just once a year, he says, though in my dictatorship we'll have La Alborada once a month. Why so often?, La Murciélaga protests, it takes the fun out of it if it's a regular thing. But at least everybody's pets will get used to it, says Julieth, looking beatific. Where to now?, Pedro asks, and my heart sinks at the question. This is over, I tell them, though the night is still booming with fireworks. I'd figured that after midnight things would start settling down, but this is like a virus spreading farther by the minute. Oh is it?, Pedro says. It's not a question but an announcement: we're not done yet.

Nobody wants to go down, everybody wants to see the show from up here. Nobody, if they don't know me, is going to take me to Medellín, and the only people who know me are refusing to let me spoil their fun. Every car's playing different music, so what I hear between the explosions is a mix of rhythms, an exasperating cacophony. The bottles of aguardiente keep being passed around. The joints go from hand to hand, and there's always somebody throwing bangers at people's feet. A drunk woman with a little-girl voice and garish makeup tells me, give me a rail and I'll suck you off. I don't have any, I say, and I get in the car, turn off the radio that's going full blast, lean my head back, and, for the first time since

I arrived, wonder why the hell I came back. It wasn't because of Libardo, and not because of Fernanda or my brother either. Maybe I came back because it was time.

La Murciélaga climbs into the car, plops down next to me, and says, "They're smoking total crap out there." She rummages in her purse and pulls out the marijuana she bought. She lights the joint and says, "They're poisoning themselves with fumigated weed. Everything that grows in the ground is contaminated—rain's full of negative radiation."

"So where does the water yours is grown with come from?" I ask.

"It's run through several filters made of volcanic rock and purified with positive ions," she replies primly. "Didn't you feel, like, this powerful cosmic perception when you smoked it?"

"No," I tell her.

"No offense, Larry, but you're not very sensitive," she tells me.

She savors every hit on the joint. She inhales slowly, as if the smoke were the air she needs to live, and she holds it and then lets it out deliberately, carefully.

"This girlfriend I had used to say the same thing," I tell her, and La Murciélaga looks at me, puzzled. "She also said I was boring."

"So why was she your girlfriend?" she asks.

"Because, according to her, I wasn't like that at first."

"Flaws appear over time."

"No way," I say, "they're always there, it's just people don't see them because they're horny." La Murciélaga passes me the joint, and I take a drag. I ask, "Do you really think I'm boring?"

"I didn't say that," she says. "I said you were insensitive."

"But I do feel things."

"Even chickens feel things," she says, "but that doesn't mean they're sensitive."

"What do you know about what chickens feel?"

"They're not human beings, Larry."

"Sure, but nobody knows to what extent they feel or how they feel. It's possible they feel even more than we do."

"More than you do, I'm sure," La Murciélaga quips.

"You don't know me."

"Oh, Larry," she sighs, "you're boring me."

"See, you do think I'm boring!"

I hold out the joint, and she takes it and pinches off the cherry, then stores the rest in a little square of aluminum foil. She sighs and looks at me. "Are you getting out," she says, "or are you going to stay in here thinking about chickens?"

"I'm going to sleep till Pedro feels like taking me home."

"Sleep?" she asks, and laughs at me.

La Murciélaga gets out, and the din comes in. She closes the car door, and part of the din leaves, but only barely, and I've already got the noise deep in my body.

I close my eyes and see flashes of light. Is that the connection with the cosmos that La Murciélaga was talking about? Effects of the hydroponic pot? What state will my head be in after tonight? Right now I wish I were in London, strolling along the river, along the Embankment, thinking about returning, imagining this moment that I'm living now. The expectation was better than the reality—it's better to wish for something than to regret doing it, better to dream than to live. Maybe I'm safer here, shut up in the car, than trapped in Fernanda's embrace.

Somebody knocks on the window, and I open my eyes and see Julieth smiling at me. I blink and see her boobs pressed against the glass, pale with dark nipples that I sucked on multiple occasions. She kisses the windowpane and her mouth deforms, she laughs, and she dances off. I close my eyes.

What if I call Julio to come get me? He must have arrived from the farm by now—the three of us had planned to be all together again, like before. It's better if he's with me when I see her again.

Something explodes beside the car door, the people outside jump, and I jump. Somebody knocks on the window again and a woman calls, Pedro, Pedro! She presses her face against the glass and realizes that I'm not Pedro. And I realize that she's got to be her, the Swedish chick.

"Isn't this Pedro's SUV?" she asks.

"It is," I say.

"So who are you?"

"Larry. A friend."

"I'm looking for Pedro."

"And he's looking for you."

"Really?" she asks, and climbs into the car. She holds out her hand. "I'm Inga."

"We went to a house to look for you," I tell her. "We thought they'd dismembered you."

"What's disme . . .?"

"Dismembered," I explain. "Chopped up, cut into pieces to eat you."

Inga laughs. She's not a pretty woman, but there's something refreshing about her laugh.

"You're such goofs," she says. "They did eat me, but not like that."

She laughs again. Little by little I'm realizing that the Swedish chick is massive; she looks cramped in the seat, and this is a big SUV.

"Where's Pedrito?" she asks.

"He was there five minutes ago."

"And why are you in here on your own?"

"Because I'm tired."

"Want some coke?"

"No, I'm practically falling asleep."

"So?"

"I want to sleep. I haven't slept in I don't know how long."

"Why not?"

"I don't know. I haven't had time, I think."

Shouts break out and mingle with the explosions. They're not shouts of joy but of surprise. Inga and I look around, trying to figure out where they're coming from. What's going on?, she asks. Something must have blown up on somebody, I say, since everybody's messing around with goddamn explosives . . . Look back there, Inga says, there's a big crowd of people. I see a commotion, some people running toward it and others running away. Look, says Inga, here comes La Murciélaga. I see her. She's running toward us, laughing. Inga opens the door. Fight, fight!, La Murciélaga shouts, really agitated. Somebody opens my door—it's Pedro. His nose is bleeding. Move, jackass!, he tells me. Pedro!, says Inga. Let's go!, says La Murciélaga, and climbs in the back. I move back there too. Inga settles in the front seat. You're bleeding, I say to Pedro. I know. What happened to you?, Inga asks, more excited than upset. Some group of assholes, Pedro says. Who? He doesn't answer. What about Julieth?, we can't leave her, says La Murciélaga. But Pedro's already got the car in reverse. Out of the knot of people, a group runs toward us. Oh, La Murciélaga exclaims, they're coming. Julieth bangs on my window. Let me in! She manages to get in before the horde reaches us and before Pedro makes the tires squeal, peeling away from the overlook in terror.

"Bastards," says Pedro. He wipes his hand under his nose and it comes away smeared with blood. "Does anybody have a tissue?"

Nobody does. Julieth, Inga, and La Murciélaga all talk at once, asking questions that nobody answers. What happened? Who were they? What did they do to you? A sign announces a road down into the city a hundred yards ahead. It's now or never.

"Turn, Pedro," I tell him.

He doesn't respond or slow down.

"Turn!" I yell.

He doesn't budge. He's plowing ahead, his face distorted with fury. But I'm even more furious.

"I said turn, motherfucker."

Ten yards, five yards. I lunge forward. The three women scream. I grab the steering wheel with all my remaining strength and spin it left. Pedro tries to straighten the car out, but I give the wheel another yank to force us onto the turnoff. Two yards. Pedro lets go of the wheel and starts punching me. The women keep screaming. Asshole, shithead, you're insane, what are you doing. I don't care what they call me, it's done. Pedro elbows me in the face. But we're heading down, on our way back. Julieth and La Murciélaga grab me by the shirt and the waistband of my pants. They pull me backward. Inga slaps me. Pedro pounds the steering wheel, irate, and brings the car to a sudden halt.

"Get out, asshole," he tells me. "Get out right now."

"I'm not getting out," I say, "and you're taking me home right now."

"Who is he?" Inga asks, referring to me.

"That's Larry," Julieth says.

"Libardo's son," La Murciélaga says.

"And who's Libardo?" Inga asks.

Pedro grits his teeth and, dripping rage and full of hatred, turns around to look at me. I'm about to answer Inga, but Pedro cuts me off. "A capo," he replies.

26

C harlie squeezed his hand, and the airplane shook furiously. The seatbelt signs lit up, and the flight attendant came on the loudspeakers to announce what was already clear to everybody: the plane was experiencing some turbulence. The people who were sleeping woke up, those who were already awake sat up straighter, and even the drugged ones shifted in their seats.

"What's going on?" Charlie asked.

"There's some turbulence."

"Yeah, I know, but why?"

Larry raised the shade to see if he might find the explanation outside, but that made things worse; the plane lights bouncing off the clouds made it seem like they were in the middle of an electrical storm.

"Shut that," Charlie ordered him.

"We're going through some clouds. That's why."

"But there aren't any clouds this high up," Charlie said.

"Then we must not be that high up."

"Oh, God," she exclaimed, and squeezed his hand tighter. Then she said, "Recite something to me."

"What?"

"Whenever I was scared, my dad used to calm me down by reciting a poem."

The plane was lurching up and down, shaking from side to side. Behind them they could hear a lot of noise. As they pitched in and out of air pockets, Charlie asked Larry for a poem.

Like I'm some kind of medieval troubadour . . .

"Please," she insisted, her fingernails digging into his arm.

"What poem?"

"Any."

"But I . . ."

Then, from somewhere in his memory, Larry remembered how his econometrics professor in London, Sean Leeson, used to end every class to clear his students' minds: *Do not go gentle into that good night, old age should burn and rave at close of day.* Closing his eyes, savoring the experience, Larry started reciting the Dylan Thomas poem he'd memorized through hearing it so often from Leeson.

It wasn't the best poem for traversing a storm in an airplane. Thomas talked about lightning, death, rage, and darkness. Maybe that's why she looked at him in bewilderment, though she did seem less scared. *Rage, rage against the dying of the light.*

The turbulence affected Larry's voice; he was trying to call up the same gravitas and power his professor had displayed, but he wasn't pulling it off. He wanted her to feel what he'd felt when he used to listen to Leeson closing out the session with his hoarse but gentle voice, after having turned their brains to mush with mathematical models and statistics. The plane lurched and dropped, the passengers screamed, and Larry, as if he were praying, continued: *Grave men, near death, who see with blinding sight.* He stopped and she asked him to keep going.

What if the poem were a premonition? . . .

He translated it in his head. They *were* those grave men near death—Larry, Charlie, and the two-hundred-odd other souls aloft in a plane that was plunging out of control.

"Go on, don't stop," Charlie insisted.

And you, my father, Larry recited, then stopped and confessed, "I can't go on."

Why a mention of the father, and in that line, in this moment? With the two of us on our way to be with our dead fathers . . .

If he'd finished the sentence, Larry would have said, *there on the sad height.*

I can't go on . . .

Charlie laid her face on his chest and started pleading to her father. And her father must have heard her, because the plane bounced on a pocket of air and rose again.

"Daddy," Charlie said, biting Larry's shirt.

The bottles and glasses crashed to the floor, and the two interlaced their fingers as the plane climbed and climbed. A spark of hope flickered in them both: higher up there would be no clouds, or wind, or lightning, only stars and sky, and her and him and, perhaps, eternity.

27

T he stalking was simple at first: somebody would call and then hang up. The call could pass for a wrong number, but then there would be five, ten more calls until late into the night. Libardo would lie sleepless with rage, and Fernanda was climbing the walls. Whoever it was didn't even give Libardo time to insult them; Fernanda got the brunt of his tirades instead. You goddamn sewer rats, I'm going to find you, I'll drag you out of your fucking holes and make you regret it, Libardo would say, but they'd already hung up before he even got to the first obscenity.

"We'll unplug the phones at night," he told us. "In this house we're going to sleep in peace. They can stay up all night on their own."

"Who is it calling?" I asked.

"The people who killed him."

"But what do they want? Why do they keep hanging up?"

"To screw with us, to scare us, but we've gone through darker times than this before," Libardo said, resolute.

It wasn't true—we'd never experienced anything like this, at least not as a family. Libardo had probably faced death many times in his life; he'd have felt it bearing down on him with a pistol in his mouth, with a chainsaw rumbling at his throat. Who knows how often he'd believed his final moment had arrived, and who knows how he kept managing to elude it. But now they were messing with his family, and Escobar wasn't around to help him out.

During the day they called every hour on the hour. Libardo had instructed us not to answer, but the endless ringing was worse than the silence on the other end of the line. It echoed like an air raid siren, like a dripping faucet on a sleepless night, like a madman's shouting on the streets or a burst of gunfire in the wee hours. More than a noise, it was an icy shock that ran to the very tip of every nerve. So it was better to pick up the handset and immediately drop it again. It would ring again only exactly sixty minutes later, like the bird in a cuckoo clock.

Fed up, Libardo managed to get our number changed and, at least as far as noise went, calm returned to the house. But the harassment didn't let up. My philosophy teacher, Mario Palacio, in a fit of self-righteousness, decided to mock Julio and me and all the other students he referred to as "cartel kids." He wouldn't name names, but he'd look at us pointedly when discussing "the corrosive epidemic of drug trafficking"; he'd stop next to us while preaching about "the mafia culture that has aggravated our city's social ills." He gave a lot of exams, and I received a failing grade on every single one, supposedly because philosophy was a way of looking at the world and, he claimed, I was blinded "by the ephemeral gleam of easy money." To make up the failed exams, he gave me an additional assignment. He handed me a small, worn red book that looked like a missal, titled *The Five Philosophical Theses of Mao Tse-tung*. And he told me, "I don't want a summary of the book, I want an examination of how each thesis can be applied to the new social and economic model of Medellín." He said it in the dogmatic tone that he used in class to convince us that his way of looking at the world was the correct one.

"Poor bastard," said Libardo when I told him about the assignment and showed him the red book. He looked at it with disgust and added, "Screw that assignment and Mao what's-his-face too. That bitter old coot isn't going to ruin your year over a completely useless class. Let me talk to him."

Of course they never talked; he sent Dengue in his stead. I never knew what was said, but in any case the Mao assignment was dropped, though I continued to do badly on the exams. What's more, other teachers made common cause with Palacio and took the same attitude toward us. My schoolyear hung in the balance.

Then one day, the phone rang again, and nobody said anything on the other end of the line. It rang again exactly sixty minutes later. And every hour every night. And the next day and the days after. We unplugged the telephones again before going to bed, but when we plugged them in the next day, they'd start ringing right on the hour once more.

Libardo cursed and hurled threats right and left. Into the void, knowing there was nothing else he could do. He could keep getting new phone numbers, and they'd find them out every single time.

Then we started getting clear, direct messages through emissaries sent by Los Pepes. They wanted our properties, the most valuable ones, and large quantities of cash.

"At least they're looking to negotiate," Fernanda said.

"Does this seem like a negotiation to you?" Libardo replied in fury.

"Well, yeah," she said. "Each side's contributing something, right?"

"They're demanding everything."

"But they're offering us peace," Fernanda said.

"Are you all out of brains or something?" Libardo said. Leaping up and pointing a finger at him, she replied, "What I am is all out of patience with you. I've had it up to here!" With the same finger she drew a line across her forehead. She stormed out and into the bedroom, slamming the door behind her.

"What a harpy," Libardo remarked.

Any spark could set us off. Somebody always ended up

slamming a door at the end of a conversation. The next day we'd hug it out, like a team before a game, and apologize, promising love, loyalty, and unity. The four of us with the water up to our necks, but clutching one another.

In any case, Libardo failed in his efforts to keep Julio and me out of everything that was going on. It was impossible not to let us be drawn in—we weren't little kids, and the whole business with the phone calls, plus the mood swings, the news stories, and the rumors, ended up pulling us right into the power struggle. Ironically, while the country believed one war was over, another was beginning, and I was an unwilling recruit to one side.

Los Pepes were out of control. There were a lot of them, and they had a lot of power. According to Libardo, all he needed to guarantee his safety in the conflict was a Pepe. That was the only thing he was looking to hook in a turbulent river. Los Pepes had been around for two years, ever since Escobar had burned the mutilated bodies of the Moncadas and the Galeanos, and now they were not only stampeding over everything in an unrestrained herd but also exhibiting a terrifying level of hatred. They murdered people and left a message with every corpse, burned properties, tortured victims with unprecedented cruelty. We were actually lucky that their attention to us had been limited to anonymous phone calls and specific demands. The question that haunted us was when they were going to take the next step.

Libardo waited for the maid to clear the plates from the table. Once we were alone, he said, "Every revolution has involved a long series of battles. The ideas that changed the world traveled winding, difficult paths. The changes we're after can't be achieved overnight. We've lost a lot of people, but we've kept going. And we're not going to stop."

It wasn't a new speech—he was always saying that Escobar was hated and persecuted for being a subversive. That in this conservative, oppressive society, his ideas were shocking because they were so revolutionary. Libardo picked up the fork that had been left for dessert, gripped it tightly in his fist, and said, "Revolutions demand sacrifices, and sooner or later this retrograde society will embrace Pablo's social message. I'm going to keep fighting for those changes, boys, so you'll be proud of me one day."

His voice cracked. While waiting for the lump in his throat to clear, he grasped the fork in both hands as if he were going to bend it. Though it was hardly the moment for it, I ventured a question: "What kind of changes, Pa?"

He looked at me and smiled. His eyes welled up. He let out a quiet laugh, and finally bent the fork. "The little squirt's a smart one, huh?" he said. "I like that." He spread his arms and said, "Come here."

I got up and approached him slowly, more alert to Julio's reaction than to Libardo's, looking for support in my brother's eyes, but Julio was as bewildered as I was.

"You too, Julio," Libardo said. "Come here."

"Me?"

"Of course, son, you come here too."

He wrapped his strong, hairy arms around us. He kissed us. He smelled like sweat and soil. His three-day beard pricked my face. I was annoyed that he and Fernanda were both trying to fix everything with a hug. Warm washcloths on foreheads. No hug has ever saved anybody from a fatal disease. Drops of herbal tinctures, floral teas to distract us from our suffering.

I tried to pull away, but he squeezed us tighter. We couldn't hear anything, couldn't perceive anything apart from his heavy breathing, until the noise of the fork crashing to the floor made us all jump.

28

L arry?"

"Hey, Ma."

Fernanda tries to sit up, adjusting the T-shirt she's using as a nightgown. She isn't wearing anything else. She's lit up by the hall light, and my shadow is falling across her face, which she scrunches up like a little girl carelessly awakened. She murmurs something, as if weighed down by her own body. I put my hand on her back, and she asks me, confused, "How did you get in?"

"Pedro unlocked the door."

"Oh, O.K.," she says, and looks around in a daze, as if she's awakened in an unfamiliar room. "What time is it?" she asks.

"Three thirty."

"Did you just get here?"

I nod, and Fernanda sits up in bed, pulls the sheet over her legs, and runs her hand through her hair. She seems surprised to discover that it's still damp. I reach out to turn on the bedside lamp, but she stops me. "No," she pleads, "I look awful."

She gazes at me a while and strokes my cheek. "Larry," she says, "I've really missed you." She grabs my hand and leans toward me. "You smell like liquor," she says, smiling.

"They refused to bring me. I've been trying to get here for a while, but Pedro told me you weren't . . ."

"I was bushed," she says, and touches her hair again. "What time did you arrive?"

"In Medellín?"

"Yeah."

"Like noon. I haven't slept at all."

"Come here, sweetie." She gestures for me to sit next to her. She leans her head on my shoulder. Her hair smells clean, but her breath smells like cigarettes.

"Where's Julio?" I ask.

"At the farm. But he said he'd come early."

She slides down the bed a little. She shakes her head and covers her ears.

"All those fireworks, Jesus Christ," she complains. "What time are they going to stop?"

She breathes in, sighs, then rests against my shoulder again.

"Did you see the apartment?" she asks.

"Yes."

"It's really small."

"I wouldn't say that."

"It's not like the house," she says.

It is smaller. The bed is half the size of the one she used to have. Instead of picture windows it's got narrow casements; there's no artwork or heavy drapes, just blinds.

"It's great," I say. "You don't need any more than this. It's bigger than my place in London."

"It isn't easy," she says, and clears her throat.

It occurs to me now that the reason she never sent me a photo of the apartment or showed it to me when we talked on Skype was more because of the mess than the size. Fernanda has never finished unpacking the things she brought from the house.

"I set up Julio's room for you," she says. "He's at the farm pretty much all the time. At any rate, it's got two beds, if it turns out he wants to stay. Hope so. It would be wonderful to be all together again." She sighs, sighs again, and clarifies, "Not beds. Cots."

"I'm so tired I could sleep on the floor," I tell her.

"Sleep here with me tonight, if that's even possible with all this noise. Are you hungry? Did you eat?"

"I'm fine. Sleepy."

I could fall asleep like this, fully clothed and with my shoes still on, leaning back against the wooden headboard, with Fernanda's damp hair as a pillow. I would plunge into sleep as soon as I close my eyes, but the overhead light suddenly flips on and blinds us.

"Why is it so dark in here?" asks Pedro, standing in the doorway.

Fernanda pulls the sheet over her head. "Jackass," she says.

"Turn off the light, dipshit," I tell him.

"I just wanted to show you the shirt I borrowed," Pedro says. He spreads his arms to show me the one he's put on in place of his bloody one. "It was the best one I found," he says. "Your clothes are butt-ugly. You've got the worst fashion sense."

"What are you doing here?" Fernanda asks.

"I brought you your son."

"Right, but why are you still here?"

"I was changing."

Now I see her in the overhead light. Her skin is red, her eyes swollen, and she has spots and wrinkles that weren't visible on the computer screen. It wasn't so long ago that I last saw her in person. It could be the hour—everybody looks like crap when they're disturbed in the middle of the night. She's still beautiful anyway; she still looks like a queen. Or is it the passing years, which destroy everything?

"What happened to your face?" she asks Pedro.

"Not too much. Sure happened to the other guy, though."

"Well, bye," I tell Pedro.

"Bye?" He laughs. "You're coming with us. Inga and the others are waiting in the car."

Fernanda laughs too, and I don't understand her reaction.

I'm irritated by the complicity in her chuckle. "What's so funny?" I ask, and the question only makes them laugh harder. Fernanda's face flushes, her nostrils flare, and a thread of spit lashes her upper teeth to her lower ones.

"I'm going to pee," she says, and gets up.

The Dictator goes gloomy, deflates when it's just me around. It's always been like that when we annoy each other. Our friendship always saves us eventually, or his willingness to turn the page as if nothing had happened. I'm not budging from here, Pedro, I tell him. It's still early, he says, let's go for a ride. I shake my head. I heard about this kickass afterparty, he says, it's going to be off the hook. No, I say. He looks at me. Fernanda flushes the toilet. I'm taking your shirt, Pedro says. I shrug, and he leaves. I feel myself nodding off. Fernanda's taking a long time. Just as I'm about to fall asleep, she says, "You stayed?"

"Uh-huh."

She gets into bed. Maybe it's me, but something about her isn't right. The sparkle and mischief in her laughter from before has gone. "Take off your shoes, Larry."

She runs her hands over the part of the bed where I'm going to lie down. She fluffs my pillow.

"Turn off the light," she instructs me, "and leave the one in the hallway on for Julio."

I see it's too late to tell her I'd rather sleep in the other room. It doesn't matter. Sleeping is what counts.

"Are you cold?" she asks.

"No."

"I am."

I float adrift on fatigue; my legs are aching. She whispers, it's so nice to have you here. I don't have the energy to respond. She presses against me, and her breathing lulls me again. I feel her trembling, and just when I think I'm finally going to slide into the abyss of sleep, Fernanda says, don't fall asleep, Larry, don't leave me alone. I stop, take a couple of steps back to hover right there, on the threshold where the fireworks are still booming. Don't go to sleep, she says again. I'm begging you, she says in anguish, stay with me, honey. Crying, she beseeches me: please, talk to me.

29

N obody said anything. Not a single grumble or sob or murmur of a prayer to be heard. Only the engines sucking in the cold air of a night that had gone, in an instant, from turbulence to calm.

"It's over," Larry whispered in her ear, though his heart was still lodged in his throat.

There was a need to confirm that they were still flesh and blood, that the stillness and silence weren't part of a new state of being, another life. It would only take a couple of seconds to verify, but the disbelief, the loss of any sense of time, the fear of another bout of turbulence had destroyed the certainty that they were still alive.

Charlie still had her head buried in his chest.

"The sky does that sometimes," Larry soothed her.

"Before I boarded this plane I wanted to die," she said, "and just now I pleaded with my dad to save me. It's weird. That's the first time I've talked to him since he died."

Larry tried to check whether she was crying, but her face was hidden behind her hair. So he kept murmuring to her: "Those first conversations are hard because you refuse to accept what's happened, but you're going to end up talking to him a lot. Sometimes more, sometimes less. Sometimes you'll complain, you'll ask for something, you'll imagine how he would have reacted to something you've achieved, or a goof-up, the birth of a child, another death."

"Will he hear me?"

"Of course, always," Larry said. "Though sometimes it's a conversation through feelings, communicating an emotion, an image, something that can't be expressed in words, like when you try to describe a dream."

Larry fell quiet, and Charlie sat up to look at him. She was a mess. Her hair was disheveled, and her nose glistened and dripped.

"Don't stop talking," she said.

"I was thinking."

"What about?"

About how the dead can surprise us when we get an answer. It's not just physical signs—the picture frame that topples over, the painting that crashes to the floor, the book that leaps off the shelf with a title that offers the answer we're seeking. It's something deeper than that, invisible, like when you feel like someone's looking at you, a rush of energy that makes us believe there is such a thing as a soul . . .

"I was thinking it's great to talk to the dead," Larry said.

Charlie leaned back in her seat and surveyed the chaos left by the turbulence. The tipped-over glasses, the little bottles scattered over the floor, the blanket tangled in the seat. She looked around and saw everybody was as uncomfortable as her, as one another.

"I have to go to the bathroom," she said, "but I don't dare."

"You can't anyway," Larry said, pointing to the illuminated seatbelt sign.

"Is it going to start up again?" Charlie asked.

"You never know. Better safe than sorry."

Feverishly, she grabbed his hand again. Finally a flight attendant appeared, pushed the curtain to one side, and walked down the aisle, looking from side to side. She smiled as if nothing had happened, as if the fear was something they'd made up.

30

We lost count of the cars Escobar blew up once he started terrorizing the country with bombs. One a day in Medellín alone, or two or even three, not including the random bombs that went off in other places. I was consumed by fear thanks to what I saw on the news, apocalyptic images that made me squeeze my eyes shut, and because I'd often pass by the site of a recent explosion and shudder at the wreckage, the dried blood. Anything might be a piece of leg, an arm; a pile of something would look like a heap of guts, and there was always a lone shoe somewhere, loose sneakers, flip-flops, boots amid the rubble.

Fernanda and Libardo weren't too worried about Escobar's bombs. I assumed it was because the man was still alive. On the run, but alive, and they must have agreed with his battle strategy. But I didn't understand why they weren't concerned that Julio and I might be nearby when a car bomb went off. Or that one of them might. At first I believed nobody was exempt from the terror, but I discovered there was one privileged group: Escobar's inner circle. They got warnings, were told the time and place. And we were among those privileged few.

Nobody came right out and told me, but at school people talked about how some people weren't allowed to go outside at particular times, and I realized we were always at home when the bombs went off. I felt a wave of dizziness when I figured it out, a shudder, an urge to vomit, to run, to cry. I asked Libardo about it that night.

"How do you figure I'd know that stuff when I don't even know where the man is?" he answered.

"But is it true?" I said.

"We're at war, son. Anything goes."

I asked Fernanda too.

"I do what your father says."

"Which is?"

"He decides how we need to look after ourselves."

"What about the other people?" I asked.

"What other people?"

"Everybody else."

Fernanda's face took on the appropriate expression, a subtle grimace in response to my naiveté. The expression that people adopt in relation to others. An expression to alleviate one's own guilt. That's what my unease was, after all: guilt at my privilege in the face of death.

Then Fernanda said, "Everybody else is a lot of people. Understand? We can't be responsible for all of them."

So it was true. Death was sending out emissaries to its friends. I also learned that the members of Escobar's group weren't the only ones who enjoyed death's favor; a lot of Medellín's elite did too. All of them must have felt the same way I did whenever an early-evening bomb went off and caused hundreds of people to die and many more to be grievously injured. Relief and guilt—that's what I felt.

But then death changed sides. That became clear when it left Escobar sprawled on a rooftop and sent harassment, persecution, and fire after us.

Four months in, they burned one of Libardo's farms. It was called El Rosal, and it was one of his favorites. The funny thing was that, despite the name, it didn't have a single rosebush; they wouldn't grow in the Magdalena Medio region's torrid climate. Even the cut roses we brought from Medellín to decorate the house didn't last more than a couple of days. By the third, they'd already dropped their petals and were drooping from the heat.

One morning the boys woke him up to let him know that El Rosal was burning. What happened?, Libardo asked the caretaker, because in the fifteen years he'd owned that farm, nothing had ever caught fire, not even during the driest summers. Not a single paddock or tree or outbuilding.

"They burned it, Don Libardo, they came and set it ablaze."

"Who?" Libardo asked mechanically, already knowing who had done it.

"They left you a letter, Don Libardo."

"What does it say?"

"I can't read, boss, but if you want I can take it to my brother—he knows how."

"No need," Libardo said, and hung up the phone before they could tell him that the arsonists had slaughtered forty head of cattle on their way out. They riddled them with bullets so they couldn't even be sold for meat.

Libardo kept to himself for two days. In the mornings, supposedly, he was still sleeping; in the afternoons he wasn't around; and at night he'd come home after we'd already gone to bed. Until one morning we found him sitting in the living room, with his eyes closed and an empty glass in his hand. He told us about the fire and the cows. His voice scratchy, he said, "I always wanted to have a daughter, a little girl, after you two, but Fernanda didn't want any more children. You know how vain she is. She said you two were enough and left me still wanting a little girl." He sighed, cleared his throat, and said, "I even had a name for her. Rosa. And I had her farm. El Rosal."

He swallowed hard and couldn't go on. He brought the glass to his lips, not noticing there was nothing in it. Julio and I, who always used to look at each other in these situations, didn't. We stood stock-still, frozen, with our heads bowed, until he said, go on to school, boys, don't be late, and remember you've got to be the best. What's going to happen, Pa?, I asked him. He blew a long puff of air, staggered as he got to his feet, adjusted his pants at the waist, and said, they're going to be sorry.

A little while later, another crime rocked the country, and when I started gathering up the shards of this story and gluing them together, I fit Deputy Attorney General Diago's murder side by side with Libardo's warning. Libardo already had Diago in his sights for his failure to fulfill his promise to Escobar. But those realizations came later. When the murder happened, I didn't want to—or simply couldn't—think about everything that was happening; all the deaths and bombs and scares left me unable to think clearly.

Fernanda and Libardo started thinking again about leaving, but every conversation ended in an argument. She'd say we should go, but all of us as a family, and Libardo would insist he couldn't, saying he wouldn't be able to defend himself in court from abroad. He suggested the three of us leave with our grandparents, and he'd come and go as needed.

"I'm not staying over there all by myself," Fernanda would say.

"You won't be by yourself," Libardo responded.

"You won't be there to make decisions."

"Well, you can just call me."

"It's not the same."

"It's only for a little while."

"How long?"

"However long it takes to finish these bastards off."

Fernanda hesitated. Though the decision involved us and was being made to protect us, they never asked us what we thought. When Fernanda looked at us, I realized she'd been wavering not because of us, but because of Libardo. Finishing off his enemies was going to require annihilating an entire country that celebrated when the capos' farms were burned or the capos themselves were captured or killed. She refrained from calling him out at the time, but a few days later, during another disagreement with the grandparents present, Fernanda exploded.

"I can't believe how stubborn you're being about staying here so you can wage war against the entire world. If it were just Los Pepes, I'd get it, but the whole world . . . it's madness. People hate us, Libardo."

"They'll calm down eventually," he said. "It's money that runs the show here. If we can hang on to our cash till everybody settles down a little, things will go on as normal."

"I'm not going to any country where they don't speak Spanish," my grandmother said.

"That's no problem," Libardo said. "It can be Spain or Argentina or wherever you want."

"I need a nurse," my grandfather said.

"He doesn't need anything," my grandmother said. "He just likes the massages."

"It helps with the pain," my grandfather said.

"That's enough," Libardo broke in. "We can decide on a place later. The important thing now is to be on the same page about what we're going to do."

"What about my nurse?" my grandfather asked.

"Shameless," my grandmother said.

"Enough!" Libardo shouted.

Nobody said anything after that. I wished I could think of something to change the subject. Julio seemed indifferent to the conversation. In the silence, I heard the rattle of ice cubes tumbling into a glass. Fernanda was making herself another drink. Libardo was visibly annoyed. Then came the sound of liquor filling the glass.

"All right," Libardo said. "Let's leave this for another day."

As he moved to get up, Fernanda spoke: "I know why you want to stay, Libardo."

"I'm not staying," he said, impatient. "I'll be coming and going."

"I know why you don't want to leave for good," she said.

We all fidgeted in our chairs, except my grandfather, who was looking back and forth between them like a lost bird.

"Fernanda," Libardo murmured.

"You want to stay here to be with that woman," she said, her voice rising with each syllable, spattering each word with fury. "That bitch must have persuaded you to get rid of us, because you know full well you've already lost this war . . ."

"Shut up, Fernanda."

"If Pablo couldn't win it, you certainly aren't going to pull it off with fewer men and less money."

"I'm going to shut you up, I'm warning you."

"You're not going to shut me up, not before I tell you a couple of hard truths."

"The two of you are setting such a great example for the boys," my grandmother commented.

Fernanda ignored her, took a swig of her drink, lifted her chin dramatically, and challenged Libardo: "Why don't you come out and say it? Why don't you just tell me you want a divorce? Is your hoochie not satisfied with that apartment you gave her?"

Libardo reached out to cover her mouth with his hand, and she turned her face away. Julio leaped up to put himself between them, my grandmother let out a high-pitched shriek, my grandfather shouted, what a goddamn mess!, and I covered my ears and curled up in a ball.

In the commotion, Fernanda's glass shattered on the floor. My grandmother shrieked again, and I don't know what happened after that.

When I looked up again, they'd separated. Libardo was huffing, sitting in the armchair; Fernanda was sobbing wearily on the floor; Julio paced back and forth, breathing heavily; my grandmother, shattered, was fanning herself with a magazine; and my grandfather, with short, slow movements, was pushing the shards of glass with his foot.

It was exactly six in the evening, and in the silence, the phone rang as usual. It was them, exulting in the chaos. Libardo let it ring four times, then picked up the handset just to silence the noise and gently set it back down. He got to his feet and said, "I'm going to the kitchen. Anybody want anything?"

31

W hat are you thinking about?" Larry asked her.
He expected to hear anything but what she said:
"About you."

Charlie noticed Larry's surprise. Her tongue was already in a tangle, or the tangle would be the secret she was about to reveal.

"I was sent to London for rehab," Charlie said, "because I was drinking alone and hiding it."

She looked at him, expecting a reaction, but his face remained impassive. Charlie waved her hands. Something in her had changed. A spark of rage, a defiance, a refusal to conform.

"So we fucked up," Larry said.

"What?"

"We drank. We're drinking. If I'd known, I wouldn't have accepted the invitation."

"I would have done it anyway," Charlie said.

"How long had it been since you'd had a drink?"

"Nineteen months and twenty days."

She told him she'd already suspected that as soon as anything tough came along, she was going to lose all the effort she'd put into recovery. They'd warned her and even prepared her for just such a moment. But it hadn't worked.

"I feel guilty," Larry said.

"No," she said.

She told him she'd never needed friends or parties to drink an entire bottle, to get falling-down drunk alone in her house, shut up in her bedroom. She drank by herself, and that was her downfall.

"But maybe today's drinks were just because of what you're going through," Larry said.

"I don't know and I don't care," she said.

"I've always believed," he said, "that a person's death either brings those who are still alive together or it pushes them apart. Grief unites people, guilt divides them, loneliness unites them, and maybe fear does too, though I think uncertainty sometimes divides them."

"The thing that really divides people is arguing about the will," said Charlie. Larry laughed, and she sat looking at him and finally said, "I know why you're here. Maybe you're the one who needs company."

Larry gulped a mouthful of air, leaned his head back, and started moving his feet in circles. The atmosphere had grown strained. It was all having an effect: the drinks, the long hours of the flight and those that still lay ahead. He was exhausted by the confinement and sleeplessness of an artificial night.

"I've got something to tell you too," he said.

She looked at him with interest, with those eyes that said everything and nothing.

"I'm Libardo's son," Larry said.

Charlie shrugged and smiled in confusion. "Who's Libardo?"

Larry searched for an answer in the tangle of his former life, looked for it in truth and falsehood, in the words he'd always avoided. Charlie kept looking at him with those eyes that said nothing and yet said everything.

"A capo," Larry said.

32

Y ou haven't answered me, Larry," Fernanda complains.
"What's the question?"
"When did you realize what your father did?"
"Julio's First Communion," I tell her. "I got really bored and
started watching people, what they were doing, the way they
laughed, what they were talking about, and I noticed it was all
just like people said they were—the capos." I manage to say it.
"The way they got portrayed in movies, the way people talked
about them at school and at the club. And, well, seeing how
Dad always carried a gun and how he used to get violent."

"But you were so little," she says remorsefully.

"Yeah, but that was when."

"Did it worry you?"

"It made me sad."

She offers me more coffee so we can keep talking, and I
stop her with a gesture.

"You should rest a little too," I say.

"They're still setting off fireworks," she says.

"What's that about?"

"It's because December starts today."

It's because they're crazy, I think, because we're still sick.
Those fireworks are just bullets in disguise, a ritual venerating
Colombia's wars.

"Let's go to sleep, Ma, please."

Her cell phone vibrates on the table. She looks at the
screen.

"It's Pedro."

"Don't answer," I say.

She runs her finger down the bridge of my nose, as if she were a blind person testing its shape.

"You don't look like him," she tells me. "You look like me."

"I know."

"Julio's more like him."

"I know."

"But you're not like me," she says.

"What are you like?"

"I'm the worst."

Sleep rebuffs me. These aren't things a son wants to know about his mother; nor is it fair for a mother to say them to her child. Nobody wants to hear these things.

"Don't say that, Ma."

"I'm a disaster, Larry."

The cell phone quivers again on the table.

"It's Pedro again," she says. "If we don't answer, he's going to keep calling till the battery's dead."

"Turn it off."

"No. Julio was going to start off from the farm at daybreak, and I want to keep track of him."

"You are a good mother, see?" I say.

"I'm not judging myself as a mother, but as a person," she says, "though I haven't been the best mother either."

"Stop it, Ma."

"I married Libardo knowing who he was and what he did. And I had you two knowing that he wasn't just still the same but actually even worse—he'd become more powerful, and I knew everything he'd done to achieve that. I had you knowing that people would point at you, exclude you, that you could never be like everybody else and would never have a normal life."

"I'll take that coffee, Ma."

She puts the water on to boil and rummages for the coffee in the cupboard. She asks, "Do you think God sets off fireworks?"

The white light of the kitchen makes us look pale, gloomy, tired; it emphasizes the lines on her face and the slackness of her thighs.

"God's too old," I tell her.

She laughs. "The only old person around here is me."

While the coffee's brewing on the stove, I pad barefoot over the tiles of the kitchen floor. In London I walked on old rugs, wearing socks or slippers to fend off the cold.

"What about Libardo?" she says. "Did he ever ask you what you thought about what he did?"

"Luckily, no," I say.

"Why luckily?"

"Because I wouldn't have known how to respond. Remember how furious he got that time I told him we were going to get killed because of him?"

"You had him in a corner," Fernanda says. The coffee rises to the upper chamber with that gurgling sound that makes a person feel at home. "I think he never asked because he was ashamed."

"Ashamed of what he did? I don't think so."

"He must have been afraid, then," she says. "Afraid of your answer."

"I think he never asked because he didn't care."

"Of course he cared. Everybody cares," Fernanda says. "Rejection's the most painful thing of all."

She offers me cookies from a tin. I take one just to be polite, because what I really want to do is vomit. A bottle rocket zips right past our window, and the whistling and sparks make us jump out of our chairs.

"It's him," Fernanda says.

"Dad?" I ask, bewildered.

"Pedro," she says.

We look out the window, and sure enough, there's Pedro the Dictator, looking up at us and laughing. He gestures for me to come down. I stick out my hand and give him the finger. He hasn't changed, I tell Fernanda. Here nobody's changed, she says.

"How's Maggie?" she asks.

"Ma," I whine.

"What?"

"I told you we broke up a long time ago."

"Really? I don't remember. What happened?"

"Ma," I whine again, and say, "I'm tired."

"I'm going to the bathroom," she says.

I go back to the window. Pedro's gone. Peace at last. I didn't pay much attention to the kitchen earlier. Something about every object confirms that Fernanda's changed, but I can't figure out how. There are dirty dishes in the sink, sugar scattered across the counter, a wineglass with lipstick on the rim, a burnt slice of bread in the toaster oven. She doesn't have domestic staff anymore to keep her house sparkling. Now it's Fernanda against the world and against herself. I hear her laugh loudly in the bathroom. What?, I ask, in case she's said something to me. Maybe she's laughing because I didn't understand, because I couldn't hear her, but no, she keeps laughing away, and I start feeling frightened. Ma, I call to her, and she comes out of the bathroom, talking on the phone. You're crazy, she says, and hangs up. That was Pedro, she tells me. I sit back down, relieved—for a minute there, I thought she was the crazy one. Is he finally going to leave us alone?, I ask, and Fernanda says no, they went off somewhere and he'll come back later. Later?, I ask, it'll be daytime later. Fernanda shrugs, sits down, and sips her coffee, still cheerful.

"How are Gran and Grandpa?" I ask.

"Ha," she says. "Speaking of crazy."

"Please, Ma."

"She doesn't tell me anything—I get all my information from Julio, who goes to visit them sometimes. Supposedly she's been deeply affected by Libardo's reappearance." Uncertain that she's been clear, she attempts to clarify: "You know what I mean. She's been crying a lot, Julio says. And your grandfather's getting worse, as you know."

"I want to see them."

"Go right ahead," she says, making no effort to hide her irritation.

They're all we have left of Libardo. The only living thing, and not for much longer.

"I'm sure they'll go to the memorial service," Fernanda says.

"When is it?"

"As soon as they hand over the remains. You and Julio are going to go claim them."

"What about you?"

"No, honey," she says, and shakes her hands. "Father Diego's expecting my call; he'll set up the service when we let him know. It's the only thing I have left to do."

"I ran into some of Dad's friends in a karaoke bar," I tell her.

"In London?" she asks, intrigued.

"Here," I say, "a few hours ago. There's this one named Nelson. I don't remember him, but he recognized me."

"Nelson Vargas?"

"I don't know," I say.

"Would you believe," she says, "I got to know your father better after his death than I ever did when he was alive. You can't imagine the stories that came out, and documents, photos—one surprise after another."

"Yeah, you told me."

"Not everything," she says, "but I'm not going to ruin your night. These fireworks are enough for that."

Fireworks or not, they're not going to ruin my life. I don't want to hear any more stories. We'll bury Libardo, as God intended, and that'll be that. We'd already settled our burdens, everything in its place—grief, guilt, rage. I'm not going to let Fernanda bring Libardo back to life to make us miserable.

"I'm going to the bathroom," she says.

"Again?"

"I'm getting a cigarette."

Another burst of explosions rattles the early hours of this first day of December. Fernanda curses on her way to the bathroom. Another burst follows, and then another and still more, as if the approach of daybreak were a challenge to those who don't want the party to end. Or as if Libardo himself, on purpose, had decided to come back on a night of fireworks.

Fernanda returns with a cigarette and goes over to the stove to light it. "What are you thinking about?" she asks.

"About how death fills the dead with life," I tell her.

Three weeks after El Rosal burned down, they set fire to another farm of ours near San Onofre. It was smaller, but the size didn't make the attack any less serious. The message was clear: all-out war. Actually, that's what Libardo had declared before he realized he'd be the one to lose that war. There was no longer any possibility of negotiating. Their demands, rather than diminishing, increased day by day. They wanted more money, more property, more enemies identified. Not to mention the pressure from the government as it started to expose Escobar's secret networks. Politicians, businessmen, athletes, military officers, and even artists and priests were unmasked to the authorities and the media. Everybody knew Escobar had such ties, but some of the new revelations were shocking. And in the eye of the hurricane was Libardo, an ally in Escobar's shadow who'd rarely been mentioned before. His photo started appearing in the newspapers and on television, with claims that made me sick. The man who'd greased the wheels of Pablo's war machine, the strategist, the man who killed without ever touching a weapon, the chess master of terror, Pablo's kindred spirit, his shadow.

"It's actual, pure, outright filthy horseshit," Libardo told us. "They're demonizing me. People are going around pointing fingers right and left. Everybody's bored with Pablo's death, so journalists are making up stories to get attention. These motherfuckers think they own the world because they've got a goddamn typewriter, but I'll shove those preening bastards'

typewriters, cameras, and their lies right down their cocksuck-
ing throats, the goddamn pricks."

"Libardo," Fernanda said, her tone calmer. "Tell the boys the
truth."

"But everybody knows the truth," Libardo replied. "They
know"—he pointed at us—"because I've never lied to them,
right, boys?"

As always, Julio and I looked at each other. Then we looked
at Fernanda, trying to read her expression, and at Libardo to
see if he was going to explode, thump the table, hurl a glass, or
cry, or scratch his head. People might think they know their
parents as well as their parents know them, but Julio and I
lacked the life experience to know ours, to understand why
they did what they did, why they were the way they were.
Libardo's real life was difficult to disguise. There was no way
to hide the guys who watched his back, the briefcases full of
money secreted around the house, the cars he switched out
every couple of months, or the threats he made, and he'd never
denied his admiration for Escobar.

"Right, boys?"

Julio and I nodded. Fernanda still wasn't satisfied.

"Tell them the truth," she said again.

"What truth, Fernanda? Everybody who knew Pablo knew
nobody made his decisions for him—he liked to control every
last detail. He made the decisions, the plans, he was the brains.
The boss gave orders, and we obeyed, simple as that. And anyone who didn't obey . . ." He paused and eventually went for
an easy explanation: "You know what happened."

He sounded sincere, but something seemed off. When
you've lived a murky, tangled life, when you don't tell lies but
you don't tell the truth either, a blanket of doubt will always
settle over you. That was what Libardo's life was like. What he
said about Escobar may have been true—after all, he was now
dead, and his family was far away—but it was what they were

saying about Libardo on the news that was keeping us awake at night.

Fernanda didn't push any further. Her expression didn't change, and she seemed unconvinced, but she didn't insist. Julio chose to believe him. Like Libardo, he knew that if we didn't hang together in such times, we'd be lost. Libardo said the same thing in other words, which happened to be pretty sensible.

"It's like this, boys." He looked at Fernanda and added, "And this goes for you too. Either you believe me and are with me, or you shillyshally and play for the other side."

Fernanda spun around. "How am I supposed to believe you, Libardo?"

"The way you've always believed me."

"Until that hussy showed up."

"Oh, here we go."

"How am I supposed to believe a liar?"

Libardo came over to us, and she stayed back, muttering to herself.

"I'm going to send more men to Caucasia so they don't do the same thing to Sorrento they did to the other farms," he told us. "I'm not going to let them burn it too. I'm going to face them down and make them regret what they've done to me."

Fernanda said, I'm leaving, and he stared after her till she disappeared from view. I don't know if her story about the other woman was true, but the expression that lingered on Libardo's face was that of a man in love. He may have had another woman, but Fernanda had Libardo's heart.

"She doesn't give a shit about the farms," he said.

"Pa," Julio said, "it doesn't matter anymore what she thinks or we think."

"I know, son," Libardo said, "but they're not going to get to me that easily. They're coming at me from the sides, trying to hem me in, but they're not going to nab me without some major effort."

The telephone rang. We stayed quiet, and it stopped after four rings.

"Pa," Julio said again, but his emotions got the better of him. His eyes welled up and his chin quivered. Seeing him like that, I fell apart.

In my eyes, Julio was the sensible person in the family, the one worthy of emulation. He was still a teenager, but Libardo and Fernanda often seemed more childish than either of us. He was my older brother, my only brother. Or he was more than that. It was distressing to see him stammering, scared to death. Libardo, too, crumbled when he saw his son sobbing. Once again, it seemed, we were going to end up in each other's arms.

"The three of us are men," Libardo said. "Tough men. They're never going to take us down." He sucked in breath between each sentence. "Three warriors."

I sensed that the hug was imminent. We were so close, we could feel Libardo's spit spray as he spoke. I wanted to run away, but Libardo's overflowing emotions forced me to stay, to be tough, a warrior, as he said.

"Three stallions," he said.

The tower that Libardo insisted on keeping upright began to sway. The large hands gripping us weren't strong enough to support us and him too.

"Three lions, three . . ."

Three somethings—he never actually said because he knew we sensed what was about to happen. He didn't even have the energy to give us a hug. His hands on our shoulders was the best he could do. If Fernanda hadn't come back, the three columns that kept Libardo's tower standing would have toppled right there in front of her as if they were made of cardboard.

"Libardo," Fernanda said, leaning against the wall with the phone in her hand.

"You were there," he said, though it was unclear whether it was a question or a statement.

"Estrada called," she said.

"Who's Estrada?"

Libardo had met him, but he'd stopped bothering to remember any names that weren't part of his war, ones he mentioned every day, ones that obsessed him and kept him up at night.

"The headmaster," Fernanda said, and looked at us with an expression of anger, or sadness, or something equally scary. "Julio and Larry can't go back to the school," she added.

"What?" Libardo asked.

"The parents and teachers had a meeting and decided it was best if the boys don't go back."

"They kicked them out?"

"No. They'll hold their spots till things get better. In the meantime . . ."

"They're kicking them out? They're putting them out on the street after everything I've done for that fucking place? I'll go after the bastards who don't want my sons to go to school."

"He said it was for their safety." Fernanda gestured toward us. "And the school's. They don't want to have the bodyguards around, they say that . . ."

"See here," Libardo interrupted, "how about instead of making excuses, those bastards come and talk to me straight?"

"Let me speak," she said, almost shouting. "They can keep studying here at home. The school's going to send assignments, and some of the teachers can come tutor them here."

"And you're O.K. with that?" Libardo asked belligerently.

"Of course not, but what can we do? Are you going to go down there and wave a gun around to force them to accept our kids?"

"Not one gun. A hundred of them, a thousand, as many as it takes to make those bastards understand."

"Perfect," said Fernanda, "and after the massacre, they'll definitely welcome us with open arms."

She was the only person in the world who talked back to Libardo. Even his mother faltered when reproaching him for something, and though Julio and I sometimes rebelled, we were always terrified. Fernanda was the only person who dared. Plus maybe his lover, if he had one, or maybe Escobar, his boss.

"No," Libardo said after a silence. "You two are going to go study at the best school in the world."

"Which one's that?" Julio asked.

"Any school, doesn't matter where, as long as it's the best, and you're going to show those dirtbags you're made for big things, not graduating from some shitty school."

"When?" I asked.

Libardo had this look on his face like he had it all worked out; he was already smiling and waving his arms, striding back and forth, talking loudly like the old Libardo. "Tomorrow if you like, or next week," he said. "We're lucky enough to be able to do whatever we want. We'll look for the best school in the United States, or Europe, and Estrada and the rest of those bastards will eat their words."

"Libardo," Fernanda broke in.

"They won't know what hit them," he continued, ignoring her.

"Libardo," she said again.

"You two are going to walk out of that shitty little school with your heads held high."

Fernanda dropped the telephone on the table, grabbed her purse, turned around, and said to Julio and me, "I'm going to the casino. I need to clear my head."

Libardo didn't hear her or see her leave; he was too caught up in his rant. "And when they find out you're graduates of the world's finest school . . ." He raised his arm, pointed his index finger, and said emphatically, "I mean it, the world's finest school—they won't know what to say; imagine their stupid faces, they'll have to eat their goddamn words."

He stopped pacing back and forth and stood still, looking at us. My head was about to explode, and I longed to run after Fernanda to get away from this madman.

"Where's your mom?" Libardo asked, looking around.

"She went out," Julio said.

"At this hour?"

"She went to the casino."

Libardo's lips moved in a silent curse. Probably he said what he used to say to her when they hated each other, during a fit of jealousy or a lover's quarrel, what the two of them would say in private.

"Go to bed," he instructed us.

He gave us a kiss, and the phone started ringing again.

"Don't worry, I'll unplug it now," he said, with the tone and expression he always used to try and delude us. To delude himself.

34

Charlie told Larry that he wasn't him, he wasn't Libardo, and it was another way of saying he wasn't to blame. In other circumstances, the comment would have bothered Larry a lot, but he didn't react, maybe because she'd said it, or because time had passed, or because reality is very strange on a plane. So strange that just when Larry sensed they were going to talk about rejection and signals, about his neuroses, about rage or uncertainty, Charlie blurted out that she still didn't know why she drank alone.

"Apparently I'm still stuck back at breastfeeding," she said. "I never got past the oral stage, had too much lithium, inherited some syndrome from my mother, or no, actually it was my father's side, I wasn't raised right . . ." She took a deep breath to continue and picked up her glass to drink. "What was clear to me, and what nobody understood, was that I enjoyed drinking alone. There wasn't anything in the world that could top the pleasure of my own company. Every drink disconnected me and took me to another reality. I was floating. It was like . . ." She couldn't think of the word. She took another drink. She looked for more words with her hands, but that wasn't any use either.

"Splitting in two?" Larry asked.

"Exactly." Charlie clapped. "Yes, exactly. I'd escape from my body and float in a warm space, and my hair would drift around my head the way it does when you're underwater." She put her fingers in her hair, closed her eyes, and moved her hands like waves rocking her tresses.

"Chill out," he said, and she looked at him in irritation.

"You don't get it either?"

"It's not that. I don't know why I said that," Larry said. Somebody raised a blind, and a ray of light streamed into the cabin. The glare smacked them, and they both squinted. It didn't last long. When they were in darkness again, Larry apologized. And he asked, "So you don't care?"

"About what?"

"About my dad."

"Oh," Charlie said. "I'd forgotten." She reclined her seat a little farther.

"If you want to sleep, I'll go back to my seat," he said.

"No, my head just feels heavy. Stay."

Her eyes were heavy, her eyelids swollen, her lashes damp, and she felt a tense knot between her eyebrows. In her hand she was holding the glass with the last drink they'd poured themselves. She nodded off, and Larry tried to take it from her so it wouldn't spill, but she clutched it tightly.

"No," she murmured without opening her eyes.

She must have fallen asleep with a glass in her hand so many times when she was drinking alone. And woken up in a puddle of booze on her binges . . .

Larry couldn't really make sense of her story. Reclining there in her seat was a very beautiful woman, and he'd always believed beautiful people didn't experience loneliness.

Beauty is like a magnet . . .

The idea that someone would have to drink alone made him sad.

He sat gazing at her for a long time during which nothing happened. No descents or ascents or turbulence or pilot announcements or flight attendants coming down the aisle. Time didn't even pass. Suddenly, Charlie spoke as if they'd only just now been chatting.

"What are you thinking about?"

"Life," he said.

She still had the glass in her hand, and her eyes closed as she lay back like a queen. Larry started thinking about life for real now, not the one you live but the one you describe.

"Life" is the only word that goes with any adjective. Happy life, sad life, high or low life, long or short, hard-knock, wild, bad, good, thunderous, transparent. Lush life, private, fake, shake, thug, bare, hollow or flat, cannibal, crazy life . . .

He was still playing around with words when Charlie came out of her trance and, touched by what she was hearing, whispered, "Bastard life, goddamn life."

35

The day breaks, and with the pink light the booming of the fireworks seems to diminish. Seems like anybody who hasn't managed to set all of theirs off already is still awake, and they won't quit till they've blown up every last cartridge. Dawn is also an excuse to say to Fernanda, it's dawn, Ma, let's go to bed. The sun that is about to rise will shine down on a Medellín that has supposedly been transformed, one that will awaken slumbering memories and illuminate Libardo's remains.

"When I was your age," Fernanda tells me, "I was terrified of daybreak. I felt enormously guilty if I was still out when the sun came up, and intense anxiety if I was still awake."

"Let's go to sleep, Ma, it's dawn now."

"Whereas Libardo loved it. He used to say it was the best time of day, the prettiest time, but of course he was always drunk by then."

Fernanda smiles, still inside the memory. I get up to make it clear that I want to rest.

"Where are you going?" she asks.

"To sleep, Ma."

"But . . ."

She is unable to find another excuse to keep me there with her. I'm going to use Julio's room, I tell her. It's your room too, she says, I always knew you'd come back. Yeah, I think, but just for a few days. I don't want to stay. I don't want to live here. Over there I'm not Libardo's son, or hers, or anybody's.

"I don't want to see him," she says.

"Who?"

"Libardo," she says. "You go with Julio; I can't see him. I don't know what kind of condition he's in. In any case, whatever they're going to show you today isn't *him*."

Her voice breaks off, and mine isn't working. I can't utter a single word. Whatever I say would come out as noise, sputtering, or a spray of spit. The Libardo I'm going to see today isn't the one I saw the last time, alive. Today's Libardo is the product of hatred and oblivion, though I'd like to put it to her another way.

"I'm not going to see him either, Ma. I'll close my eyes. Besides, Julio and I won't be able to tell whether it's Dad. They can decide that when they run their tests."

"They already ran them—it's him," Fernanda says.

"Then the man we see will be somebody who is still changing, just like we all change, Ma."

She shakes her head and starts to cry.

"We're all going to end up like that someday," I tell her. "There's nothing abnormal about the father they're going to give us."

"He didn't used to be like that," she insists.

"That's death, Ma." I sit down across from her and take her hands.

"No, Larry, it's not. They found him in a garbage dump—he was rotting alone for twelve years under heaps of trash. He deserved better."

"Let's not kid ourselves. We loved him a lot but . . ."

She can believe whatever she wants—her love for him was different. She chose him, she accepted him as he was. Not me. It's obvious to me that Libardo couldn't have died any other way.

"Last night, when I ran into Dad's friends," I say, still holding her hands, "as I was watching them sing, I thought how he could be there with them. But something didn't sit right: I couldn't picture him old and potbellied, singing out of tune at a karaoke bar."

Fernanda nods with her head bowed, sniffles, and gradually stops crying.

"Who knows," I say, "maybe you wouldn't have been able to stand being married to a retired capo."

"But he'd be alive," she says.

"Sure, but maybe you'd hate him."

Fernanda looks at me as if she were trying to read something in my face and the words were blurry, illegible. I try to pull my hand away.

"Did you hate him, Larry?"

I've asked myself that question many times, but I've never been able to come up with a satisfactory answer. For starters, what did hate mean? Wanting Libardo to die? No, I never thought that. Wishing him every ill and misfortune? Not that either—his well-being was my well-being. Did hating him mean rising above him, surpassing him to be better, superior, greater than him? No, I never wanted to be like him, not even a little bit. So was hating him wanting him far away from me, not having any kind of relationship with him? Yes, a thousand times yes, countless times I'd longed to live in another world where there was no such thing as Libardo, or his story, or his shadow.

"I couldn't hate him," I reply. "I tried, but I couldn't. You can't hate and love at the same time. When you hate someone, it's for keeps. You know?"

"Of course," she says, and looks toward the window. There are flashes in the sky outside.

"Now I really am going to sleep, Ma."

The stool scrapes as I push it back. Just another noise in this cacophonous night. She stares out, lit only dimly under the white light of the kitchen. I stand up, and she says, "Larry."

"What, Ma?"

As if she were attempting to shoo my exhaustion away, or to make it stay and destroy me, or to fuck up my life, or because that's how she is, or because it's simply the right time to say it, Fernanda says, without turning to look at me, "Larry, do you know you have a sister?"

After the threats, the hourly phone calls, the fires at the farms, and the extortion, the day eventually came when Libardo disappeared. It started like any other. He got up at five in the morning and made himself coffee. The bodyguards patrolled the yard and, as always, woke us up with their walkie-talkies. Fernanda got up late, as she did every day. After breakfast, Julio and I did the homework our teachers were going to review that afternoon when they came to the house. It was a seemingly normal day in the last phase of our routine life.

Nobody can say that Libardo was uneasy that day, different, as if he sensed it would be the last day he spent with us. He was exactly as uncomfortable and anxious as he'd been since December 3, when Escobar was killed. Nobody had a premonitory dream; there were no supernatural omens that might have alerted us. The phone started ringing early, as soon as he plugged it in, but we were getting used to it. At one point when I went out to the backyard for some air, I heard him in his study talking on the phone with somebody. Every time I wipe my ass I'm going to remember you, Libardo told him, but that didn't seem strange either. That's how he talked, that's how he did his business. And so it continued to be a morning like any other.

Sometime before noon we saw him and Fernanda talking in hushed voices, shut up in the study. Nothing strange, nothing that didn't happen every day, even before that December.

"I'm going to take a shower," she said afterward, almost like she wanted everyone to hear. He followed her into the bedroom and closed the door.

After a while, Fernanda came out wearing a sweatsuit and without makeup. That was how she dressed when she had to run an errand that didn't require her to get out of the car. She used to get fixed up even to go to the grocery store, just in case she ran into somebody, she said. Libardo emerged wearing the same clothes he'd had on all day. I hadn't noticed it, but when we realized he was missing, his clothing became the most important information we could provide. Blue jeans, a gray long-sleeved shirt, brown loafers with rubber soles, and his gray leather briefcase, whose contents he never told us. He didn't let us snoop in there or even get near it, though later it was easy to guess what he'd been carrying. That's what people talked about when he disappeared: Libardo had been armed that day too.

He and Fernanda left the house together, just as they'd done innumerable times, all their lives. Bye, boys, she called from downstairs, and the two of us responded with a mechanical bye from our rooms. See you soon, Libardo said on his way out, and we didn't reply at all. Fernanda returned two hours later to organize lunch. We didn't ask and she didn't say where Libardo was. It was all so natural, so routine, that explanations were unnecessary. It was only at six in the evening that we started to feel things stirring at the house. I was getting a physics lesson in the dining room, and Julio was in his room with the humanities teacher, and suddenly the bodyguards started bustling around like they did whenever Libardo arrived, but this time he wasn't there. Or at least I didn't see or hear him anywhere. But I did see the bodyguards in the yard, talking quietly to each other with worried looks on their faces. In any case, Fernanda didn't interrupt our classes, so it was only when we finished, as soon as the teachers left, that she told us, "Your dad's missing."

It was then we learned she'd dropped him off at a building on Avenida El Poblado, practically in Envigado. She had a dermatologist appointment, and he was going to stay there with his bodyguards. He ordered them to wait outside and went in alone, they didn't know where—an office building, but he didn't say where he was going.

The lunch hour passed, and then two more hours; it was three o'clock, then four, and they started getting worried. They didn't know what to do. Dengue tried to ask the doorman, but apart from Libardo's full name, they didn't have much information. They didn't know what office he'd gone to, and Libardo didn't appear on the list of people who'd entered the building. They decided that three of them would wait there in case Libardo came out, and Dengue and another bodyguard came home to inform Fernanda.

She started pounding them with her fists. She moaned and cursed them, accusing them of falling down on the job. Dengue insisted that they'd followed Libardo's orders.

"He can do whatever he wants, but you can't take your eyes off him," Fernanda said.

"Sometimes Don Libardo wants his privacy," Dengue objected.

She pondered a moment. She took a deep breath and went over to a chair to sit down.

"Maybe it's nothing, ma'am, but it's my duty to let you know."

"Ramírez," she said, "did you check that tramp's place already?"

Dengue lowered his head and nodded silently. Fernanda leaped out of her chair and grabbed him by the shoulders.

"Yes, what, damn it?"

"We talked to her," Dengue stammered.

Fernanda waited angrily for him to say something else.

"He hasn't been there all day," Dengue said, and she started pounding him with her fists again. She was hitting him so hard, he had to grab her by the wrists and tell her to calm down. He practically dragged her to the chair and didn't let go of her until he felt her stop struggling. Then he told her, "I need your authorization, ma'am."

"To do what?" she asked, her whole body tense.

"To proceed."

None of the bodyguards had ever asked her for instructions. At most, some household task—the groceries, an order to take Julio and me somewhere or pick us up, the simple matters of everyday life. What Dengue was asking for now had to do with things that Libardo normally dealt with. She said, "Do what he would have done."

They went back to the building and two men took each floor. Another man kept a gun pointed at the doorman. They entered each office by whatever means were necessary, depending on the reception they got. They forced anyone they encountered to get down on the floor; they shot two people in the hand who tried to go for the phone; and another man who tried to run ended up getting shot in both legs. They ransacked every room they entered, searching wildly, suite by suite and floor by floor, for a man they already knew they weren't going to find. An hour later, they left in defeat; an hour after that, the police arrived, and according to the news reports, six people had been wounded but none were killed.

Given the uproar, there was no way the country wasn't going to find out that Libardo had disappeared. But nobody paid much attention. Ever since the war between Escobar and Los Pepes had begun, everybody had grown accustomed to each group displaying the other side's casualties like trophies. Especially the people who'd taken my father.

We didn't sleep that night. We were still hoping we might get a phone call. It had happened before with a few who'd gone missing and were later traded for money or people. That's what Benito, who'd set up in Libardo's study to organize a search, reassured us. Later, my grandmother arrived alone. She didn't intend to tell her husband anything until we knew for sure what had happened. She blamed all of us, but she lashed out at Fernanda.

"You left him alone," she told her. "You left him alone right when he needed support most. You made him worry wherever he went. You poisoned his sons against him and made his life more difficult."

Fernanda replied, "Out of respect for Libardo and for my children, shut your mouth."

"I'm not going to shut up. He's my son."

"Gran, we still don't know anything," Julio said, trying to calm her.

"So go screech at somebody in your own home," Fernanda said, "but you're going to respect mine."

She went up to her room and called down to me and Julio. She started weeping on the bed, and my brother and I sat on either side of her, awkward and sad. I was the one who should have been sandwiched between the two of them, sobbing. I was the youngest; they should have comforted me, but I was the first one to reach out my hand and place it on Fernanda's back. I let it rest there, not moving, just so she'd feel that she wasn't alone. She'd stayed strong till our grandmother arrived; she'd cried but hadn't collapsed.

But then the situation overcame me. Fear advanced. I lifted my feet onto the bed because I could no longer feel the floor. I leaned against Fernanda, clung to her. I stuck out my arm and sought Julio's fingers with my other hand. He hesitated but finally took it, and also moved closer to Fernanda, and we all became a single body with three wounds.

37

The cabin was still in darkness, though the clinking of glasses and cutlery and the murmurs of the flight attendants preparing breakfast for the first-class passengers could be heard. It smelled like coffee and confinement; the dry air was scratchy, and more than one passenger had red eyes from sleeplessness and fatigue. Charlie was resting in the fetal position, her head on Larry's shoulder. He was following their route on the map, with the feeling that the plane was not following the line progressing across the screen. Time was going at a different speed, as if they were moving slowly to a swift beat, and the strange sensation of flying against the clock became increasingly surreal as the end of the trip approached. They were flying over some islands in the Caribbean, Saint-Martin and Antigua—it had to be those two. Larry knew the hours were ticking down till he'd have to return to his seat, arrive in Colombia, end his encounter with Charlie.

Larry and Charlie—sounds like a movie title . . .

That was what the whole experience felt like: an airplane movie that would end before they landed.

Charlie lifted her tousled head and looked at Larry, dazed, and saw him staring at the map on the screen.

"How long to go?" she asked, her voice hoarse.

"An hour," he replied.

She looked at her watch and tried to shift in her seat but found she was tangled in the blanket. She kicked until she managed to wriggle free.

"Did you sleep?" Larry asked.

"No."

"Me neither."

"My head hurts."

"I've got some pills in my bag."

"No," she said, and grabbed his forearm. "Don't leave."

Larry placed his hand on hers and said, "We're both afraid to get there, huh?"

Charlie nodded, untangled the knot of their hands, sat up, and said, "Wait for me just a minute. I'm going to freshen up."

She staggered to her feet.

She gazed at herself in the mirror. There was nothing left of the woman who'd left her apartment on King's Road. She looked more like the Charlie who used to drink until she passed out. The one who, in front of the mirror, used to work to disguise the addiction nobody knew she had. There in the plane, though, she had little desire to do anything for that Charlie. She just washed her hands, swished some water around to relieve her parched mouth, and tidied her hair a little.

When she returned to her seat, she was startled, breathless, to find that Larry wasn't there. In his place, he'd left the blanket neatly folded.

38

D aylight streams in through the blinds and fills the room where Fernanda has set up two cots for us, even though we no longer live with her. It's been confirmed now: living with Fernanda is impossible. It seems that even she realizes it, and prepared this room for us merely out of obligation. Everything in here lacks any indication of real desire, like a movie set to which Julio and I, the actors, will have to give meaning. Every object is there to fulfill a requirement, but our mother is nowhere to be found; nothing in here reflects her love.

With the daylight now illuminating every detail, I toss and turn in bed, trying to digest the surprise, the explosive announcement with which Fernanda sent me to bed. A sister. A half-sister, she clarified, launching into, or continuing, a withering diatribe against the young girl who, like me, was Libardo's daughter. A little sister, eleven years old, that woman's daughter, Fernanda claimed, giving me the news with tears in her eyes as fireworks continued to boom around us. Didn't you know, Larry? Julio never told you? And why didn't you tell me? How long have you known? I told you about that bitch, Larry. Yeah, Ma, but the daughter . . . I wasn't sure, Larry. I ran into that woman in the supermarket one day and she was with a little girl, pushing her in a stroller, and it had been three years since your father . . . well, and I tried to get closer to see the baby, but she recognized me and took off in the other direction.

Fernanda put her face in her hands and wept gently. A long while. I was wide awake now. I wanted to know everything—

what she was like, whom she resembled, whether the girl knew about us, about me and Julio.

"But how do you know she's his daughter?" I asked.

"Your grandmother confirmed it."

"Gran knew?"

"Worse than that," she said. "She accepts her, welcomes her, has photos of that little brat all over the place, talks about her constantly."

She said it angrily, with that same old jealousy she hasn't managed to overcome despite having been a widow for so many years.

"So you haven't seen her again?" I asked.

"To be honest, Larry, I never met her. All I saw that one time, in the stroller, was a sleeping bundle."

"What's her name?"

"I don't know and I don't care."

"Do you know where she lives?"

"Don't even think about it, Larry."

With that warning, I retreated to the bedroom to imagine my life with another sibling. It's ironic that I've returned to Colombia to collect my father's remains and found somebody I didn't know existed who carries his blood, my own blood. It seems like a prank Libardo's playing, or a message, a legacy— or it's nothing, simply the result of an indiscretion. Though what the hell do I know about what Libardo felt or thought.

But all at once I recall that he wanted a little girl. A daughter. He told us so several times, when he was drunk and feeling sentimental. Little girls bring joy to a house. He even wept with yearning for the daughter he didn't have, that he hadn't yet had. Life denied her to him—though he was a father, he never met her. And she never met him either. She will make her way without her father's shadow darkening her path.

There is one more listless explosion in the street and, inside, the sound of a door closing. Fernanda shutting herself in her room? The wind slamming doors in the early dawn? I hear footsteps in the hallway, a gait I know by heart. I hear him speak to Fernanda and my heart starts racing. The only man I love. My guide for many years, my shield, my buttress.

The voices breach the walls as if they were made of cardboard. Fernanda says, he's in your room, she asks if he's hungry, if he's had breakfast. Julio doesn't answer or maybe gestures. Instead, he opens my door and asks tenderly, "Little Bro?"

"Big Bro," I say, and he turns on the light.

We don't fool around with hugs or airport mushiness; he bumps his fist against mine. Fernanda yells from her bed, shut my door, Julio!, and he obeys. He must have gotten up a long time ago to make it here at dawn—it's a two-hour trip or longer—but he still smells clean, unlike me, who smells like shit.

"How did it go?" he asks.

"All right, but I haven't slept a wink."

"You picked a bad day to arrive. La Alborada."

"It's not just that," I whine, and ask, "Are you going to sleep a little?"

"No, I've slept enough. At the farm I go to bed at eight."

He sits on the other bed, leaning against the headboard. With one foot he removes a shoe, and then with the bare foot removes the other. He whispers something I don't catch. He points to the wall between us and Fernanda. I can't hear you, I say. I said did you talk to her, he hisses. About what?, I ask. About everything, he says. She told me about Dad's daughter. Oh, he says. Is it true?, I ask. I think so. Do you know her? No, I've just seen photos. What's she like? Julio shrugs. Who does she look like? A little bit like Dad. What's her name? I don't know, I don't remember, I think Valentina or something like that. Aren't you interested in meeting her? I'm really busy, Larry, I've got a lot of work at the farm, things have been really rocky, and I have to be on top of everything. But she's our sister, I say. Apparently so, he says, though he doesn't sound terribly convinced. A feeble rocket seems to announce the end of the festivities. Goddammit, that's enough, Fernanda shouts from her room. I tell Julio she's been complaining about the fireworks since I arrived.

"Well, she was friends with the guy who came up with all this," he says.

I don't understand. I sit up, and Julio sees in my face that I have no idea what he's talking about.

"La Alborada," he says. "Don Berna was the one who started it. Do you remember him?"

"Not a clue."

"Hang on to your hat, then," he says. "She met him when Dad was alive. Then this war kicked off between two street gangs, Berna's guys against the Double Zeroes, and one November 30 the bloodbath ended up turning into a celebration with fireworks. And now they claim it's about welcoming December, the jackasses."

"I don't get it," I say.

"It's pointless anyway," he says.

"I had to endure the whole thing, from beginning to end."

"December gets on my tits," Julio says. "Luckily, on the farm it's like nothing is happening. Well"—he laughs—"actually everything happens there, but fireworks aren't allowed so bullets can't catch you by surprise."

"Are you going to stay a few days?"

"No. I'm going back today. Tonight."

"What about her?" I gesture toward Fernanda's room. Julio shrugs to indicate he doesn't care.

"I've spent plenty of Christmases with her," he says quietly. "And New Year's Eves. And do you know what we'd do?"

"I was always with you on Skype."

"You were with us for a little bit, kid, but she couldn't wait to hang up so she could get on the computer and sit there playing whatever with people from all over the world."

"Playing?"

"Cards. Poker. I don't know what all," he says, unable to

mask his rage. "Every so often I have to top up her credit card. She doesn't give a shit how much money she's throwing away."

I feel my chest crack open, and pain and nausea rush in. It hurts to imagine Fernanda the way Julio describes her, and it hurts even more to hear the tone he uses to talk about her.

"Doesn't she ever win?" I ask.

"Drinkers get drunk, and gamblers lose," he recites, and then asks, "How long are you staying?"

"I've got a ticket for January 2."

Julio snorts.

"What?" I ask.

"Nothing," he says.

We sit in silence, hearing a noise from her room. As if she'd bumped into something, or dropped something. What's up since Maggie?, Julio asks. Nothing, I say. Are you going to get back together? No. You haven't met anybody? Yes, I say, but I don't know. What don't you know? I don't know what's going to happen, don't even know if I'm going to see her again. Does she live there? Yeah, but she's from here, and I don't know if she'll go back to London, I say, though I don't dare tell him that I met her on the plane. What about you?, I ask. Bah, he says, there's nobody good in that town, just whores, nobody worth dating.

"What are you talking about, boys?" Fernanda surprises us, leaning in the doorway. She's got on a short robe now, more modest than the T-shirt she wears to bed.

"Just catching up," Julio says.

"You're going to need hours," she says.

"Well, we'll do what we can today," Julio says. "I'm going back tonight."

"What? What about your father?"

"That's this morning."

"Yes, but . . ." Fernanda hesitates. "Weren't we going to have a mass for him?"

"Another one?" Julio complains.

"That was when we didn't know anything," Fernanda points out. "Now there should be one for his death."

"He was always dead," Julio says.

Fernanda sits on the foot of my bed. She sniffs as if she's been crying or is about to. I wonder who will want to attend a service for Libardo, all these years later.

"Did you tell Julio what I told you?" Fernanda asks me.

"About what, Ma?"

"That I'm not going to see your father. You two can go get him, not me."

Julio, indifferent, shrugs again.

"Is Gran going?" I ask.

"I asked her not to," Julio says. "There's no need for her to go. Plus, she wants to keep him."

"What?" Fernanda exclaims, horrified.

"She wants Dad's remains to stay at her house."

Fernanda's face, hands, and posture express her thoughts clearly. "Oh no," she says. "She'd better not even think about keeping him."

"You want him here?" Julio asks.

"Of course not," she says. "He needs to rest with the other dead, he needs to be in a cemetery. We already decided that."

"Well, talk to Gran about it."

"You know I don't talk to her."

Fernanda gets up and cranks the window open to look outside. Heathens, she says when she sees that people are still setting off fireworks around Medellín, and adds, there will be a mass and Libardo's going to a cemetery. Period. But who's going to go to the mass, Ma?, Julio asks. Anyone who feels like it, she says, still looking outside. Defeated, Julio closes his eyes, still leaning back against the headboard. Something explodes in the distance, and Fernanda says again, heathens.

From that day on, everything changed for us. First of all, there weren't four of us sitting around the table anymore, just three. Our habits changed; routine turned into apprehension, and sleep into insomnia. Gone was our sense of calm and safety. It changed our appearance, our gaze, our appetite, our character, even our digestion.

Fernanda attempted to soothe us with a lie: "As long as they don't find him dead, he could still be alive."

But things didn't work that way in Libardo's world. There, death was a message to the enemy. The way a man died was a message, a warning. Disappearance was the worst punishment of all: perpetual uncertainty, preempted mourning. We told Fernanda that, but she kept saying that she'd believe it when she saw him dead. That was the only thing she agreed with our grandmother on. Whereas our grandfather, wandering lost in who knows what labyrinth in his brain, one of the few times he spoke, said, "The man must be buried deeper than a cassava root."

The doctor put me and Julio on bromazepam, which sometimes made us giggle uncontrollably. Fernanda had already been taking all sorts of things for years—her body was used to it—whereas for us, in addition to the laughter, it caused extreme thirst and lethargy. Only two things in our lives remained intact: our classes with our teachers at home and the telephone that kept ringing every hour on the hour. Regarding the classes, Fernanda insisted we mustn't fall behind; no matter what, we couldn't fail our last year. And as for the phone, she wouldn't let anybody change the number or unplug the devices for even a moment.

"Somebody might call," she'd say. "He himself might even call."

On one of those phone calls, somebody spoke. He asked for Fernanda and demanded seven or eight hundred million pesos, some astronomical amount she couldn't even remember because she'd been so nervous. She asked to have till the next day so she could look into things.

"You see? I knew it, he's alive, he's been kidnapped, but he's alive."

Benito asked, "Did they tell you they had him?"

"They called asking for money, Benito. That's all they're interested in," she said. You know Libardo was paying them for a long time."

"But did they tell you they had him?"

Fernanda hesitated. "No."

"Did they tell you they'd return him if you paid?" Benito asked.

"No." She faltered again. "But what's the problem? Obviously they have him—they're asking for money in exchange."

Benito told her that when they called again, she should demand proof of life, and if they really have him, he said, we'll negotiate.

"Negotiate what?" Fernanda asked.

"That's a lot of money," Benito said. "Libardo would never agree to pay that much."

"But we can afford it," Fernanda said, and Benito shrugged.

Our pulses changed; our hearts beat faster now, sped up for no reason. Our tastes changed, as did our preferences. The air in the house and the light that came in through the window changed too. And so did the way we walked and carried ourselves. Our patience evaporated, and irritability was a constant companion.

Dengue and his men were still looking. Their way. The way Libardo had taught them, the way Escobar had taught Libardo, and the way the devil had taught Escobar. All they managed to do was stir things up even more, and all their investigations led back to the same place: Los Pepes. A devastating truth that dashed our hopes.

"Keep looking," Fernanda ordered.

Our grandmother was there one afternoon when Dengue arrived with the same news as always. Right in front of Fernanda, she asked him, "And why isn't your boss here helping you look for him?"

"I don't know what you mean, Carmenza," Fernanda said.

Without looking at her, as if Fernanda weren't there, Gran said to Dengue, "She was the last person who was with him, the last one to see him. She left this house with Libardo still alive."

Fernanda stood in front of her so my grandmother was forced to look at her. Gran looked defenseless with Fernanda towering over her.

"What are you implying?" Fernanda asked.

"What we're all thinking. You were the last one who saw him."

"I've already discussed that with them," Fernanda said, gesturing to Dengue, "and with you and my children. I don't know why you're coming at me with this now, Carmenza. I don't know what you're insinuating."

"Libardo was tired," Gran said.

"Of me?" Fernanda asked defiantly.

"Of your tantrums, your gambling, your whining."

"He told you that?"

Gran looked over at us. Dengue was staring at the floor. Fernanda was still poised for attack, standing upright, her breasts aimed at Gran's face.

"Did he tell you that, or are you making things up, Carmenza?"

"This isn't a topic to discuss in front of your boys."

"Who started it?" Fernanda said. "Besides, they've been filled in already. I imagine Libardo told you about his tramp, right?"

Gran pressed her lips together, her body trembled slightly, and she even clenched her fists as if she weren't afraid of Fernanda.

"Ma," I said, "that's enough. Stop."

"Carmenza," Fernanda said, "I don't ever want to see you in my house again. If you want news about Libardo, you can call your grandsons or call him." She pointed to Dengue again. "Or ask Libardo's goddamn hussy, or check the newspapers, but I don't want to see you here again for as long as I live, understand?"

"Fine for now," my grandmother replied, "but my son will have the final say on that once he returns." Turning to Dengue, she said, "I'll leave you to ponder that question." Then she looked at Julio and me: "You're always welcome at my house, boys. Come over whenever you like."

Fernanda led us to the kitchen, asked for water, took out three bromazepam, and passed the pills around. It was our daily communion against reality. She downed her dose with a beer and shut herself in her room for the rest of the day. She answered the phone whenever it rang. And when they didn't call again for several days we were left feeling both depressed and elated.

"They're probably getting ready," Benito predicted, and, when they were alone, warned Fernanda, "The next move is to go after the widow."

"That's only when there's a dead body," she said.

Benito shook his head. "No," he said. "They come after you so you'll give them everything."

"I'm not a widow, Benito."

"Your husband isn't here, Fernanda. Alive or dead. It's awful, but that's the situation. And the only way they'll leave

you and your sons alone is if you give them what they're asking for."

"And if I don't?" she asked.

Benito's expression was unambiguous. She sat down to cry,
and when he tried to place a hand on her shoulder, Fernanda
swiftly brushed him away. He hovered nearby, waiting.

"So they're not going to hand him over to us?" Fernanda
asked.

"If they haven't said so, then no."

That night, she relayed the conversation and added that
she'd lost faith in Benito. But he's family, Julio said. That's no
guarantee of anything, Fernanda said. So what now?, I asked.
She was quiet, then said, I need to think.

Though she didn't get fixed up like she used to, she
changed her clothes and put on lipstick. She pulled a wad of
bills out of an old purse that was hanging in the dressing room
like any other. She called for two bodyguards and went to the
casino on Calle Oriental near Avenida La Playa, where she
wasn't so well known. It didn't matter that we begged her not
to go out, not to make things worse. I even said, what if something happens to you, Ma, what will we do? Nothing's going to
happen, I won't be long, she said, I need to think, she insisted.
We told Benito, because who else.

"Don't worry, I'll have them keep an eye on her without her
noticing," he told us, but we remained worried, especially
since we'd absorbed some of Fernanda's suspicions about
Benito.

Ever since I can remember I've felt like I was condemned
to loneliness. I was never actually alone—the house was always
full of people, there were always parties full of Fernanda and
Libardo's friends, always other children to keep me company,
and later friends from school or other people who were
around—but even though my world was bustling and
crowded, I still had the sense it was all a setup to mask my

solitude. And not just mine but all of ours, a solitude that suffocated Libardo, Fernanda, Julio, everyone who inhabited that criminal underworld where everything was a lie. But I'd never felt so alone as I did that night when I realized that we had no one left we could trust, and that at that very moment Fernanda was deciding our future in front of a slot machine.

40

C harlie waited three minutes to make sure Larry hadn't gone to the bathroom too, or maybe was in the back looking for something for her headache. But five, fifteen minutes passed, and Larry didn't show. He'd left his seat so tidy, it looked like it had been unoccupied for the entire flight. Pillow, blanket, headphones all neatly in place. She turned around to look for him a few times but couldn't see the back rows. When she decided to go find him, she was blocked by the carts handing out breakfast. A flight attendant pulled down her tray table, and Charlie told her she didn't want breakfast.

"Not even coffee?" the flight attendant asked. Charlie shook her head.

All I want is a drink . . .

And she wanted Larry by her side; she wasn't ready to land in Colombia alone.

What was it that chased him away? Did my alcoholic past scare him off? . . .

For the first time the whole flight, she thought about Flynn and recalled that at one point she'd nearly invited him to come with her on this trip. She'd decided against it because she was becoming increasingly doubtful about her feelings for him. It was best to put some land between them, or ocean, at least for a while. But she wanted him by her side now, wished he were there to console her, to face the arrival with her and help her make her connecting flight to Medellín, to do for her what she felt unable to do herself.

He wouldn't have let me drink, and I wouldn't be wanting so badly to have another one . . .

She felt rage. It felt unfair that Larry had left. Larry wasn't Flynn, but he was somebody. She looked back again, and the service carts were still in the way. She brought a glass to her lips; it was empty, full only of fingerprints. From one of the seat pockets she pulled out two mini bottles of gin, two among the many they'd drunk, but they were empty too. Not a dreg, not a drop—even the smell had evaporated.

She lifted her feet, wrapped her arms around her knees, and cried a good long while. Her neighbors glanced at her a few times while finishing their breakfasts. Images and sounds of her father when he was alive kept flooding her memory. Him with her, with her mother, alone, with the whole family. More and more memories that caged her in grief and despair. She decided to go get a glass of wine, anything, even if she had to beg the flight attendant. But when she tried to get up, she couldn't. Her feet didn't respond, nor her arms to support her, nor her voice to ask for help. With effort, she was able to move her eyes, and when she looked across the aisle she saw her neighbor cleaning up a bit of egg that had fallen on his shirt. She saw the white lights on the ceiling, and where the fasten-seatbelt sign was supposed to be, there was another one that kept flashing, intermittently, from red to black, and it said, best not do that, Charlie. Best not do that.

41

At about eight in the morning we see Libardo again, twelve years after, scattered across a tray. There are fewer bones than I'd expected. Some of them aren't even whole. The official from the National Institute of Legal Medicine separates them with a large pair of tongs, as if he were manning a grill. Libardo's skull catches my attention. There's still hair on it.

"Well, here you are," the official says from behind a surgical mask.

"That's it?" I ask.

"The earth consumes everything else," he replies.

"Are you sure it's him?" Julio asks.

"That's what the necropsy says," the official answers, and adds irritably, "That's not my job."

My brother crosses himself; I don't know whether to imitate him. Julio approaches the tray and picks up the skull. He examines it on all sides, like when you're buying an avocado.

"Look," he says, "it's intact."

"If you're going to take him, you have to sign these forms," the man says.

The comment sparks my curiosity. "What if we don't want him?" I ask.

"He'll go to the medical school," he informs me.

"Of course we're going to take him," Julio says, looking at me with annoyance. "That's why we're here."

The official asks us to wait a moment. Julio returns the skull to the tray and picks up another bone. A long one, maybe a femur. Poor Dad, he says, holding the bone in both hands. He holds it out to me, like a scepter being passed from one king to another. No, I say, I don't want to touch it. It's Dad, Julio says. I know, I say, but I don't want to, I can't. Julio goes over to the forms the official left on the counter and flips through them. A wave of nausea washes over me; I look for a chair and sit in the first one I find. Julio doesn't even notice. This is what I came back for, then, to collect a heap of bones, to root around in the wound that had already closed and formed a scar, to undo the steps of our past. The ceiling light starts flickering like in a horror movie.

"This doesn't specify how he died," Julio tells me, examining the papers.

"He was murdered," I say, and I taste the nausea in my spit.

Julio looks at me gravely and says, "Really? No kidding."

I burp, and a retching convulses my body. I'm enveloped in a vapor of rum and ether. I struggle to my feet and run for the door.

"Where are you going?" Julio asks.

I see my reflection in the water in the toilet bowl. Nothing comes out, though it feels like my eyes are about to bug out of my skull with every spasm of my stomach. I puke up groans, spit, rage, grief, pain, and memories.

"You O.K., Little Bro?" Julio asks from the other side of the door.

"Yeah," I say, just so he'll stop asking.

"Let's go then," he says. "We're all set."

Outside he's got a red bag with the name Libardo scrawled on it. He's holding it as if he were carrying a baby in his arms. The official looks at me and chuckles. "Pretty much everybody vomits," he says. "Some people even shit themselves."

I don't have the strength to protest.

"You look pale, Little Bro," Julio says. "We should go."

"I'll go with you," the official says.

We exit the room, go upstairs, walk down hallways. The official drops off copies of the form, in different colors, at various doorways. Outside, at last, we encounter daylight, natural light, and the air still smells of fireworks. The official says goodbye.

"How many bones does a body have?" I ask.

"Two hundred and six, give or take. Not counting the teeth," he replies.

I don't understand the "give or take," as if some people had more or fewer bones than others. I don't have the energy to ask; I barely manage to wave.

"Let's get some breakfast," Julio says. "That's why you're feeling weak."

"What about Dad?" I ask, still staring at the bag.

"He's coming with us," Julio says, already heading toward the car.

Out in the streets, city maintenance workers are gathering up the ravages of La Alborada. Sticks from bottle rockets, candles from sky lanterns, charred remains of black powder, aguardiente bottles, bags of food, condoms, shoes, and dead birds.

"The three of us together again," Julio muses as he drives. "The men of the house."

Libardo's riding in the backseat in the red bag. Julio glances back every once in a while. Now we're the ones taking care of him. As much as he told us, we're three invincible warriors, three tigers, three stallions, still all we've got is the little of him they managed to gather up.

"The guy told me we can't cremate him yet," Julio tells me. "We've got to wait till the attorney general's office issues some document."

"There's no need anyway," I say.

"Fernanda wanted to," Julio says.

She doesn't realize how little of him is left. We can stick him in an urn just as he is.

The men picking up the trash toss a couple of dead dogs into the garbage truck. Stray dogs that didn't survive last night's battle, and seeing them tumble on top of the rubbish, I think about Libardo dumped in a landfill. The image isn't a new one. I've pictured it a million times and dreamed it, with impeccable clarity, in every nightmare I've had. Libardo rotting among other corpses, a dream I stopped dreaming only recently.

Julio parks near a restaurant. By now the sun is shining brightly, and the dazzling light only adds to my sleepless exhaustion. Julio opens the back door and takes out the bag of remains.

"What are you doing?" I ask.

"Taking him with us," he says.

"You're nuts."

"If I leave him here, somebody might think there's something in the bag and break in and steal it."

"But . . ." Julio's already locking the car. I persist: "Why don't you put him in the trunk?"

Julio gives me a big-brother look and says, "What's up with you?" He holds the bag out toward me with both hands and says, "It's Dad, Little Bro, this is Dad."

So the three of us head into the restaurant. Julio insists I carry the bag, and I insist that I don't want to. Bring this man a strong cup of coffee—he hasn't slept for I don't know how long, Julio tells the waitress. She looks at me pityingly and jots down Julio's order for two breakfast platters. Scrambled eggs, chorizo, an arepa, and cheese. Is it just going to be you two?, the waitress asks. Julio nods, and she gathers up the extra place settings. Libardo's in the other chair, but he won't be eating.

"Well," Julio says, "it's the end of an era. We know where

he is, and given what Mom wants to do with him, we'll always know where he is."

I yawn and apologize. Julio grimaces at the waitress and points at me so she'll hurry up with the coffee.

"According to those papers I was reading," he tells me, "Dad may have died ten or twelve years ago."

"So they don't say anything," I say.

"Ten or twelve years, don't you get it?"

"Well yeah, but which date are we going to use?"

The waitress arrives with our coffees. Julio is pensive. I'll be right back with your food, she says. Julio stirs the sugar into his cup and keeps thinking. He lowers his head, puts his hand on his forehead, and starts to cry.

"Hey . . ." I say. I swallow the coffee and the knot that rises in my throat at seeing him cry.

Julio raises his other hand to signal to me not to say anything, to let him be, it'll pass. He cries a little longer, wipes his drippy nose with a paper napkin, looks at me, and smiles. I return his smile, feeling that I love him now more than ever.

"We'll use today's date," he says. "This is the date we saw him again, the only one we're sure of."

I grab his hand across the table, and that's how the waitress finds us, like two men in love. Smiling as well, she sets down our plates. Here's your eggs, sweetie, she says to me. And yours, she says to Julio. Don't let the arepas get cold, they're best hot, she tells us both, gives us a tender look, and leaves.

"This looks great," Julio says, and tucks into his eggs with gusto.

42

With every day that went by, Libardo was even more dead. The government had no interest in finding him. They claimed to be looking for him, but in fact they'd have been thrilled to have one less drug trafficker to deal with. They condemned vigilante justice—that's what institutions were for, they said, and we needed to trust in the authorities. They kept giving us speeches when it was clear to everybody that Libardo had disappeared—had been disappeared, as Fernanda emphasized to them, even though she knew they wouldn't do anything to find him.

The few friends he had didn't do anything either, apart from making some noise. His absence must have suited them too. It meant one less person sharing the pie, or the portion they had left, since the Cali capos, the Norte del Valle guys, Los Pepes, and others had steadily filled the vacuum that Escobar left in the drug trade. So the only ones who missed Libardo were us.

Our grandmother didn't come back to the house after her confrontation with Fernanda. We used to go visit her, and she'd always insinuate that the last person who'd been with Libardo and seen him alive was Fernanda. She said it a lot, to the point that Julio had to shut her down. That's enough, Gran, he said, Ma had nothing to do with it, she adores him, she wouldn't have let anybody hurt him. Gran scowled, annoyed by Julio's tone, and stared at our grandfather, who was probably off orbiting Saturn's moons.

But the others kept calling. Not on the hour anymore but several times a day, and sometimes when they felt like it they'd ask for Fernanda. They demanded money in exchange for information, and though Benito warned her it might be a scam, Fernanda got sucked in. She was talking with a guy named Rómulo who, he claimed, was the spokesperson for the group that had Libardo. Fernanda asked for proof of life, but Rómulo put her off with excuses. He claimed they were holding him in an isolated area and that for Libardo's safety and theirs, it was best not to take photos of the place. Fernanda tried to put up a strong front, there's no deal without proof, she told Rómulo many times, but they wouldn't give in.

Dengue, who was battle-hungry, urged Fernanda to negotiate. We'll get him one of these days, ma'am, he told her, we've got to maintain contact with them, we can't let them disappear, Dengue said, his hitman adrenaline pumping.

Benito brought Julio and me together and said, "You all are going to end up in the street. Talk to her. Libardo's assets belong to you too, and those people are looking to clean you out."

Obediently, the two of us attempted to talk with Fernanda, as if we were adults, men of the sort who could fill Libardo's shoes, confident and aggressive. We talked, and then she said, "There's no reason for me to be negotiating with those murderers in the first place. I would have thought Libardo was enough of a man that by now the two of you would have learned something and would know what to do in these situations. But no. So now, since I'm trying to save him, I'm the bad guy."

"Ma."

"Let me finish. I'll remind you that Libardo's blood is running through your veins too. You are Libardo. What happens to him happens to all of us."

Just as it seemed like her lecture was hitting its stride, Fernanda let out a shriek of terror. We were sure they'd come after us and we were dead meat. But she'd cried out because a bat had flown in through the sliding doors in the living room and was circling above us, above her. She screamed every time the bat brushed against her head. Julio tossed a sofa cushion at it, but that only made it more frantic. Two of the guys burst in through the same door where the bat had come in. They had their pistols drawn, ready to let off a hail of bullets. One of them made Fernanda get down on the floor while Julio and I kept hurling cushions at the bat.

"Duck down," one of the guys said, raising his gun.

"No," Fernanda shrieked. "The light, the light." She was referring to the twelve-arm crystal chandelier that hung in the middle of the room. But the bodyguard didn't put away his gun, and in the confusion shot not the chandelier or the ceiling or even the bat, which managed to find the exit before it took a bullet, but a Botero painting, the one Libardo used to say was worth more than any of us.

Fernanda got up from the floor, furious with the bodyguards and with us. She chased them out of the house with another scream. Julio stuck two fingers in the gash that the bullet had left in the thigh of a fat woman playing cards in the buff. Holy shit, he said, and Fernanda yelled for us to get out.

That single shot gave the neighbors an excuse to complain to the authorities that there'd been a gunfight at our house. A patrol car pulled up out front, and from my room I saw the bodyguards talking with the police for a long time. Fernanda found me glued to the window when she came upstairs to have us all pray together. For a long time, ever since I found out what Libardo did, I'd believed it was presumptuous to ask God for anything. I didn't feel deserving of his protection or his favors. And I still believed it in that moment when Fernanda took our hands, Julio's and mine, and with her eyes closed asked for Libardo to return safe and sound as soon as possible. She asked for that every night, clinging to us, convinced that God protected capos too. In that tense atmosphere, I would burst into uncontrollable laughter every time I remembered the mayhem the bat caused.

That night, Pedro came to visit me. He was one of the few school friends who still came around. That last year was when we started calling him "the Dictator." He was a complete tool, but he was also caring and loyal, especially with me. Probably because he'd been obsessed with money ever since he was a kid, but I didn't care about that: there he was whenever I needed him, or surprising me with late-night visits with a bottle of liquor, though he might also just steal one from Libardo's study so we could sit around and drink and talk.

"Did you write your will?" Pedro asked.

"Don't joke about that."

"Everybody's saying you're going to get killed."

"Maybe," I say. "I don't care anymore."

"Leave everything to me, man," Pedro said.

"What's everything?"

"The Rolex, your stereo, your motorcycles . . ."

"Don't be an ass."

"Everybody's getting killed, Larry."

"Then maybe you will too."

He took a swig from a bottle of brandy and passed it to me. We both coughed as the alcohol hit our throats.

"You're so lucky," he said. "Not having to go to school. That's the life."

"Actually, it's hell here, Pedro."

He shrugged, unconcerned.

"It's hell everywhere."

We drank again, and again coughed and shuddered at the brandy. We were quiet, staring at the bottle, until I said, "I'm going to leave you everything."

"Really?" he asked excitedly.

I nodded, and he smiled.

"In writing?" he asked.

"In writing," I said.

He leaped toward the desk, rummaged for some paper, and grabbed a pen. He handed them to me and started dictating:

"Medellín, April 2, 1994 . . ."

43

L ibardo? Is that you, honey?" our grandmother asks.
"No, Gran, it's Julio."
Gran, standing in the doorway, blocks the entrance and looks at us warily. "Oh, sweetie, you scared me," she says. "Come in, come in. Why are you here so early?"

"Early?" Julio looks at his watch and kisses her on the cheek. "It's ten, Gran."

Our grandmother holds out her hand to me and says, good morning, young man, come in. Julio stops. Don't you recognize him, Gran?, he asks. She looks me up and down and says to Julio, you never come by, especially not with friends. I'm Larry, Gran, I say. She goes pale. It's Larry, Gran, Julio says, and she brings one hand to her heart and the other to her mouth. Oh, honey, she asks me, what are you doing here, what happened, what are you two not telling me? The house smells of damp, of confinement, of old age. It's the house they moved to after the Libardo situation, but inside it's the same as ever, frozen in time.

"Dear God," our grandmother says. "Come in, come in. Have you had breakfast?"

"Yes, Gran, thank you."

"What's going on? Why are you here, Larry? Are you back for good?"

"No, Gran, I just came because of Dad."

"Dear God."

The curtains are the same, heavier now with accumulated dust. The furniture is the same Louis XV stuff that Gran always used to impress visitors. They're French, supposedly from that Louis fellow, she'd say, the real deal. The only new thing I spot is the shrine, which may not actually be so new, but I've never seen it before. In a gold-framed photo is Libardo, smiling and lit by church candles, perfumed with white flowers. I get goosebumps, and my breakfast stops short on its journey through my guts.

"Oh, honey, what a tragedy," Gran says, grabbing my hands. Her eyes well up and her voice is nasal and sad.

"Yes, Gran," I say, "but at least now . . ."

Now he's dead? Or now we know he's dead? What can I say to her that won't bring her more torment? What can I tell myself to assuage my guilt over the peace it's brought me? She must have hoped for another outcome, that after a dozen years we'd be informed that Libardo was alive, that he'd survived Los Pepes' attacks and been hiding out all this time, and that she wasn't confused and in fact it was Libardo, and not Julio, who'd appeared a few moments earlier at her door.

"What's wrong, Larry?" Gran asks, and says to Julio, "Sit him down over there, Julito, before he falls over." She points to an armchair and asks again, "Are you sure you've eaten? I bought pastries yesterday."

I just need air, that's all. There's not a single window open. The candles and flowers smell like death.

"I'll bring you some blackberry juice," Gran says, and then complains to Julio, "You didn't bring me any guavas or cheese from the farm, honey." She frowns and says, "Or won't your mother let you bring me anything?"

"No, Gran," Julio says. "It's been a hard summer."

She makes a face like she doesn't believe him and heads for the kitchen.

I ask Julio where our grandfather is, and he shrugs. She doesn't like for him to come out, he says. I want to say hi, I say. He's not going to recognize you, Julio says. How long has it been since she set this up?, I ask, nodding toward the shrine. Years, Julio says. I've never seen that photo before, I say. I hadn't either, he says, she gave it to me so I could get it blown up, it's a photo of a photo. I'm going to open a window, I tell Julio, and I go over to the sliding glass doors that lead out to the balcony. Behind the drapes is a sheer that used to be white. The door is locked, the balcony crammed with flowerpots of parched plants. Gran appears with a tray loaded with a plate of cookies and two glasses of blackberry juice.

"All right, boys," she says. "Here you go." She stares at Julio and asks, "What have you got there, honey? Set that bag down and have some juice."

Julio looks over at me. The question in his eyes is, do I tell Gran we've got her son here? My response is a look that says nothing. She sets the glasses and plate on the coffee table. Her hand shakes as she deposits each thing, but she makes sure it's all arranged neatly. I take the plunge and say, "I'm hot, Gran, could we open the window?"

"Oh, I don't know where I put the darn key. I haven't even been able to water the plants, so they're dying on me." She thinks a moment and then adds, "I think that old coot lost it."

The old coot is our grandfather.

"No worries, Gran."

"I'll open the dining room window, but drink your juice. It's cold—it'll be refreshing." To Julio she says, "Put down that bag, honey, and come over here."

"Gran," Julio says, and looks at me.

Now I'm the one who's shaking. I grab the glass and sip the juice, just to have something to do.

Julio continues: "This is Dad." He raises the bag a little. Gran doesn't understand and stares at him, puzzled.

"This is your son," Julio says.

It sounds pathetic; it sounds biblical, absurd, awkward. Julio holds out the red bag and she asks, "Where? Where is he?"

"Here."

"There?"

When they told her Libardo's remains had been found, she'd pushed back right from the start. How do I know it's him? They've analyzed the data. What data?, she asked. The DNA. What's that? It's like a kind of ID that all human beings have in their bodies. Where do we have it?, she'd asked. In the body— skin, hair, bones. Well, to be sure it's him, I need to see him. But maybe there isn't anything, Julio tried to explain, we have to trust the DNA, I gave them a sample of mine so they could do the analysis in case he was ever found. Oh, sweetie, don't confuse me with that stuff, Gran said, bewildered, and added, if I can just see him, I'll know if it's him, after all he's my son.

"Here he is, Gran," Julio says, and holds out the bag as if he were giving her a present.

Our grandmother wobbles; she doesn't know what to do with her hands, whether to bring them to her mouth, or press them to her chest, or fan herself with them, or wipe away her tears, or use them to prop herself up so she doesn't collapse on the floor. She goes quiet, her own words stifling her. Julio takes a step toward her and she steps back.

"Are you O.K., Gran?"

She shakes her head and points to the red bag. She tries to speak, Li, Li, Li. I hold her up and try to lead her to a chair. Suddenly, from somewhere, a voice booms out, saying, where's Carmenza the Dense-a? Where's Carmenza the Dense-a?

"Where is he?" Julio asks.

"In the kitchen," Gran says.

Julio starts to go off to look for him, but I gesture to him to let me go instead. And there I find him. He's in pajamas, and his hair is a mess, as if he's just gotten out of bed. He slaps the table in the breakfast nook and chants, where's Carmenza the Dense-a?, but as soon as he sees me he goes quiet, watching me with his yellow eyes. He blinks with difficulty because of the pterygia growing over his corneas, which have left him almost blind. Nevertheless he smiles at me.

"Hi, Grandpa," I say.

He laughs. He doesn't have a single tooth. Maybe he never did. I mean, maybe he was using dentures before and now he doesn't bother. He's drooling. There are stains of dripped food on his pajama top. He stops laughing, but he keeps studying me up and down.

"I'm Larry, Grandpa."

He raises his eyebrows, opens his mouth a little, and burps. He utters something that sounds like my name. In some corner of his memory, my face or my voice must have set something off that tells him, it's Larry, Libardo's kid.

"I arrived yesterday from London," I tell him.

Grandpa slowly lifts his arm and points to the cupboards. I don't see anything worth notice, just jars, battered cookpots, a pile of dirty dishes, a basket full of blackened bananas.

"Do you need something?" I ask.

The nail on his finger is long and untrimmed. His hand trembles, and his voice isn't able to pull together what he wants to tell me. The glibness with which he'd been taunting my grandmother is gone. Now he looks like a spoiled child who's trying to get attention by using baby talk.

"What do you want, Grandpa?"

He's not even trying to talk now. He looks like a tragedy mask; he groans, still pointing, looking back and forth between me and the cupboards.

"Do you want something to eat?"

His groan sounds like a complaint. His old finger looks like the one God points when issuing punishment. His eyes glare at me as if in warning. I go over to the cabinets next to the stove and ask, "Here?"

Grandpa shakes his head. I point to the lower cabinets and he again says no. He tries to lift his arm a little higher, and I point to the upper cabinet. He nods. I open the doors and find only old glass and metal containers full of unidentifiable substances, full of food and time.

"In the back," he says, quite clearly, with perfect pronunciation.

I push the jars aside to look in the back and there, in the shadows, I see an old revolver that doesn't even have a cylinder. I look at my grandfather, and he looks back at me with his eyes very wide open, translucent and full of fear.

"Whose is it?" I ask, and close the cupboard.

My grandfather looks toward the living room, where Julio and my grandmother are murmuring over a bag of bones.

"She's going to kill me," he says quietly.

Now he uses his finger to signal me not to say anything. Or maybe, from having lived with her so long, he knows what's going to happen, that she, her curiosity piqued by our silence, will come in right at that moment, as she in fact does, and asks, "What's going on?"

"Nothing, Gran. Just saying hi to Grandpa."

"Did he recognize you?" she asks, not caring that he's right there.

"Of course, Gran."

"See?" she says. "He's faking it to manipulate us." Her tone changes and she pleads, "Larry, come tell your brother to leave your dad here. He's insisting on taking him to that woman."

That woman is Fernanda. Gran not only demeans my mother by referring to her without saying her name, but she also makes a contemptuous face that hurts my heart. Julio walks in with the bag.

"No, Gran, stop making things up," he says. He looks at me and says, "I just want to take him so I can find something decent to put him in."

Gran crosses her arms. "I wasn't born yesterday."

"I can't leave him here." Julio tries to convince her. "I have to take him to make sure he'll fit. Dad deserves something dig-nified and comfortable."

"What's more comfortable than his own home?" Gran asks defiantly. She defies all of us by ignoring the fact that Libardo's real home was our house, the one he built for us.

The tension intensifies with the din of stool legs scraping against the floor. Grandpa has gotten to his feet and, again with the same finger, points at the red bag Julio's carrying.

"Is that him?" he asks Julio.

"Hi, Grandpa," my brother says, as if he's just spotted him.

"Don't listen to him," Gran says. "He doesn't understand what's happening."

"Is that Libardo?" Grandpa asks again.

Gran turns to him and tells him to go to his room, to leave her in peace, to stop bothering her; she says he stinks to high heaven, tells him to take a bath, shave, go to bed, die. I look at my grandfather and think about the revolver she's got hidden. He looks at me, and at Julio too, and in that rheumy gaze I read a litany of complaints and humiliations. And I ponder, I won-der how Grandpa figured out we were talking about Libardo and discussing where to put his remains, and how he guessed that the plastic bag contained his son, the one he'd mourned, when Gran insists he has no idea what is going on.

"Gran," Julio says gently, "you're going to be able to be with him forever, but I need to take him with me right now . . ."

"He's my son," Grandpa breaks in.

"We're going to look for a container for him, something worthy of him," says Julio, who's gradually losing his compo-sure.

"Where are you going to put him, huh?" Gran asks, and Julio loses his shit.

"How the hell do I know?" he says. "This is the first time I've had a father die on me. I don't know what to do with the dead, but we can't leave him in this bag. A box, a chest, an urn, what do I know . . ."

"Julio . . ." I try to soothe him.

"What, what, what?" he yells, balling up a fist.

"Calm down."

"My son," Grandpa says, the sad-mask expression on his face once more.

Julio goes off like a rocket without a fuse, as if it were I or Fernanda or somebody else complaining about dead Libardo's return to the land of the living.

"A cardboard box or a trash can!" Julio yells. "As far as I'm concerned, they should have left him in the dump where they found him—that's where he always should have been."

I turn my back on him so I don't have to deal with his tantrum. Until I hear a blow that shuts him up, a sharp slap, and a my God from our grandmother that causes me to turn around and find that it wasn't her who hit Julio but our grandfather. My brother looks at him in bewilderment, and our grandfather stares back at him, irate. He's returned from another planet, or from the galaxy to which our grandmother banished him, to scold his grandson:

"Show your father some respect, damn it."

44

The photo arrived of Benito riddled with bullets, as if the single gunshot between the eyes hadn't been enough. And beside him a spiteful little calling card accusing him of being a murderer, an ass-kisser, a snitch, though it was that last accusation that indicated the real reason he'd been killed: for being a friend of Pablo's. Miraculously, or because they'd run out of room, they didn't write "and Libardo's."

Benito had adored my dad, and he'd felt the same way about Benito, so it was also possible they'd made a pact never to rat each other out; Benito would have been targeted for his closeness to Escobar alone. But by sending us the photo—and sending it a few days before the police found his corpse—the message was clear: they were aware of not only Benito's ties with the boss but also his ties with Libardo. Still, it seemed strange that the only person who never turned up, either dead or alive, was Libardo, not even in the bloodcurdling photos his enemies used to boast of their acts of vengeance.

For Fernanda, it was a cruel blow. She'd always complained about Benito because he encouraged Libardo's affairs; she'd cursed at him, kicked him out of the house, and in recent days had even become suspicious of him. Deep down, though, she knew the two men were like brothers and that Benito was the only person she could trust now. Once she'd managed to stop crying, Fernanda told us, "I'm going to look for them and ask them what more they want. I'll give them everything we've got if they let us live, since after this the only thing left will be to come after us."

"Who are you going to talk to?" Julio asked.

"Them."

"Who's them?"

"The people who've been calling. Next time I'm going to be crystal clear with them."

"We don't even know if the people calling actually have him," I said.

"Look," she said, "that's what Benito thought, and they killed him."

"How do you know it was them?"

Fernanda clutched her hair with both hands as if she were going to pull it out. She howled with fury and stomped her feet, like a little girl having a temper tantrum, but in fact she was terrified. We were terrified. She felt alone. She was overwhelmed by powerlessness or the burden of having to fight with her two sons, though she didn't suspect that, for a long time now, Julio and I had had no idea how to fight with her. None of us—not her or Julio or me—knew what to do, and that's what scared us, that's what they wanted, that's what they achieved.

The mess didn't stop there. The man Fernanda was talking to, Rómulo, didn't know what she was talking about when she brought up the photo of Benito. He didn't even know who Benito was. And he even turned it around on her: don't try to confuse me, ma'am, he said, I've just got your husband, and I can do whatever I want with him; I can release him if you give me what I'm asking for, or I can kill him if you don't work with me. How can I pay you when you haven't sent me proof of life?, Fernanda objected. I've got the cops breathing down my neck, Rómulo replied, but I'll finish him off before they catch me, he said, and hung up.

No other friend of Libardo's inspired any confidence in Fernanda. She would invite them in and hear what they had to say, but she never told them what she was thinking. She, Julio, and I were the ones who'd discuss the plans, though there really weren't any plans. There was just us thinking out loud.

Fernanda decided to look for a way out in Libardo's study. She emptied the drawers, pulled the letters out of their envelopes and the documents out of their folders. She gathered the billing statements in one stack, invoices and receipts in another, and she set aside the notes written in Libardo's crude handwriting. Suspicious, she put the business cards in a pile—the culprit, the informant, the snitch, the killer might be among them. She organized the objects—every item, every knick-knack, all the crap Libardo had in drawers or on shelves. And the guns Libardo had kept locked away for our sakes. The Luger sold to him by a Russian collector, another that kind of looked like only half a pistol because it didn't have a barrel, plus two more new-school ones: one with a silencer, and the other with the initials *LV*.

Everything was exposed, and there wasn't a single spot of bare floor in Libardo's study. She went around barefoot so she could step on the papers without ruining them. Julio and I didn't need to look at each other to share our thoughts or feelings. Especially since one corner of the desk held a sparkling glass, full of ice and something else, maybe vodka or gin or light rum, that made her totter as she hopped over the piles of papers, repeating, "It's all here, boys, the truth, the answers we're looking for."

There on the floor was part of Libardo's untidy life. Papers like pieces of a puzzle that only he could have put together. I took off my shoes and walked among the mounds of documents, getting a bird's-eye view of numbers, names, letterheads, strangers' signatures next to his, fingerprints signing agreements, maps, scraps of paper with notes, and even stray napkins with phone numbers. Nothing told me anything. Nothing was familiar except the guns, which, though I'd never seen them before, were like seeing Libardo's toothbrush.

"Did you find anything weird?" Julio asked Fernanda.

She took a drink, waved her hand in the air as if she were shooing a fly away, and said, "To be honest, everything's weird."

Something crunched beneath my foot, under a yellow receipt, and for a moment I thought Libardo was sending me a sign. The answer, my son, is there, under your big toe. I stooped down and picked up the piece of paper, hoping to find in it the solution to the current state of affairs, but what had crunched was a pair of reading glasses, the kind Libardo used to keep all over the place because he always forgot where he'd left them. The lenses had shattered, and one arm had broken off.

Fernanda scolded me. "What did you do?"

"I didn't see them. They were covered up."

Though Libardo hadn't sent me a sign, I did experience a flash of lucidity; I realized that the things heaped up in that room weren't going to contribute anything new to what we already understood. The information might be useful in the future, if we ever had to sell some asset to get by, but when it came to Libardo's situation, nothing in those piles was going to help us.

"Ma," I said, "there isn't anything here."

"You've barely looked, you twerp."

"If what you want is to find him, he's not here."

"Larry's right, Ma," Julio said. "We've known who's got him from the start."

Fernanda took a drink. She shook her hair back, haughty, ready to defend the task she'd been toiling away at in that study for an entire week. She perched on the edge of the desk and said, "I hadn't realized my boys knew so much. I'm just going to go rest, and you two can wake me up when your dad comes home."

"Ma," I said, "it's one thing for us to know who has him and something totally different to be able to get him back."

"There's definitely important information in these papers," Julio said, "but what we need is to get in touch with one of those people who's a real heavyweight."

"Oh, a heavyweight," Fernanda said.

"Yes, you must know one of them."

Fernanda drained her glass. She held her breath a moment and then blew it out. She must have felt useless, nothing but a former beauty queen.

"Remember, it wasn't so long ago they were all the same, they were on the same side," I said.

"And the one who's calling you isn't the one who's got Dad," Julio said.

"Oh no?" Fernanda said. "What else can you two know-it-alls tell me?"

Julio and I looked at each other and realized it would be better to wait till she wasn't drinking. Though I knew, just as she and Julio did, that every minute we let pass was one less minute of life for Libardo.

45

Gran serves linden tea to calm our nerves. She has a cup too, and pours the last of the pot for Grandpa. Libardo, in the bag, rests on another armchair. Gran tells us she used to have a silver pitcher, just lovely, that she used only to serve tea, but she's had to hock all of her silver over the years to get by and pay for Grandpa's treatments. She pouts and twists her lips to point at him, but he's lost in thought, staring into the bottom of his cup. Julio takes the hint when she mentions her money problems.

"The situation's really complicated, Gran," he says. "Not only is it summer, we've been having law enforcement issues too. Getting rid of those guerrillas has been a nightmare, but what are you going to do."

"I'm not trying to put you down, honey," our grandmother says, "but your father would have solved that problem in an instant."

"We're working on it, Gran; we've got some tough people on our side, but we have to handle things delicately."

"I know, honey."

"Nothing is easy, Gran."

"Except gaining weight," she says.

Grandpa laughs and tells us, as if revealing a secret, "Carmenza's a whale."

Gran shushes him.

I get up to see if we can put an end to this reunion. I haven't come to bring them Libardo's remains. I go over to a bookcase and pick up a large picture frame with a photo of a little girl who's looking out the way Libardo used to do.

"What's her name?" I ask Gran.

"Put that down, Larry," Julio tells me.

"Rosa Marcela," our grandmother responds, and then asks in surprise, "You didn't know?"

"I found out today," I say.

"Larry," Julio says again.

"Bug off," I tell him.

"Doesn't she look just like him?" Gran asks me.

I study the photo again and say, "They've got the same eyes."

"And the same laugh," Gran says, her voice sweet.

"Do you know where she lives?"

"Larry."

"Lay off, Julio, he has the right to know about it too," Gran says. She turns to me. "Of course I do, sweetie, I visit a lot, and she comes here too, though she's frightened of him." Again she points at our grandfather with her mouth and adds, "And Vanesa's a sweetheart too."

"Who's Vanesa?" I ask.

"Rosa Marcela's mother. You didn't know that either?"

Gran's eyes gleam. She's never said anything like that to Fernanda. Julio stands up and sets his cup on the coffee table. Gran sips her tea as if it were ambrosia.

"We're leaving, Gran," Julio says.

"Do you want to go see her?" she asks me. Julio looks at me angrily.

"I do."

"Hold on," she says, and gets up. She moves gently, like a sweet little grandmother who's trying hard to indulge her grandson, and goes into the kitchen.

Julio says, "Drop the bullshit, Larry, we've got to go. We've still got a lot to do."

"It's just for a minute," I tell him.

"Don't get Gran wound up," he says. "You don't realize how much this game of yours could cost us."

"Cost us?"

"Yeah, dumbass, a lot," he tells me, his temper flaring. "Are you ready to share the little that Libardo left us with that brat? Her mother's behind this, in case you didn't know that either."

Gran emerges from the kitchen, fanning herself with a sheet of pink paper and smiling vibrantly.

"Here you go," she says, "and I wrote down the phone number too, just in case."

I look at the information to see where they live. Julio grabs the bag. Gran steps in front of him.

"Where are you taking him?" she asks.

"I told you. We're going to look for something to keep him in."

"He's not leaving here," she says firmly.

"Do we have to go through all that again?" Julio replies.

She lifts her hand to her chest and says, "I can't take this."

"I'll bring him to you this afternoon," Julio says.

Meanwhile, Grandpa has fallen asleep, his teacup between his legs.

"I can't take this, boys," Gran says again.

Julio doesn't do anything. I go over and ask her to sit down.

"Let's go, Larry," Julio says, and strides toward the door.

"Oh, honey, oh dear."

Gran tries to catch her breath. Julio looks for a way out. I wish for the earth to swallow me. Julio turns around and looks at me. He gives me a commanding gesture. I walk by our grandfather and stroke his sparse, matted hair, pick up his cup, and place it on the table. I look at the photo of Rosa Marcela, at our grandmother collapsed in an armchair, at our snoring grandfather, at my brother, who's heading out with Libardo under his arm. And I follow him because, as they say, in the land of the blind, the one-eyed man is king.

46

Out of the blue, men we'd never seen before started showing up at the house. Fernanda said they were prominent lawyers or people who knew that sphere well. I wasn't sure whether she meant the legal sphere or the drug trafficking one. I preferred not to ask. As long as Libardo returned, I didn't care what she had to do. I would have welcomed the devil himself into our home to get Libardo back. I was still hoping that if he reappeared, we'd go live in another country and start a different life. But the news we were hearing about the Escobar family suggested that it wasn't so easy to shed the past. Of course, Escobar was Escobar; dead or alive, his name had split Colombian history in two. Whereas Libardo was a secondary character; they wouldn't even know who he was in other countries, and that fueled my hope. But men came, they went, they called, and my dad still didn't come back.

Fernanda also decided to remove Dengue from his position as head of security. She didn't fire him, but instead assigned him to watch the house and named another man, Albeiro, as her personal bodyguard.

"I still don't understand why Dengue left Libardo alone that day," she told us, and her breath ran out when she said "that day."

Dengue, for his part, since he was hanging around the house, took the opportunity to vent to us. Or, rather, to confuse us, because he got us second-guessing Fernanda's decisions. He claimed he could get in touch with the men who were holding

Libardo, that he'd been given firsthand information, that he still had some pull with the police, that if our mother had let him finish his work, Libardo would already be with us. He sought me out to complain to more than he did Julio. I seized on his desperation to soothe my own. I was sick of being cooped up—I wasn't even allowed to go outside. So I told Dengue, "I can talk to her, but I need a favor from you. I need to go out, see my friends; I've got to get out of this house for a little while every day."

Dengue was as tired of being cooped up as I was, so as soon as Fernanda went out, I'd hop in the backseat and head out with him to patrol Medellín. I went to visit Henríquez, Posada, and many others, but the only person who was happy to see me was Pedro, the Dictator.

"Don't you have a girlfriend too?" Dengue asked, looking at me in the rearview mirror.

I didn't have a girlfriend and didn't want one. Dengue hinted that if I wanted women, he could take me to the best ones in town.

"You must be full up from tamping down your urges for months," he said.

It was true, but this was no time for hookers. Especially not the kind Dengue slept with. I settled for going to visit Pedro, who'd greet me with a hug, and invite him to climb into the SUV and drive around with us. We used to buy aguardiente and sit in the back drinking, gossiping, looking out through the windows at Medellín falling apart around us.

Dengue made sure to keep tabs on Fernanda so we always got back before her. She never caught me or realized I was coming home drunk. I'd retreat to my room, and she didn't find it at all unusual. Poor kids, she'd say, they're so depressed. Dengue told me that Julio did the same thing, but he always dropped my brother off at his girlfriend's house. As far as I knew, Julio didn't have a girlfriend, but I didn't ask and didn't care.

A few weeks later, Dengue refused to take me anywhere. He told me he couldn't, offering no explanation, but I knew what was going on: he was demanding I hold up my end of the bargain and persuade Fernanda to let him rejoin the search for Libardo. So I tried.

"Ma," I said, "Dengue really loves Dad and he's been looking into things, and, well, I was thinking . . ."

She removed the glasses she was wearing to read a document, and that gesture alone told me I shouldn't say anything else. "What are you doing talking to a crook like Dengue?" she asked, shaking her head.

"He works for us."

"Yes, because when your father comes home, Dengue has to be here, but if it were up to me . . ." She went back to reading and, without looking at me, added, "Libardo has to find everything just as he left it."

"Do you really think he'll come back?"

"Of course," she said, lost in the document again.

The days became denser and slower; every passing hour was stickier than the last. Without realizing it, our schedule shifted. We spent more time awake at night and got up late every morning. During the few hours I managed to sleep, I would dream about Libardo. Strange dreams, as dreams always are. Fernanda and Julio dreamed about him too, but we didn't share. One of us would just say, I dreamed about him last night. That was all. Given our day-to-day reality, there was no need to make things even more complicated. Fernanda decided to increase our dose of bromazepam. We went from taking half a pill a day to a whole one, so we'd sleep better, she said. She'd already increased her own dose a while back.

We stopped talking to one another. Fernanda spent her days shut up in Libardo's study, looking at papers with her "lawyers." I would do schoolwork sporadically and watch TV, but mostly I just stared at the ceiling. Late at night we'd exchange a few sentences; Julio and I would try to get Fernanda to catch us up on what was happening. She would say the same thing as always—everything's going to be O.K., boys, God willing. In other words, she was waiting for a miracle.

This was confirmed one afternoon when Fernanda came home with a man who was quite different from all the others. He was short and ugly. She introduced him and said, "Keep doing what you're doing. Iván's going to be around, working alone."

There had been so many strangers in the house that it didn't strike me as weird that a new one would be prowling around— that is, until we saw him waving a torch that was giving off black smoke, ringing a bell with his other hand, and reciting prayers in some unfamiliar language. Suffocated by the smoke, the maids, the bodyguards, and my brother and I went out into the backyard for some air. Julio whispered to me, Ma's crazy, and she told all of us, "Go back inside. Iván needs to be alone in the backyard."

We watched him walk around, swinging a pendulum, until he stopped and crouched down. He started digging with a trowel, kneeling on the grass. Pretty soon he signaled Fernanda over. He showed her something, and she raised her hands to her mouth. Julio and I went out to see what Iván had found: a burial, a tiny bundle full of old coins and hair. I asked if the hair was Libardo's. Probably he said. And what are those coins?, Julio asked. Somebody wants to do you a lot of harm, Iván said. They already have, I said, and Fernanda shot me a furious look. Then she asked, "What now?"

"Now we burn this so Don Libardo will come back soon," he said, picking up the little packet.

The house filled with a nauseating odor, and the ceilings were stained by the smoke from the torch. For days, ashes kept falling. But I have to admit that the holy smoke and the burning of the charm were successful, though much later than we'd been promised. Libardo did come back, even if he was dead and it was twelve long years after Iván's visit.

47

I'll be right out, Fernanda yells from her room, and Julio and I wait for her in the living room, which is crammed with boxes that haven't been unpacked. From the previous house, she brought a loveseat and the armchair that had been in Libardo's study. There's also a TV, a telephone, and the laptop she uses to talk to me, and a jumble of things that seem not to have found their places. Right next to that is a small dining set. We hear clacking footsteps, and Julio and I look at each other. Fernanda appears in a tight-fitting blue dress and high heels.

"Where is he?" she asks, surprised. "You didn't leave him at your grandmother's place."

"He's in the car," Julio replies.

"Oh, O.K.," Fernanda says, and sits down next to me on the sofa. "What are you going to do with him?"

"We've got to find something for him," Julio says. "He's in a bag at the moment."

Fernanda takes a deep breath, as if trying not to cry. She's wearing makeup—she's got eyeliner on, and she fans her eyes with her hand.

"And how is he?" she asks hesitantly. "Did you see him?"

"Yes," I say.

"He's not all there," Julio says.

"Jesus," Fernanda says, unable to contain her tears.

"If it makes you feel better, there were no signs of violence on what they gave us," Julio says.

"Don't tell me any more," Fernanda pleads. She dabs her

eyes and checks her fingers to see if they're smeared with mascara. She says, "I haven't been able to arrange the mass yet. Father Diego isn't answering me, but I already left him a message."

"I'm leaving tonight," Julio says.

Fernanda raises her voice: "You're not going anywhere till we give him the sendoff he deserves."

"Dad didn't go to mass," Julio objects.

"But he was a devout believer," Fernanda says.

"In whom?" Julio asks. "Or what? The only thing he believed in was money."

"Stop it," I say.

They fall silent like chastised children. Fernanda gets up, rummages in a cardboard box, and pulls out a pack of cigarettes.

"Have you had breakfast?" she asks us.

We nod. She says she's going to make coffee anyway and clacks off to the kitchen. Julio says in a low voice, she's been in this apartment four years and she's still got all these taped-up boxes. What's in them?, I ask. Her things, he says, house stuff. Does she need help?, I ask. She's got help, Julio says, there's a lady who comes in three times a week and I've offered too. Plus, he adds, she's in got more boxes out at the farm. Maybe now that I'm here . . . , I say. Fernanda is humming a song in the kitchen, a romantic song from the eighties. What does she do all day?, I ask Julio. Huh, he says, and shrugs. All I know is she's always asking me for money, he adds. And do you give it to her? As much as I can, he says, I give her a set amount each month, but she claims it's not enough.

"Are you talking about me?" Fernanda asks.

We don't hear her footsteps; she appears there like a cat.

"I was telling Julio that while I'm here I can help you unpack these boxes."

"Thank you, sweetheart," she says, "the problem isn't unpacking them but where to put what's in them. Did you see how small the closets are? The kitchen doesn't even have a pantry."

"So why don't you sell all this?" Julio asks. "Why keep it?"

"Darling, there are things in there it's impossible to get anymore," Fernanda says, and then asks, "Who wants coffee?"

She doesn't even wait for a response. She spins around and leaves, like when she used to parade down the catwalks, Miss Medellín 1973.

All these years, all this time, and yet everything's exactly the same. Or worse. An aging beauty queen, a brother who's hiding out on a farm that he's made his little fiefdom, a city that's repeating its own history, a non-viable country that's marching backward, and a world full of hate and war. A dead father who refuses to die, a dumbass who falls in love with a stranger on a plane. It all makes me want to throw up, to just stop existing.

But it smells like coffee, and the aroma brings me back. When it comes down to it, London isn't so bad. I used to have Maggie, and I've still got a job waiting for me. A small apartment in a nice neighborhood—the bus passes nearby, the market isn't too far away, I can walk to Finsbury Park, and on Sunday afternoons I can walk a little farther to see movies at the Everyman in Hampstead. I can fall in love again with an English girl, a Russian, an Indian, or a Serb. If Maggie loved me, somebody else can too. What I need now is to get some sleep. Fernanda can keep drinking her coffee and plan the mass, Julio can refuse and leave, or he can stay and we can sleep side by side the way we sometimes did as kids, Medellín can rot, Colombia can end up being devoured by hate, the world can explode. Fernanda is laughing loudly, alone in the kitchen. Alone? I'm going to sleep; I've been awake for more hours than anybody can endure.

"Shall we head out?" Julio asks me.

"Where to?"

"To find something for Dad."

"Where are we supposed to go for that? What are you look-ing for?"

Julio shrugs. Fernanda laughs again, and he can't take it anymore and stands up.

"Let's get out of here."

I go to the kitchen to say goodbye to Fernanda and find her with her back to me, talking on the phone. She's scratching one calf with the tip of her foot. You're crazy, she tells somebody. She laughs and says again, crazy.

"Ma."

She turns around, looks at me, opens a cupboard, and takes out three mugs. Larry's here, she tells the person she's talking to, I've got to go.

"It's just now finished," she tells me, meaning the coffee. That aroma.

"What are we going to do with Dad?" I ask. She pours the cof-fee. "I'm not having any," I say. "I'm going to lie down a little."

"What about Julio?"

"He's going out. What do you think we should put Dad in?"

"We've got to give Libardo a Christian burial."

"You want to bury him?"

For a moment I consider pointing out that Libardo was buried for twelve years.

"Nobody gets buried in those circumstances," I tell her. "They get dug up and taken somewhere else. To an ossuary or something, I don't know, anywhere."

"But he didn't have a Christian burial," she moans, and I start to get irritated with how she keeps saying "Christian bur-ial," as if she were a priest.

"The most practical thing is to cremate him," I say.

"Most practical? Are you talking about your father?" she asks me indignantly, then yells, "Julio! Are you having coffee?" Julio walks in and Fernanda says, "Your brother tells me the most practical thing is to cremate Libardo."

"Ma," I try to interject.

"Makes no difference to me," Julio says. "But we'll have to wait if we want to cremate him because we need a document from the attorney general's office."

Fernanda holds out a cup of coffee but Julio refuses it. She offers it to me, and I say no. But that aroma. I take the cup and lift it to my nose.

"Libardo hasn't been able to rest properly," Fernanda says. "He deserves for us to give him a Christian burial."

"Stop saying that, please," I say.

"Stop saying what?"

"Just say we have to bury him, full stop."

"But weren't you just saying we should cremate him?"

This aroma that perfumes my exhaustion. This sleepiness that's got me so I can barely stand. A mother who calls somebody crazy and laughs. The attorney general's office that won't let us cremate Libardo yet. An exasperated brother. A sip of coffee that warms my mouth, that cajoles my tongue and scrambles my neurons. The scorched smell of fireworks coming in through the window, the mountains like a backdrop. If I could die right now, I would.

"They can decide that afterward," Julio tells us. "I'm going to buy him something before I take off. You coming?" he asks.

I'm only halfway through my coffee. I haven't yet regained the strength to stand up. There are still a few people out there with the energy to keep setting off fireworks.

Julio looks at Fernanda, and she says firmly, "I can't, I've got an appointment."

"Where are you going?" I ask.

"I've got a lunch."

Who's the makeup and high heels for? Who makes her laugh? Why is she still worshiping Libardo?

"And I'm going to go to Father Diego's church," she says.

"You coming, Little Bro?" Julio asks.

If I lie down, I don't know if I'll see him again. He'll go to his farm, and I don't know if I'll go visit him. If I want to spend a little more time with my brother, I have no choice but to go with him.

"Let me finish my coffee," I say.

"I'm going to the bathroom," Fernanda says.

"I'll wait downstairs," Julio says.

I sit alone with this aroma and this flavor that remind me of what I never should have been: a human being. And the mountains outside confirm to me the place where I never should have been born. I breathe in the sulfurous air of the city I never should have returned to. I think about the father who, for dignity's sake, should never have had children, and about a country that should be wiped off the map. A failed species on the earth. A drowsiness. A fatigue.

I toss back the rest of the coffee, leaving the grounds in which fortune-tellers read the future. For the moment, mine will be to look for a container for Libardo's bones.

I put the mug in the sink next to other dirty dishes. Fernanda has left her cell phone on the counter. This curiosity that killed more than the cat. I pick it up to look at the record of the last call. "Pedro," it says.

This confusion, this spasm.

48

The cold from up in the mountains collided with the hot, moist air rising from the sea, and the plane started shaking. It was the announcement of their arrival in the New World. What was visible through the windows was no longer blue but rather green and brown. The mountains, the jungles, the plains, the tropical forests, the textures of a gestating continent. And a sky full of clouds in the shapes of monsters and demons so travelers would understand, once and for all, that they were entering a cursed realm.

Charlie hadn't raised the blind. A little earlier, once she could move her legs again, she'd curled up in her seat and stayed like that, waiting for Larry to return. She no longer felt the urge to go looking for him. She dozed until she was awakened by the announcement to fasten seatbelts. She was dying of thirst. She looked back, toward the rear of the plane, trying to catch a glimpse of him. In the snarl of her hangover, she tried to find an explanation for why Larry had fled.

Did I say something I shouldn't have? . . .

She didn't remember everything they'd talked about or every detail of what she'd done, and apart from having started drinking again, she had no other regrets. But it had always been like this in the past—she'd wake up believing that nothing had happened, when in fact all kinds of things had happened.

She pressed the button to summon a flight attendant. Charlie requested a glass of water with lots of ice. A pang in

her upper abdomen reminded her that she hadn't eaten anything. The drinks she was having now were making her feel
sick, and churning along with everything else was her sadness
over her dead father. She cried as she drank her ice water.

The airplane kept shaking gently, the passengers unfazed.
The flight attendants' bustling suggested that the plane would
be landing soon.

They passed out the immigration form, and she took the
opportunity to ask for more water. With her feet, she grabbed
the purse she'd placed on the floor and dragged it toward her.
She hunted through the jumble for a pen and an ibuprofen for
her headache, but didn't find either. She looked at the form,
and it seemed to ask too many questions. There wasn't room
for all four of her given names. There's never room for me,
she'd once told a psychiatrist, I don't even fit on forms, my full
name won't fit on a credit card. I'm not one person, I'm four,
she told that psychiatrist, still drunk and burping rum.

She borrowed a pen from the man in the other seat. He
passed her a cheap ballpoint with a hotel logo.

What happened to the Montblanc you used to fill out yours?

She thanked him with a smile. Even writing her names in
tiny letters, she spilled out of the boxes.

I spilled out of boxes . . .

She answered no to all the questions, signed, and paused as
she was about to put the date. What's today?, she asked her
neighbor, and he replied, November 30. As she wrote it down,
Charlie knew she'd remember that date for the rest of her life.

There are some amounts of time that for whatever reason feel round, so we use them in stories to take inventory. A week ago, people say, or a month ago, or three, or six. They're useful for tallying either sadnesses or joys, but we tend to use them most often for keeping an account of hardships. Especially absences. Fernanda, the dramatic one in the family, was the one who kept measure of the time since Libardo's disappearance. It's been a week, she'd say, a month now, it's been three months since they took him.

Julio and I would keep quiet, assessing the seriousness of what Fernanda had said, waiting for the pain to pass—though it wasn't passing—practicing patience so we could go on with our lives. Though the days went by, some swift and others slow, only an uneasiness persisted beyond wondering what had happened to Libardo, one that came from not knowing what we were going to do, what was going to happen to us. Again we considered the possibility of leaving, but to all three of us it felt like a betrayal. We were oppressed still by the hope that he might be alive. Even if staying meant being cooped up in our house, frightened, under the pressure of threats and financial difficulties. Worse still, being at the mercy of Fernanda's harsh commentary. She was convinced that money would get Libardo back to us, but she was also spending loads of it whenever she went to the casino to "clear her head."

She was sharing her decisions less and less, confiding instead in the men she was meeting with, the purported lawyers, the spiritual advisers, the important people who, she claimed, were helping her.

She reviewed every sheet of paper she found in Libardo's study, and instead of clarifying things, each discovery confused her more. Did you ever hear your dad talk about a piece of land in Montelíbano? There's some guy named Roberto Mahecha who owes your father three hundred thousand dollars. Who do you suppose Mister X is? Is this López Benedetti the same one who was a government minister? Boys, did you know that Don Luis Gustavo—can't remember his last name—the president of Colautos, who was supposedly so respectable and honest, did business with Libardo? No, Ma, we didn't know anything about that, Dad didn't talk much about his stuff. I, at least, never found out, or maybe didn't want to know—I preferred to remain ignorant of Libardo's world.

"All I care about is the farms," Julio told her, and said, "Don't hand those over, don't negotiate with them—they're our future."

Julio was more and more determined that as soon as we graduated from high school, he was going to start running the farms, despite Fernanda's insistence that he go to college. He told her, I'm not going to waste time learning what I already know. She retorted, if you don't study, you're going to be just another peon. They argued a lot, and never resolved anything.

Six months after Libardo disappeared, I started organizing parties at our house. At first they were small gatherings on Friday nights, which Pedro the Dictator would attend with a couple of friends, nobody from school, just his friends from around town. We used to drink a couple of bottles of aguardiente, watch music videos, talk tough—it helped me blow off steam. Then they started bringing girls, their friends, loose chicks who'd get drunk right along with us. We would dance, watch more videos; we'd grope the girls and they'd get us all horny, but it never went anywhere. Julio would hang out with us some nights, though he almost always took off to visit his mystery girlfriend. Fernanda was understanding at first and put up with the noise and the music, but when she saw the chicks, she told me, "I don't want those girls in this house."

"Why not?"

"Just look at them."

"What's wrong?"

"Look, Pedro is welcome whenever you like, but tell him not to bring those girls."

"They're my guests. I invite them," I said.

"Well, don't."

"If you don't want them here, let me go out."

"No."

"Then I'm going to keep bringing them."

"Absolutely not."

"It's my house," I said defiantly.

"And mine too," she said, "and Julio's and your father's. So you're going to respect it."

"Who respects a drug lord's house?"

Fernanda raised her hand and gave me a slap that practically knocked me off my feet. She pointed at the bedroom door and told me, "Get out, you ungrateful brat."

That weekend I didn't have anybody over. I told Pedro I was sick and sat drinking alone in my room, cursing and crying. At midnight I came out, geared up to lash out at Fernanda about how miserable I was, but she was nowhere to be found. Julio wasn't there either. Only the two maids, four aggressive dogs, and six bodyguards were around. I vomited up the aguardiente I'd drunk and the next day awoke sprawled on the floor, curled up next to the toilet.

Fernanda didn't talk to me all week and Julio reprimanded me for what I'd said. I was fed up, I said. You were out of hand, Julio said. She's the one who was out of hand, I said, and showed him the red blotch that still marked my cheek. Watch what you say, Little Bro, Julio warned me.

The next Friday I invited everybody again, both guys and girls. I gave Pedro money so they could buy aguardiente; I didn't want Fernanda throwing it in my face that we were drinking the house's liquor. But she never said anything about my parties again, not about the girls or our benders. I guess since she was going out at night, she didn't feel like she had the right to scold me.

At another party I met Julieth, and I slept with her that same night. At a certain point we turned out the light, and the glow from the videos provided enough light to keep pouring ourselves drinks. Taking advantage of the darkness, I felt her up and found she was already as wet as an oyster. She was the one who suggested we go to the bedroom. I went upstairs with her without checking whether Julio and Fernanda were home. I didn't care what they might think.

Julieth and I devoured each other. I had been in forced abstinence for months, and she was lusty by nature. Pedro told me afterward that they could hear my moans downstairs, even with the music turned all the way up. She emptied me all the way out, I told him, and I thanked him, instead of thanking Julieth.

On another Friday night, when we'd already downed an entire bottle, Pedro tossed a folded dollar bill on the table and looked at me, waiting for my reaction. The others clapped, including Julieth. I smiled to oblige them.

"We're doing coke," Pedro said.

I kept smiling.

"Want some?" he asked.

One of the guys unfolded the bill to reveal the white powder. He touched it and then sucked his finger. He flung himself backward and fell to the floor, faking a fit of emotion. Everybody laughed, and Pedro pulled his ID card out of his wallet. In the video we were watching, two stout gentlemen were dancing and singing *Macarena, Macarena, Macarena.*

"Want some, buddy?"

I glanced over at Julieth, and she shot back a look full of uninhibited desire. Pedro put the corner of the ID with a bit of coke under her nose. Julieth sniffed. It looked like her lips were going to explode, like she was about to come. Before it got to me, everybody took a hit. And then Pedro was standing in front of me, digging in the bill with the corner of his ID. Under my nose was my history, Libardo's, the Pandora's box of Colombia, the force that made the world go 'round. Every particle of that powder contained a war, but who was I to judge? A victim? The victimizer? A standard bearer for morality, or the bad apple? Everybody was watching me to see if I'd take that hit. The son of a capo doesn't do drugs?

"Come on, man," Pedro urged me.

In reply, I told him—told myself—"I don't give a shit."

50

D o you think Mom has a boyfriend?" I ask Julio.
"I have no fucking clue," he replies.
"Don't you care?"

"What would be the point? She does whatever she feels like anyway."

"She's still pretty," I say. "I wouldn't be surprised if she were seeing somebody."

"You talk to her more than I do. You know a lot more about her."

"I think there's somebody who knows more than the two of us."

"Who?"

"Pedro."

Julio makes a face I can't decipher.

"What are we doing here?" I ask.

"Where else can we go?" he replies.

It's the first time in my life that I've been to a funeral home, and I hope it's the last, at least while I'm alive.

"Wooden PJs for our eternal rest," Julio remarks, standing in front of the array of caskets in different styles and colors.

A salesman in a black suit and a tie offers his assistance. He speaks in a quiet voice, his tone grief-stricken, as if he were the bereaved one.

"We need something for my dad," Julio says.

"My condolences," the salesman says.

"It's a special case," Julio explains.

"Of course," the man murmurs. "No problem. Come and I'll show you."

It smells a little like flowers and a little like wood. There's celestial music in the background, a choir of angels providing atmosphere.

"Actually, you should take a look at my dad," Julio says, and raises the red bag in front of the face of the salesman, who clears his throat awkwardly.

"Right," he says. "Let's go to my office instead."

He gives us each a business card. The salesman is an adviser, the card says. He offers us coffee and calls to Marinita, a woman who's wiping down a casket.

"I imagine your late father has undergone an exhumation process."

We don't respond.

"In that case," he continues, "an urn rather than a casket is the more suitable choice."

"Will he fit in an urn?" I ask.

"I can offer our cremation service," the adviser says.

"Dad's got a matter pending with the attorney general's office," Julio explains. "We can't cremate him yet."

"Right," the adviser says, and the cleaning woman deposits the cups of coffee in front of us. "Bring me one too, Marinita," the man says.

"We don't have all of him," Julio says, "and I think there . . ." He hesitates, then plunges on. "There are some parts that are really long."

"Of course," the adviser says, "that's why I suggested the cremation service, which comes with a plan that includes the urn."

"My grandmother wants to keep him," I say.

"In that case, the most appropriate choice is definitely a box."

He slides a catalogue with photos of wooden boxes across the desk.

"These are specially for storing remains. We have them ranging in size from twenty-eight to forty inches long," he explains, "and we can also have them custom-made according to your particular needs."

There are boxes made from various kinds of wood, simple or ornate, and he says we can put whatever inscription we want on it.

"Like an epitaph?" I ask.

Julio looks at me oddly and asks, "What's that?"

"What's written on gravestones," I say.

"But he isn't going to have a gravestone."

The adviser breaks in. "Maybe a twenty-eight-inch one would be large enough for your grandmother to keep him in." He shows us the photos of the smallest boxes. "But we can make them to order too," he says again.

"Gran might like one of these," I tell Julio. The adviser sips his coffee. Julio and I start looking through the photos again from the beginning. The salesman tells us to take as long as we need, afterward he'll show us the funeral plans for this kind of situation.

"What kind of situation?" I ask.

Does he suspect how Libardo died? Are there special services for burying cartel capos?

"We offer ceremonies for the final resting place," he adds, "as in your father's situation."

"This one," Julio says, and puts his finger on one of the boxes. He looks at me, seeking my approval.

"That one's quite sober," the adviser says. "Exactly right for someone who's deeply loved. It has a timeless, traditional design."

"Do you like it?" Julio asks me.

"Yes," I say. "Let's get this over with."

"We have it in stock," the adviser says.

"How much is it?" Julio asks.

"That's one of the larger ones. It costs two hundred thousand pesos, and we do offer financing," the adviser says.

Julio wants to pay in cash, with no payments or interest to worry about; like me, he wants to put this behind us now and not have to think about yet another of Libardo's debts every month.

"What's next, Little Bro?" Julio asks.

He means what are we going to do with the remains. Put them in the box now? Carry them in the bag until we find the right time and place to transfer them?

"Do you offer that service?" I ask the adviser, and then clarify. "Without cremation, of course."

"You're referring to . . . ?" He moves his hands from the bag to the box and back again. "Of course," he says. "We have a very special plan in which our mortuary technicians, with the utmost compassion and professionalism, prepare your loved . . ."

"Plan?" Julio interrupts. "It's an additional cost?"

"Three hundred twenty thousand pesos, which can also be financed via the credit options I mentioned."

"Let's go, Little Bro," Julio tells me. He grabs the bag and stands up. He signals to me to take charge of the box.

In the car, he remarks that if Libardo had known how expensive it is to die, he would have stayed alive. He was such a tightwad, Julio says. It's not like he decided to die, I point out. I know, Julio says, but if he'd known how much it costs, maybe he would have left some kind of instructions.

The box is in the back, on the floor, and the bag is on the seat. Julio looks irritated. It's a risk, but I decide to say it. "I need a favor."

"What?"

"Can you take me to this address?"

I show him the pink slip of paper that Gran gave me.

"What is that? What's there?" Julio asks.

How can I say it without it being the end of the world? I'm already regretting bringing it up. I could have gone on my own, without telling anyone about it. This overwhelming exhaustion has got me making bad decisions.

"Rosa Marcela lives there," I say.

"Who?"

"Our sister."

Julio shakes his head. He doesn't look at me. The muscles in his jaw tense. I attempt to smooth things over.

"Is it far from here? Does it take you out of your way?"

"What part of this do you not get?" he asks slowly.

"It's natural for me to want to meet her," I say. "It's not her fault. Like us, she has nothing to do with this."

"I don't get you," Julio says, still looking straight ahead, driving without heading anywhere in particular. "If she doesn't have anything to do with this, why do you want to get her involved?"

"Because she's our half-sister and I want to meet her."

Julio tries to shift gears, but he doesn't press the clutch down far enough and the gear sticks, grinds, and the car bucks.

"Look, Little Bro. Dad's back. There's no more mystery, no more waiting. The next step is the inheritance process. If the government doesn't confiscate whatever's left, our portion is going to be very small. And you want to share that small portion with a little brat we don't even know."

"For me it's not about money, it's about kin. She's family too," I say. "Very much so."

"Well, it's going to be about money for the judge. He doesn't give a shit about kin."

It's like Libardo's alive. He's still generating discord, still causing problems. He's still ruling over us survivors as well as among the dead.

"Is it a long way away?" I ask again.

"A long way from where?" he asks. "It's a super long way from New York. Paris too. It's even a long way from the farm."

It's too late now to put out this fire I've started, but even if it's my fault I have no intention of getting burned.

"I can go by cab," I say.

Julio looks at me and pulls over without checking whether anyone's coming up on our right.

"Go ahead," he says. "Good luck with your bullshit."

"I don't have any money," I tell him. "Colombian money. Can you change a few pounds?"

Julio lets out a furious laugh. Change, he repeats, change, he mutters. He pulls out his wallet and hands me two bills.

"Where are you going?" I ask.

"No fucking clue," he says. "But I do know where you're going. You're going off a cliff, Larry, and you're going to take me and Mom with you."

A sharp pang silences me. Dejected, I heave open the car door and get out. He's my brother, and it hurts. Why am I doing what I'm doing? Could I live in peace if I didn't?

51

Fernanda shoved everything off the desk—binders, papers, notebooks, all the information she'd been reviewing for weeks now—and spread out a blueprint of the house on the bare surface.

"There's something here," she told us, placing her finger on the backyard area.

I was fascinated by the blueprint. I'd never seen the house in this dimension. It was like seeing it from the air, but intimately. The bedrooms, the kitchen, the bathrooms and toilets—even plates and mugs had been drawn in the dining room. In the backyard were green plants, the rectangle of the pool, sun loungers, an umbrella, and several Xs marked with a pencil that were different from the architect's lines. According to Fernanda, those Xs contained the mystery.

"Your dad doesn't trust anybody," she said. "He doesn't keep all his money in the bank or in the safe—and here, boys, look here." She opened a school notebook, full of figures, names, scribbles, all written in pencil.

"What's that, Ma?"

"Cash. Money your dad received, a lot more than is in his bank accounts."

"He must have spent it," Julio said.

"Not all of it," she said. "I'm sure he hid part of it."

That was where the backyard came in. Those Xs, marked by Libardo, she claimed, must be hiding places, spots where he might have buried a lot of money. I looked at Julio to read his expression.

Fernanda's theory wasn't completely out there. We knew that ever since Escobar died, random citizens had been trespassing on his estates and other properties to search for false walls, tunnels, underground caches where they hoped to find vast sums of cash. Even the prison he'd had built for himself in Envigado was being plundered and destroyed, little by little, by those hoping to come across a hidden stash.

"Nobody," Fernanda emphasized, "absolutely nobody can find out about this." And once more she put her finger on the Xs on the blueprint.

To keep everybody from suspecting anything, she gave the maids a day off, and since the bodyguards refused to leave the house unprotected, Fernanda demanded that they remain outside in their vehicles, claiming she wanted to spend a day as a family, with no outsiders.

That night, like tomb raiders, we armed ourselves with picks, shovels, and flashlights and started digging approximately where the marks indicated. I didn't believe there was money buried in the backyard, but I loved the absurdity of the situation. Doing anything different was an adventure.

"If Dad buried something here, it must have been a long time ago," Julio said, and added, "There aren't any marks in the grass."

"He was a real wiz at hiding things," Fernanda said, laboriously prodding the hard soil with her shovel.

Julio was the one who had experience with this kind of thing. When we used to go out to the farms, he'd turn into a laborer. He built corrals, mended fences, dug wells, had breakfast with the hands, forgot he was the boss's son. There, in the backyard, he was the only one who was producing results. Fernanda and I had barely managed to remove the top layer of lawn. With power and precision, Julio was burying his pick in the earth and removing large quantities of soil.

"How far down do you suppose it is?" I asked.

"If he was just hiding it, I doubt it's buried very deep," Julio said.

Fernanda let out a shriek of terror.

"What's wrong?" Julio asked, running to her.

"Worms," Fernanda said.

Julio moved them aside with his shovel and admonished her for yelling.

"They're so gross," she said.

Julio suggested she keep digging in the hole he'd started while he continued with hers.

"Wouldn't it be more efficient to go over everything with a metal detector first?" I asked.

"What, you think Dad hid piggy banks full of coins, dumbass?"

Fernanda reprimanded him. "What did I say about treating each other better?"

"I didn't say anything," I defended myself.

"I don't care," she said. "It goes for both of you."

Julio finished digging the three holes. Fernanda took smoke breaks, and half an hour after we'd started, she poured herself a glass of gin. Julio and I removed our shirts. We were soaked with sweat, and nothing was emerging from the earth.

"Maybe we didn't gauge the marks correctly," Fernanda said.

Julio huffed.

"Maybe we're off by a couple of feet," she said, sitting on one of the benches.

"That's a problem," Julio said.

"We've still got two left," I said.

"We should keep making these bigger," he suggested.

"Look," I said, "we've got an audience."

Several people were watching us from a neighboring building. Julio yelled at them, lose something, assholes?, but, unfazed, they didn't budge. I'm going to turn out the pool light, Fernanda said. Tomorrow everybody's going to know we're looking for something, I said. So what?, said Julio, anybody who ventures in here is going to end up in one of these holes, he added.

Fernanda started walking around our excavations. She was shining the flashlight on the grass and using her foot to shove fallen leaves aside. We didn't ask what she was looking for because she didn't know herself. Any clue, a scar on the lawn, an odd mound, some mark that Libardo left so we could unbury what had been buried.

By three in the morning, I could no longer feel my hands. Fernanda was struggling to remove the soil that Julio had loosened. He looked obdurate, though from time to time he massaged his arms.

"Let's call it a night and finish tomorrow," I suggested, and the three of us looked at one another with frustration.

"We can't leave things like this, boys," Fernanda said.

"Why not?"

"Well, look at it," she said, gesturing to the heaps of earth, the holes, the entire backyard torn apart.

"So what do we do?" Julio asked.

Fernanda, tired and shaking, lit another cigarette. I don't know if it was from the smoke, but it looked like her eyes were watering. If she was going to cry, it was no surprise. We'd imagined we'd brandish the shovel a few times and strike a plastic bin full of US dollars. Plus, what good would that money do us, if it existed? What would being richer get us? Would it bring Libardo back? If Fernanda was going to cry, the cigarette dispelled her weeping. With her fingers, she squeezed the top of her nose between her eyebrows.

"What if those Xs aren't what we're thinking?" I asked.

"I'm sure there's something here."

"Well, today wasn't the day," I said, and dropped my shovel next to the hole. When I put on my shirt, my whole body ached.

"What are we going to tell the boys?" Fernanda asked. "And the help?"

"This area is off-limits," Julio said. "Anyone who sets foot here gets shot. And anyone who asks about it can go to hell."

It was dark, but I could tell Fernanda was shocked by Julio's comment. It might have been Libardo talking. I was alarmed but also felt comforted. At least somebody was starting to show some authority in this whole business. And what scared me wasn't that Julio was talking like Libardo, but that he might meet the same fate.

"Why not tell them the truth?" I said.

"That there are hidden stashes?" Fernanda asked.

"No," I said. "That there isn't anything."

"Well, I'm going to keep looking till I've dug up the entire backyard," she said.

"Let's go to bed," Julio said.

Before heading up to our rooms, we looked over the work we'd done, the wasted effort in every pile of earth and every hole. And we saw her, defeated, lost, inhaling on a cigarette as if it were the only thing she had left in this world.

52

As soon as the airplane wheels touched the runway, the magic of flying lost its divine, mythic, defiant quality and became the mundane act of endlessly taxiing. Charlie felt as if she were falling apart when the engines roared in reverse to brake. In touching down, that plane was forcing her to set foot on the soil where her father had just died. For the thousandth time, she sobbed, until they came to a complete stop.

Again she looked back, searching for Larry, but the crowd had gotten to their feet even before the announcement that it was O.K. to stand up. The only people still seated were the flight attendants; everybody else was opening overhead compartments, calling across the rows as if they were in a market. They smelled of fatigue and sleeplessness, and in the commotion, Charlie harbored the hope of finding Larry so he could be with her during the torturous ordeal of returning to Colombia.

She turned on her cell phone, and a message from Cristina, her sister, appeared, saying that everything was all set for her arrival. Salgado from the Bogotá office will be waiting for you, he'll take care of everything, look for him. And just as she was finishing reading it the phone rang, from an unidentified number, but she answered because she knew who it was.

"Salgado just called to tell me you've landed," Cristina said. "How was the flight?"

"Oh, Cris," Charlie sobbed.

"I know. It's awful."

Charlie collapsed in tears, and Cristina told her, get off that plane right now, Salgado's got your ticket to Medellín, we're waiting for you. How's Mom?, Charlie asked. She just can't talk right now, Cristina replied, when you're with Salgado call me back on his phone. O.K., Charlie said, then wiped her tears and stood up, but she had to sit down immediately.

I'm going to throw up . . .

"I don't feel good, Cris."

"You need to get off that plane right now," her sister said, and hung up.

The discomfort was simply her body rejecting the drinks she'd had. A secret that, for the time being, she'd again have to hide.

He's the only one who knows . . .

She tried to stand up once more, slower this time, and leaned on the seat back and asked another passenger to help her with the suitcase she'd stashed in the overhead compartment.

The first-class passengers were filing out, and those in coach were being told to wait by a flight attendant. Charlie let inertia carry her off the plane, though she threw one last glance toward the rear.

Nothing . . .

Just hundreds of frazzled faces. She put one foot in her country and then the other. She pulled her suitcase along, and almost immediately ran into a young man who said, "María Carlota, I'm Rubén Salgado, assistant director of human resources."

Her surprise was visible.

"How were you able to get in here?" she asked.

"The minister of foreign affairs has been very helpful. He's smoothed things out for us."

They were standing in the middle of the ramp, with the passengers squeezing past. Salgado grabbed the suitcase and said, "Come on, let's go. You've got just enough time to catch your flight to Medellín."

They moved down the jet bridge, but Charlie stopped to look back.

"Are you waiting for somebody?" Salgado asked.

"Yes," she replied, then corrected herself. "No, nobody."

She tried to keep up with Salgado. She pulled her sunglasses out of her purse and put them on.

"I'm really sorry about your father's death," Salgado said. "Working for him has been one of the most enriching experiences of my life. He was a remarkable person. He'll be missed here in Colombia."

Charlie thanked him in a tiny voice. She'd have to get used to it. From now on people were going to be constantly imparting their condolences. She looked back again but saw only the herd also heading for the passport control area.

"I need you to give me your baggage claim slips," Salgado said.

"What?" Charlie asked, distracted.

"The slips for your suitcases. They're probably not going to make it onto your flight. I'll claim them for you."

"But . . ."

"Don't worry. I'll bring them to you on the next flight," Salgado explained, and then his voice darkened. "I'm going to the funeral too."

He put his hand gently on her shoulder to urge her to walk faster.

Charlie was out of breath when they reached passport control. Salgado apologized to her and said again that if they didn't rush, she wouldn't make her connection. He spoke with an airport worker, showed him a piece of paper, and then told Charlie that they could use the line reserved for diplomats. Salgado took care of everything. He showed the official her passport, answered the questions for her, explained once more why they'd used that line, all in hand.

Meanwhile, Charlie was eyeing every passenger who reached the spiral that was growing behind her. Until finally, way in the back, he came into view. He was walking slowly and carrying a backpack. A powerful emotion swept through her. She smiled. She raised her hand, but Larry didn't see her. He was moving forward, his mind elsewhere, in the huge line that had formed.

"All right. Let's go," Salgado said, suddenly heading off with the suitcase bumping along behind him.

"Yes," Charlie said.

Before leaving, she looked back at Larry again. He was standing still, his passport in hand, and he was looking at her, the way you look at something in a shop window that you can't afford. Charlie raised her hand again, more timidly now, almost fearful. Larry did the same. Her hand and his, barely raised, insecure, vague, like two accomplices in a crime.

53

M y new sister lives in a gated community where all the houses are identical, small with lots of exposed brick. The guard stops me at the gate and scrutinizes me with guard-like suspicion. I ask for Rosa Marcela, and he thinks a moment. Maybe I should give her mother's name, Vanesa, because my sister might still be at school. But the guard picks up the phone and waits. I think about Julio and Fernanda; if she finds out I'm here, she'll kill me. He must hate me right now and will definitely tell her. I'm a dead man, or at least exiled; I can just see myself having to seek refuge at Gran's house.

"What's your name?" the guard asks.

"Larry," I tell him.

"Larry's here asking for Rosa Marcela," the guard says to the person who answered. Then he asks me, "Larry who?"

The usual, of course, the only way anybody ever recognizes me in this country.

"Larry, Libardo's son."

The guard repeats what I've said and endless seconds go by. I think again about Fernanda and Julio and this choice I've made that already tastes like betrayal.

"The little girl isn't home yet, but go on in," the guard tells me.

The facades are all the same, even the doors are the same; the only thing that changes is the curtain color and what I can see of the inside. So what happened here? Why does one of Libardo's lovers live in this kind of neighborhood? And what about her daughter? Did he consider her to be different from Julio and me? Did they lose their fortune, like us? There it is, in any case, here I am: in front of number 23. The bell jangles all through the neighborhood, in every nerve in my body, in my neurons that wig out when they hear footsteps approaching.

"Hello."

"Vanesa?"

"Yes. Larry?"

"Yes, I'm Larry, Libardo's son."

"Come in, Larry. Welcome."

I go in, and the first thing I see is him. His felonious smile, twisted and wicked, the glinting gaze of a man who revels in his sinning.

"Weren't you abroad?" Vanesa asks me.

"I arrived yesterday."

"Do you want something to drink?"

"No, thanks."

Next to the photo of Libardo are photos of the little girl at different ages. Vanesa signals for to me to sit down, but I continue to be distracted by everything I see.

"Has something happened?" she asks anxiously.

"They found my dad."

"Yes. Doña Carmenza told me."

We look at each other in silence, furtively studying each other. All I see is a young woman, just a few years older than me, attractive, uncertain, on the defensive.

"I thought . . ." she says, and stops.

"It was only just now," I tell her, "I found out she existed." I gesture toward one of the picture frames with my head.

"Oh, Rosi," she says, and smiles.

"I didn't know," I say.

"Nobody knew. Just Libardo, but since . . ."

It's so hard to call things by their name, especially when they refer to pain, tragedy, guilt. But I make no attempt to finish her sentence. I nod so she knows I understand.

"He never met her," Vanesa says. "He just saw her in the ultrasounds. He cried when he found out she was a girl."

"He always wanted a daughter, I know that."

Her eyes well up, and she hugs herself and looks at me with embarrassment. She shrugs and says, "Well, that's life."

I go over to the photos and compare Rosa Marcela to Libardo. She looks a lot like him, especially her smile. She's got some of both of you, I tell Vanesa.

"She's got his personality," she says, and laughs.

"Is that good or bad?" I ask. She laughs again.

"I liked the way he was," she says. "Your grandmother says they're exactly alike."

"Do the two of you see her often?"

"She used to visit us more regularly. She's been really busy with Don Alonso lately, but she's very generous with us. She helps us a lot."

I tremble just imagining Julio and Fernanda finding out that Gran has been sharing the money they send her.

"She pays Rosi's tuition. She's a saint," Vanesa says.

"Don't tell me," I say, but she doesn't hear me.

"I barely earn enough to cover our insurance and things for the house. Oh, the house is ours, he . . ."

"Don't tell me," I interrupt her. "There's no need."

How can I explain that my rudeness is born of fear? Didn't she ever learn how the cartels work? The less you know, the longer you live. Vanesa looks at me in confusion, and I apologize.

"I'm sorry, I haven't slept for two days."

"I can imagine," she says. "This must be very hard for all of you. It certainly is for me."

"No," I say. "Don't take this the wrong way, but it doesn't hurt anymore."

A chill pierces my chest when I see Libardo and Vanesa together, embracing, kissing, every photo displaying a love story. That's what the photos Fernanda has in her room look like, with that same lavish outlay of affection. I don't know if they're from the same time period or if they're from after Libardo got fed up. The two women don't seem to fit. Right up to the end, Libardo was always affectionate with Fernanda. There are photos confirming his love for her too.

"I always wanted you all to meet Rosa Marcela," Vanesa says. "Ultimately, she's . . ." I gesture again to indicate that I understand. If she doesn't feel able to call things by their names, she shouldn't. "She knows about you," she says, "because Doña Carmenza tells her stories. I would have liked to, but Doña Fernanda . . . You know, Larry."

"I do know," I say, "and she's going to cut off my balls when she finds out I'm here."

Vanesa looks down. I go over to her and say, "Can I ask you a favor?"

"Of course."

"I'm so exhausted I can barely function. Would it be O.K. if I lie down for a little bit? Right here, on the sofa, is fine."

She stands up, smiles candidly, and says, "No, please, not here. Come and rest in Rosi's room. She'll be coming home from school any minute, but I'll tell her not to disturb you."

I follow her upstairs and go into Rosa Marcela's room, an unfamiliar world. A doll house, the smell of flowers, life inside a rainbow.

"Lie down," Vanesa tells me. "I'll bring you a blanket."

"No, there's no need."

"Of course there is. This room doesn't get any sun, so it's pretty chilly."

She goes out, leaving me surrounded by unblinking gazes and fixed smiles. A menagerie of stuffed animals, a deluge of hearts in the unicorn kingdom.

"Here you go," Vanesa says, and hands me a blanket. "Shall I close the curtain?"

"It's fine. Thank you."

"You sure?"

"I'm sure. I'm just going to rest for a minute, so I can make it till tonight."

"You probably didn't get to sleep with all the fireworks, huh?" she says.

"Nope."

"I'll be around," she says, and closes the door gently, as if I were already asleep.

I take off my shoes, lie back on the pillow, pull the blanket over me, turn on my side, and find myself eye to eye with a pink gorilla. It smiles at me, and I smile back. I reach out my hand, and we hug. It must be a girl, I think when I smell its musky fragrance.

54

The backyard looked like a freshly bombed field. Fernanda locked the doors leading out to it and made it a no-go zone. The threat to anyone who went in was not banishment but death. She got the whole staff together and warned them. Not even the gardener could go out there. To drive the idea home, Julio stood next to her, holding Libardo's pistol, and said, "And anybody who doesn't like this rule can leave."

Julio and Fernanda had just put a price on our lives, and they might well turn out to be worth nothing since we'd found nothing in the backyard so far.

"Our own people are going to kill us," I said. "They're going to get greedy for what might be buried there." From a distance, the guards and maids eyed the mounds of soil and the holes that Fernanda and Julio were still digging, now in broad daylight.

"Or the neighbors," I added.

Sometimes I helped dig, not because I wanted to but because I couldn't stand Fernanda's withering looks. Or her rude comments, like the one she offered when I suggested, Ma, don't you think we should tell the guards we're going to give them part of what we find. She replied with another question: how did you turn out such a moron, Larry? It's so they won't kill us, Ma. She glared at me and left. My fear did make an impression, though; I found out she'd gone to a notary to file an extrajudicial statement saying that if anything happened to us, our employees were the ones responsible, and she left a list of all the people who worked for us and their addresses. Then she brought them back together to tell them she'd done so.

"You're going to have to keep an even closer watch on us now," she said.

We dug for a couple more weeks. We no longer limited ourselves to the Xs marked on the map, instead excavating wherever we thought we might find something. We'd destroyed every growing thing in the yard, and even the pool was cloudy with earth. The gleaming marble was obscured at the bottom and on the edges. The motor and filters jammed, and the murky water filled with bubbles and frogs. Fernanda cried at the end of every day, and Julio did what he could to calm her.

"It's not the end of the world, Ma. We've still got enough money to last a long time. Plus, if Dad comes back . . ."

Any remark about Libardo's return always trailed off. Reduced to a gesture. A sigh, a shrug.

"We need cash," Fernanda would say. "It's our only insurance. They can freeze our accounts, confiscate our assets; now they're saying something about forfeiture."

We smelled like earth, us and the whole house, just like the backyard and farmhands did. We got blisters from digging, but Fernanda didn't let anybody else help.

The people who claimed to have Libardo had stopped calling, and the silence had Fernanda on the verge of despair. Until one day she answered a call from a guy named Eloy, who asked, without saying hello, if the digging in the backyard was about what they assumed it was. Fernanda didn't respond and asked for the other guy, Rómulo, and said she wouldn't talk to anyone but him. Irate, she hung up and went to interrogate the employees. They all swore they hadn't leaked word of our search. Even so, Fernanda fired several. Of the seven body-guards, she kept only three, along with the two maids.

On our last day of digging, we heard a bloodcurdling scream from Fernanda. We thought she'd finally found something. We ran to her and found her writhing in pain in the hole. She'd fallen and hit her head on the shovel, and her forehead was bleeding. And she was crying, of course. We took her to the emergency room despite her objections. Luckily the wound was not serious or deep. The doctors cleaned and dressed it, unaware that the real injury was to her spirit and her pride. When we got home, I put my foot down.

"No more of this treasure hunt bullshit. There's nothing there. We should think about what we're going to do instead. It's been six months since they took Dad, and we're still in the exact same place."

"What else can we do?" Fernanda asked. "We've looked for him, I've tried to negotiate, I've given them money. I've given anything they've asked for to get him back—I know Libardo can start over from scratch, what matters is that he's alive. But I don't know what to think anymore."

She wept, and the swelling on her forehead grew larger. She covered her face with her hands, her fingernails black with soil as if she'd been digging with them. Julio and I looked at each other, disconcerted; he had dirt on his face, on his neck, and I must be just as filthy, just as anxious. Suddenly, I saw it all clearly: we weren't digging to find some cache that Libardo had hidden. We were digging to exhume him, to have him with us, dead or alive. We were desperately defying God, life, time, with what, for the world and for us, Libardo represented: money. We were looking for anything we could to assuage our guilt over doing nothing for him, keeping quiet. I thought all this but didn't say it, just as I didn't dare suggest that we needed to go on with our lives, to pick up our stories where we'd left off when he disappeared.

A month later, I went to spend a weekend at Pedro's house, and when I got back on Sunday evening I saw that the holes in the yard had been filled in and the pool cleaned. I felt a wave of relief when I saw the house looking like it used to. Though there was no grass, I knew it would grow back.

Another day, Eloy called again and asked Fernanda why we'd stopped digging. This time she played along and told him we'd found what we were looking for. You did?, Eloy exclaimed, so how much did you find? Enough for you to release Libardo and leave us alone, Fernanda said, and hung up. She called us to her bedroom and told us, "I've been thinking."

We looked at each other, afraid of what was coming.

"Don't look at me like that," she said. "There's still one way out we haven't considered."

"Which is . . ." Julio said.

"The right one," Fernanda finished his sentence. "The justice system, the police, the attorney general's office."

"But they already know," I said.

"Yes, but we haven't gotten them involved," she said. "It's time to ask for their help."

Fernanda was always surprising us. We didn't say anything about her proposal; it wasn't rash like some of her other decisions, but I, for one, needed to consider it a little more. All I said was, "They know everything we're doing already. They've got to be keeping an eye on us from one of those buildings." I gestured around us and said, "We need to move."

"Not yet," Fernanda said firmly. "What if they set him free or he escapes, where will he go? How will he find us?"

"He can go to Gran's, and she'll tell him where we went," I said.

Fernanda let out a wild laugh. That's great, she said, out of the frying pan and into the fire. She shut herself in the bathroom, and we could still hear her fake, sarcastic, venomous ha, ha, ha. Whenever she reacted like that, I felt like I was sitting in front of one of the slot machines where she squandered her time and our money.

55

The conveyer belt spat suitcases out onto the baggage carousel, and passengers emerged from the crush to retrieve the ones that belonged to them. Many returned a suitcase after confirming it wasn't theirs; their energy waning, all they wanted was to leave the airport as soon as possible and bring their trip to an end. Larry wandered around the carousel a few times, looking not for his luggage but for Charlie among the mob. He walked slowly, studying the travelers' tired faces, the agonized expressions of people struggling to heap suitcases and parcels onto carts. Larry was looking for her in a daze, as if he didn't want to find her. He was also watching the revolving suitcases, trying to imagine which one might be hers. Hard-sided, oversized, with an emblazoned brand name—it could be any of them, or none of them, because if he didn't see Charlie then her suitcase wouldn't be on the carousel either.

I don't want her to see me looking for her . . .

He wanted and at the same time didn't want to find her. There was still the possibility they might run into each other again on the flight to Medellín. Truthfully, the only thing Larry wanted at that moment was to figure out what he wanted.

To not return to Medellín. Not find her. Find her and not return . . .

He sat down across from the carousel on a row of seats. He placed his backpack between his legs and leaned his head back. He took a deep breath, and the air felt as heavy as it had inside the plane. Pilots and flight attendants went by, laughing as if they hadn't been crammed inside a plane for far too long. Passengers from other flights, chatting animatedly as if they didn't realize what returning meant. People went by, people arrived, other people left, and Charlie never appeared. With every blink, Larry felt as if he might fall asleep. He had an hour to make his connection to Medellín. An hour till he returned. His stomach growled, his guts writhed, the monster in his intestines attacked.

No way. Not here, please . . .

He looked around for the bathroom sign. The monster reared up. Charlie could be in the bathroom too—she could be crying, washing her face, changing her clothes, stashing her colorful outfit and putting on something black, maybe that's why he couldn't find her. The monster quaked.

Damn it . . .

He hoisted the backpack and raced for the restrooms.

Shit doesn't follow orders . . .

The restroom stank. It was full of travelers who were also in urgent intestinal need. Larry shut himself in a filthy stall; luckily, it had toilet paper. Everything else was routine.

Even Queen Elizabeth has to do it . . .

56

The eyes looking at me were so large and so black that I thought they were part of a dream and felt happy. I'm finally asleep, I said to myself in that same dream, but with my next blink I realized it was her, the little girl from the photos, Libardo's daughter, my sister.

"Hi," I say, and she runs to hide behind an armchair. Her face is hidden, but her legs are sticking out. She's wearing a school uniform and a pair of dirty sneakers. I'm still hugging the stuffed gorilla. "Rosa Marcela," I call to her, and she doesn't answer. She tries to draw her legs back, but there's no room. I imitate a couple of growls and get ready to waggle the gorilla in case she peeks out.

"Rosi," her mother calls from the other end of the house.

"Rosi," I call quietly, and ask, "What's this gorilla's name?"

"Nasty."

"What?"

"Her name's Nasty," she says, without poking her head out.

"Why'd you name it that?"

She giggles mirthfully. Maybe she's mocking my silly question. I sit up, uncertain how long I've slept. Or whether I've slept at all. I look at the gorilla's smiling face and tell Rosa Marcela, "Well, it's been very nice to me."

"She's a girl," she clarifies.

"Yes, I knew that," I say.

Vanesa peeks in the door and shakes her head. "Did she wake you up?" she asks. "Where is she? I told her not to bother you."

I point to the armchair where she's hiding. Rosa Marcela tries to conceal her legs.

"Get out from there, young lady," Vanesa says firmly. She apologizes to me. "I don't know when she slipped away from me."

Rosa Marcela peers out slowly; she looks at her mother and then at me with a guilty expression on her face. I recall the saying: more alike than a bastard child. She's a little-girl version of Libardo, made more beautiful by affection.

"No worries," I tell Vanesa, "I wasn't sleeping."

"But she didn't let you rest, and she disobeyed me," she says, gesturing for Rosa Marcela to get up. "Why didn't you listen to me?" she asks.

"I wanted to meet him," Rosa Marcela says.

"Really, Vanesa, it's no problem," I say, though I'd have liked to keep sleeping till the next morning.

"Let's go," she says to Rosa Marcela, grabbing her hand. "Keep resting, Larry," she tells me. "I promise she won't bother you again."

"No," I say. "I want to talk to her."

"Are you sure?" Vanesa asks.

"Absolutely," I say.

Rosa Marcela races out of the room. As I put on my shoes, I remark to Vanesa, she looks just like him, more than Julio and I do. Vanesa smiles and nods. She doesn't say anything.

"Do you tell her about him?"

"Yeah, tons. And she's been asking lots of questions lately."

"Does she know everything?"

"What's everything?" she asks.

"Well, what happened." I'm quiet a moment, then say, "What he was."

"Why would I tell her that? Maybe if we were rich or had that kind of lifestyle," she says. "She's not going to understand it now, much less later on."

"You're right. Sorry," I say.

"I get it," she says. "You must have gone through that, but you all had a different kind of life. Rosi asks me what happened to her daddy, and I tell her he got lost and couldn't come back." She swallows and blinks rapidly. "She tells me she's going to look for him till she finds him."

Now I'm the one who's choked up. I wobble as soon as I stand. My feet are still swollen, and my shoes are tight. Vanesa says, "Rosi's going to have something to eat. Do you want to join us?"

In the kitchen, Rosa Marcela's at a small table eating an arepa with cheese. She looks down when she sees me. Vanesa tells me to have a seat, asks what I want to eat while she pours hot chocolate for Rosa Marcela.

"Same thing," I say.

"Hot chocolate?"

"Yes, and an arepa."

Vanesa smiles at me. She's got an innocent, almost ingenuous expression. It's impossible not to compare her to Fernanda. Vanesa is much younger, which is why she looks so vibrant, but I can't help seeing Fernanda at the other end.

"Why were you sleeping in my bed?" Rosa Marcela asks me.

"Rosi," her mother admonishes her.

"Because I heard it was the best bed in the house," I say.

"Who told you that?" she asks, looking at Vanesa.

"Nasty, your gorilla."

"No way," she says. "You didn't even know her name."

"But she told me," I say.

She looks at me, unconvinced. She drinks her chocolate and ends up with a brown mustache. Now she really does look more like Libardo.

"Don't you have a home?" she asks me.

"That's enough, Rosi," Vanesa says. "Stop asking silly questions and eat."

"You said he didn't have a place to sleep and that's why he lay down in my bed," Rosa Marcela tells her accusingly.

"It's true," I say. "I don't have a home right now."

She opens her eyes as wide as the mug she's holding in her hands. Vanesa looks at me dubiously, unsure whether I'm joking or telling the truth.

"Are you going to live with us?" Rosa Marcela asks me.

"Wipe your mouth," her mother says.

"No," I say, "but I wanted to meet you. Do you know who I am?"

She nods and drinks her chocolate again. Then she asks, "Did you know my daddy?"

"Yes, really well."

"What was he like?"

"He looked at lot like you," I tell her, "though you're prettier."

Rosa Marcela blushes and takes refuge in her mug. One day I'll tell her she didn't miss much not knowing him, though I know everybody feels a father's absence. Even when Libardo was alive, I felt his. Vanesa pours me some hot chocolate. Her hands shake as she places it on the table.

"You can sleep in my bed," Rosa Marcela tells me. "I'll let you borrow it."

Libardo would have been mesmerized by this child. Maybe she would have saved him. She would have saved all of us with those large black eyes, which sparkle with all the tenderness in this goddamn world.

"Thanks, Rosi," I say, "but I have to go in a little bit."

Her gaze dims, and even so we all fit inside it. Is it the power of blood that has caused us to love each other already? But why doesn't Julio want to have anything to do with her?

Vanesa puts a steaming arepa in front of me. It's bathed in butter and covered with slices of cheese.

"I almost burned it trying to keep an eye on Little Miss Mischief here," she says.

"It looks delicious," I say.

Vanesa pulls a stool over and sits down next to us. I take a bite of the arepa and the two of them watch me, waiting for my reaction. I make a noise of pleasure, of enjoyment, though inside my soul is shattered. The arepa tastes like home, like family, like love—it tastes like life.

"It's delicious," I say, and they both smile. "But it's really hot, I burned my tongue," I say, to explain away my watering eyes.

57

F ernanda had decided to make her biggest gamble, not in a casino but on the battlefield, betting Libardo's life and even her own. We don't know how she ended up getting in touch with a regional prosecutor, Jorge Cubides, but she met with him and claimed the following, half truth, half falsehood: that Libardo had been considering turning himself in to the authorities in exchange for a reduced sentence, but his enemies, Los Pepes, had learned of his plan and kidnapped him. She no longer had the power or resources to stand up to them and rescue Libardo. She was reaching out to the attorney general's office at the moment because they were the only ones equipped to confront Los Pepes, who were the prosecutors' enemies too. She updated Cubides on the progress of her most recent conversations with the people who were supposedly holding Libardo. She offered to turn over documents, invoices, letters, everything she'd found in Libardo's study.

According to Fernanda, the attorney general's office would win this two-sided conflict, finding Libardo and dealing a major blow to Los Pepes. And we'd win too, getting our father back.

"What if Dad doesn't want to rat anybody out?" I asked. "What's that going to do to your relationship with the attorney general's office?"

"Well, if he doesn't want to do it, he can rot in prison," she said, "but at least he'll be alive."

"And what if Los Pepes don't have him?" Julio asked.

"At least we'll get rid of them," she said.

Julio sat thinking for a moment, then said, "It seems like a lot of trouble for not very much gain."

"We'll only know that for sure when the operation's over," she said.

I thought about Libardo's reaction. He would come out of a kidnapping and head straight to prison. It wasn't ideal, but he'd have us close by, his life wouldn't be in danger, and if he really was able to negotiate his sentence, maybe after a few years he'd be released. That was on the one hand. On the other, given the silence of the past few months, I'd started thinking Libardo might already be dead.

"Ma, there are a lot of things I don't understand," Julio said. "If you're not going to give them anything, how do you expect them to return Dad? You give them a suitcase full of trash and they just let him go?"

"What do you not get?" she asked. "I'll give them the money they're asking for, but it won't be ours."

"Where are you going to get it from?"

"I'll explain in a minute," she said, "but pour me a drink while I go to the bathroom."

Julio told me he was going to make it a stiff one to loosen her tongue, and I reminded him how dangerous Fernanda was when she got talkative. Holding her drink, Fernanda sat down to explain, not as a mother but as a criminal.

"Libardo's friends are going to put up the money, both those who are still free and the ones in prison. The deal with the prosecutor is that Libardo will talk, but he won't snitch on anybody who helps us."

"And how are you so sure they're going to give us the money?" Julio asked.

"First, because they're his friends. Second, because it's a loan. Jorge tells me they'll get the money back."

"Is Jorge the prosecutor?" I asked.

She didn't reply.

"Each person will contribute just, like, fifty billion pesos, which is practically nothing," she said. She smiled and savored her drink.

"I don't know," I said. "You're making decisions for Dad. We don't know what he'd think about this."

"Of course I am," she said. "Have you not noticed he's not around?"

That same day, a crew from the CTI showed up to install a call-recording system that, when it came down to it, looked just like the recorder we already had connected to the telephone. This is different, Fernanda told me, now they can listen in from over there, she said, referring to the attorney general's office. Are they going to listen to all our calls?, I asked, horrified. Well yeah, that's the whole point, she said. Yours, mine, Julio's, all of them?, I asked again. Oh, Larry, she said, annoyed, stop freaking out.

We exchanged one madness for another. It was no longer the witch doctor unearthing buried things, or us digging in the backyard like a chain gang day and night, or the stress of pitting our wits against the people who called. Now the madness had a name, Jorge Cubides, and it was serious, really serious, because Fernanda was smiling from ear to ear as she told us her plans.

58

L arry scanned the waiting area for the flight to Medellín, and she wasn't there either. All that talking, and they hadn't arranged to meet again.

I don't have her phone number, her email address, nothing I could use to find her.

He sat down to wait for the boarding call and to think. He wasn't seeing anything clearly. Charlie must have taken another flight, or would be leaving later; after all, there was no point in rushing on the way to somebody who was already dead. Or maybe she was wandering around lost in another terminal of the airport, confused amid the throngs, praying for a familiar face.

Looking for me . . .

Or in the VIP lounge, where she should be, and she might show up to board the plane later, shielded behind a pair of sunglasses, like someone who doesn't know what she's doing, just letting herself be carried along.

Above the gate a screen read "Medellín." Between his sleepiness and his hangover, Larry felt the life draining out of him. A knot of strange emotions he could not define and did not dare call by their real name: fear. He took a deep breath and let it out slowly, as he'd been taught in the therapy he'd done so he could cope with life. Inhaling and exhaling until his soul returned to his body.

Even so, he remained on alert for every passenger who arrived at the gate.

I'd like to have her cry on my shoulder again, drink more gin with her, have turbulence bind us together once more; I'd like for her to appear, for her not to appear, for her to vanish, for it all to have been a hallucination . . .

The Avianca worker arrived at the counter, straightened some papers, turned on the microphone, cleared her throat, and loudly announced, good morning, ladies and gentlemen.

A line formed in front of the gate, everybody eager to board the plane, except Larry, who was still seated, clutching his backpack and hoping Charlie would show up.

Fingers crossed she comes, fingers crossed she doesn't come, fingers crossed this plane doesn't take off, the sky slams shut, the world ends, my legs obey so I can walk . . .

The line slowly advanced.

I know what I want now, Larry said to himself.

And though he did it unconsciously, he got to his feet.

59

December 1. Two days from now would be yet another anniversary of the beginning of this mess, the story that started with a dead man on a rooftop. The fall of an empire built of dominoes, where the first brought down the second, and the second the third, until the line of tiles swept us away—Libardo, Fernanda, Julio, me: pieces in the sinister game of dominoes Escobar had played.

"Hey, tell me something. Has this all changed?" I ask the taxi driver who takes me to Fernanda's apartment.

"In what way, buddy?" he asks, looking at me in the rearview mirror.

"I mean, compared to the Escobar era," I say, as if I didn't know anything.

"Well, what can I say," he says, and thinks a moment.

The radio is playing December music, the same stuff it's played all my life, monotonous rhythms that my grandparents and parents used to dance to, and that will play on every station till early January, till our eardrums burst, till the last Christmas bender.

"Look, buddy," the taxi driver says, "when it comes to changes in this city, the changes a person sees, or when people ask what's changed, I mean, in terms of those things, man, how can I put it . . ."

Though he can't find the words for it, there have been changes. A glance out the window makes that clear enough. Where there used to be a tree is now a building, and there are coffee shops, clothing boutiques, restaurants, gyms, clinics, pharmacies, hotels, bars; there are acrobats at the traffic lights, you can still see a cluster of mangos growing behind a wall here or there, and even a man who comes up to the cab selling a titi monkey. The driver asks him, and why would the gentleman here want a monkey? I mean, 'cause they're awesome, the man says just as the light turns green and we start off. Maybe the taxi driver doesn't dare answer me because he knows what I mean. Not the things I see but instead what is not visible: what is gloomy, forbidden, sordid.

"Well, buddy," he says. "To be honest, because there's no point in burying your head in the sand when pretty much everything's in plain sight, or even if it's not, everybody knows about it anyway, because there are no secrets in this city, or if there are, they don't last long, if you know what I mean."

Of course I do. That's how we've always seen things, starting with the "it's all relative" we used that allowed us to justify our miseries and our crimes. That's the only way we could survive and break free from what I'm trying to pin down with the taxi driver: how things used to be.

"See, if we put our hands on our hearts," he says, and lifts his to his chest, "and tell it like it is, and we don't go around lying to each other, man, because even though we're known for being straight shooters, we haven't had the balls to call a spade a spade. And a society, any society, if it can't do a little critical self-examination," he adds, "is a failed society, yes siree."

"Can you turn the radio down a tad?" I ask.

"Are you kidding, man?" he says in astonishment, and sings along: *Joyous December is here, month of festivities and cheer.* He laughs and asks, "This place you're going to, is there a soccer field with stands there?"

"Yes indeed," I tell him.

"I think I dropped someone else there not so long ago, and

there was a really nice little pitch—it even had lights for night games. Anyway, buddy, like I was saying . . ."

A number of places spin through my memory—a house that hasn't been demolished yet, the bakery we went to all my life, the pharmacy where we always got our shots, the lot where we used to play soccer and that is now a proper field with lights and bleachers, places that, for whatever reason, are still there.

"It's that lack of community spirit I was talking about earlier, which you've probably noticed when someone says something's not working out and everybody refuses to admit it and they all say, what? Everything's just fine, there's no problem here. There are thousands of those people, man, not just thousands, millions, because they're not just here in Medellín, but all over the goddamn country," he says.

His babbling dishevels my fatigue; I'm fading in the sweltering afternoon, drifting away.

"We're almost there, it's real close."

I open my eyes and ask, "O.K., so where did we land? Has this changed or not?"

He thinks a while, looks at me again in the rearview mirror, smiles, and says, "What can I tell you, man."

From down below I see Fernanda lounging next to the window in her apartment, gazing out.

"How much do I owe you?" I ask.

He looks at the meter, mumbles a calculation, and says, "Just seven thousand pesos, buddy."

Fernanda sees me get out of the cab and quickly moves away from the window. Maybe she already knows where I'm coming from and is getting ready to attack. And I, the traitorous son, am arriving without any defense, with only the emotion of knowing I have a sweet, wonderful sister.

60

Larry was the last to board. He no longer had Charlie leaning on his shoulder and would be flying not over the ocean but over the mountains and valleys between Bogotá and Medellín. His anxiety increased as the minutes passed and the distance shrank.

In the first-class cabin there were twelve seats that were already occupied. Charlie wasn't in any of them. He walked to the back, scanning the seat numbers and looking at the passengers, hoping to find her, reassured knowing he probably wouldn't. He reached 24A, his assigned window seat. She's not here, he said to himself sadly. She's not here, he repeated, relieved. Charlie's face began to dissolve in a fog, the way things do at the start of a magic spell.

What if I didn't recognize her? And what if she didn't recognize me either and we're now traveling on the same plane like two strangers? . . .

The crew announced that the door was closing. The flight attendants walked up and down, preparing for takeoff. The pilot spoke, his neighbor crossed herself, a flight attendant spoke, and a child cried at the top of his lungs. Larry put on his headphones, but he didn't know what music he wanted to listen to, what would be fitting for the moment, since he didn't even know what sort of moment he was experiencing.

The plane took off and pierced the clouds at a speed that defied reason. Larry stared out at the white sky, and the chaos of the city shrank away. Then he pushed his seat back as far as it would go, which wasn't much. He considered sleeping for the thirty minutes, though it wouldn't be enough to catch up on all the hours he'd been awake, but he didn't want to become disconnected from places and names: Medellín, Fernanda, Julio, Pedro, El Poblado, Charlie. Especially her. He closed his eyes and let the music play at random. Anything that would also muffle the airplane engines.

Just as he felt himself starting to drift in his seat, afloat on exhaustion, the flight attendant offered him boxed juice, water, or coffee. Hating her, he accepted a cup of water. He looked out at the cushion of gray and white clouds, with a pale blanket above that hid the sky. He closed his eyes again, and mingling with the music he heard the names that were keeping him awake: Fernanda, Medellín, Pedro, Libardo, Julio, Charlie. Especially hers.

Suddenly, he felt as if he were falling and started in his seat. He clutched the armrests. He thought they'd hit an air pocket or maybe he was falling like when a person is just dozing off. But the bump was only the call of the earth. Down below, very close now, were the mountains. Larry pressed his face against the window. The massive, dramatic peaks heralded the inevitable.

61

T he first time the prosecutor Jorge Cubides came to the house, I thought he was another of Libardo's friends. He was wearing a sweatshirt and seemed too young, too muscular to be a prosecutor. When I opened the door, he asked for Fernanda, smiling broadly, very sure of himself.

When she appeared, he said, "Sorry for showing up like this—I'm all sweaty. I was leaving the gym, and since it's close to here, I figured I'd come by." She invited him in and offered him juice and fruit salad. From their conversation, I was able to gather that he was interested in our case because it could help him obtain the promotion he was angling for. Jorge Cubides had set his sights high: he wanted to be deputy attorney general for all of Colombia.

"That Eloy guy is calling you from payphones around the city," he added. "But we haven't been able to confirm that he's a member of Los Pepes."

"There's nobody else who'd be holding him," Fernanda said.

"But we have to confirm it to be able to take the next step. You told me you'd talked to another guy before," Cubides said.

"Yes, Rómulo," Fernanda replied, and he wrote down the name in a notebook.

"Two things," he said. "First, you have to find out from them what happened to Rómulo. Ideally, you'd start talking to him again. Second, you have to insist they send you proof of life for Libardo."

"I ask for it every time they call," she said.

"As for the money they're demanding," the prosecutor said, "are you able to get your hands on that much?"

"We're working on it," Fernanda said.

She was working on it. She was setting up meetings with Libardo's business partners, visiting those who were in prison, meeting late at night with those who were on the run, talking with wives or front men. She was always elegantly dressed, though she'd been biting her nails a lot.

The next time Eloy called, Fernanda told him, I've got the money, I've got it right here, but I can't give you anything without proof of life. Eloy was quiet for a bit, she asked if he was still there, and he responded that he was going to run it by the others. Fernanda gave us a victory sign. Before hanging up, she said, Eloy, Eloy, don't hang up, I need to ask you something. What is it, Doña Fernanda? What happened to Rómulo?, she asked. Rómulo?, Eloy repeated, and again fell silent. Eloy?, Fernanda asked. Ma'am, he said, Rómulo was killed.

Fernanda met with Cubides, and they celebrated the fact that, for the first time, the supposed captor had agreed to consider providing proof of life. In the prosecutor's view, they couldn't assume that the information about the man known as Rómulo was true. Maybe Eloy's lying and doesn't even know him, he said.

It was life that was lying, conspiring with liars or with circumstances that made it more likely that deception would bear fruit. At dawn the next day, the telephone rang. Fernanda answered sleepily, and on the other end of the line she heard a whisper saying, Fernanda, darling, it's me. She sat up, her heart about to explode. Libardo?, she asked. She heard the whisper ask, how are the boys? She told him, speak up, I can't hear you. I can't, the whisper said. Where are you? Fernanda asked. With the people who are holding me, I can't say any more, tell me how the boys are. Speak louder, Fernanda insisted. I have to hang up, the whisper said, give them what they're asking for, I'm desperate. Talk louder, I can barely hear you, Fernanda pleaded, angry, but then Eloy came on the line and said, there's your proof, ma'am, we held up our end, I'll call you later to set up the handoff. He hung up, and Fernanda was left screaming into the handset, don't hang up, Eloy, I need to speak to him, just for a second, Eloy, please! Hearing her shouts, Julio and I rushed into the room and found her clutching the telephone and piteously weeping.

We sat on the bed as day broke, speculating and making her go back over every word of the conversation.

"But was it him or wasn't it?" I kept asking.

"How do I know," Fernanda said. "Sometimes yes and sometimes not. When you hear the recording, you'll know."

"But how could you not recognize Dad?"

"I haven't heard his voice for a long time, and I already told you I could barely hear him."

"Maybe they talked like that so you wouldn't recognize him," Julio said.

"Maybe," she said, "but he's also been a prisoner for months, you know, not talking to anybody; who knows what kind of condition he's in. A person could even forget how to talk."

Again and again we asked her the same questions, and she gave us the same answers. All we could do was wait a little before contacting Cubides and reviewing the recording of the call.

Whether it was Libardo or not, I was scared stiff to hear that voice.

62

Fernanda's still in the blue dress she was wearing this morning, though she's got on slippers now, not heels. From the smile she gives me, I gather she doesn't know anything yet, or she's faking it so she can unload her wrath at just the right moment. I look around for Julio and don't see him. She asks if I've had lunch. I tell her I have, and she doesn't ask where.

"How about you?" I ask.

"Yeah, I did too," she says. "I had a business lunch."

"What business?"

"Nothing yet," she says, "but I want to do something. I'm sick of depending on Julio."

She offers me coffee, and I say I don't want any. What kind of business could Fernanda do? I don't want to pester her with questions, at least not until it's clear she doesn't know about my visit to Rosa Marcela.

"Where's Julio?" I ask. "Hasn't he been around?"

"He came and then left again. He was furious. He took your dad with him."

"What happened?"

"I'm not going to let Libardo stay with your grandmother. Plus I hated that hideous box you two chose. Don't say anything—I don't feel like rehashing that argument with you. But your dad deserved something more luxurious. You let that woman influence you."

"She had nothing to do with it," I say.

"I know, so Julio said, and I'm not going to discuss it again with you." She lights a cigarette and says, "We're all dependent on Julio, on whatever he feels like giving us. Every month I have to humiliate myself and ask for a little more. And look at you— you could have finished your degree, but no, Julio told you there wasn't enough for that, but he lives like a king out there."

"Where did he go?"

"To the farm."

"What about Dad?"

"You never listen to me, Larry. He took him. He said he's going to bury him out there and that you agreed."

So Julio didn't tattle on me to Fernanda, but he did use me to settle Libardo's fate. He left without saying goodbye, without letting me tell him what had happened with our sister, what meeting her had been like, what I think of her.

"Is he not coming back?" I ask Fernanda.

She shrugs and takes a long drag on her cigarette. "Ultimately I think it's a good idea," she says. "Libardo loved his farms—they were his life. It's O.K. for him to have his final resting place on the only one we've got left. Plus, Julio's so much like Libardo . . . It's better for them to be close."

I know her. Her satisfaction is only from having won this round with Gran. She would have tossed Libardo down a sewer grate to avoid handing him over to her. I'm hurt that my brother has left. There won't be a mass or a funeral now. There's no reason for me to be here.

"You and I should think about setting up some kind of enterprise. We'd make good partners, and we wouldn't need to depend on your brother," she says, stubbing out her cigarette in an ashtray.

"I'll be leaving, Ma."

"Where to?"

"Back to London. I've got a job, an apartment—my life is there."

"The only thing you've got there is a salary," she tells me.

"Well, here I don't even have that," I say.

"Because you don't put in the effort, because you're satisfied with nothing. They took everything from us, and you haven't lifted a finger to try to get any of it back."

"Get what back?"

"A lot of the people who killed your father are dead too, or no longer active. It's been a long time, Larry. We could do something—the three of us could start over. You and Julio have got Libardo's blood, and I spent more than half my life with him."

"Start over?"

"Rebuild, Larry, raise up what they knocked down. You're smart, Julio's ambitious, and we've still got friends who could help us . . ."

"Friends from the cartel?" I ask.

Fernanda lifts her hand to her forehead and slowly inhales. She pulls her feet out of her slippers and puts them up on the seat. She runs her fingers through her hair to comb it back. One lock tumbles back down and covers half her face.

"They've moved on to other things now," she says in a more deliberate tone. "We could too."

"Ma, everything Dad was involved with was illegal, including his friends. I don't understand what it is you're looking to rebuild."

"I want things to be like before," she says. "Get out of this rattrap. The other house still exists. It's standing empty, but it's there. With some good lawyers, we could get it back."

"How much money have you already thrown away on lawyers?" I ask.

"Well, thanks to those lawyers we didn't lose the farm where Julio's living, and I was able to get this apartment."

"You just called it a rattrap a minute ago."

She challenges me with her gaze, with her body, with the

tone of her voice as she raises it to say, "Yes, Larry, because we deserve to live somewhere better, another neighborhood, with better status. We didn't bring you up to be a nobody."

My head boils and my vision blurs. When did this pointless quarrel start? The argument would have made sense twelve years ago, but now? I look at the unopened boxes, the stacks of paintings, the mound of curtains that she's never bothered to hang up. It seems like she doesn't even sweep. Growing hazy, I say, "I think your life is the real rattrap."

Fernanda grabs the ashtray and hurls it at me in a fury. She storms off to her bedroom, slams the door, and lets out a howl like a wounded beast. I shake off the ashes and butts. It was a vicious blow. Mine and hers both. The only thing that occurs to me in all this chaos is to take a shower.

63

At the foot of the escalator, to the right, was Larry's last chance to find her. If she'd taken the previous flight and was still in the baggage claim area, if she was still outside with her family, weeping with them over her father's death, if he managed to ask for her phone number, if this or if that . . . He reached the escalator but didn't ride down, instead taking the stairs next to it. On his own two feet.

Let her be there, let her not be there. Let her be gone, let her have just arrived.

He watched the carousel as he descended; the room was crowded with people, and those waiting milled around on the other side of the glass. He was afraid to see his mother older now; he had some idea of what she looked like via Skype, but what would it be like to be inches away from her, to touch her, to study her from head to toe? Some people age overnight.

Fernanda. Charlie. I hope there's nobody here to pick me up yet, and not her either. I hope Fernanda's here to save me, or nobody, I hope they leave me alone . . .

Farther along was another carousel, empty but moving. Larry looked at the people in the room and the ones waiting outside, beyond the glass. Charlie wasn't on this side, and Fernanda wasn't on the other. An alarm announced the suitcases' arrival. The passengers swarmed as if somebody were handing out food or money. Larry stood still, searching for what he wasn't going to find, either inside or out.

People started moving off with carts full of luggage. They

looked like bumper cars. Little by little, the carousel was left alone, with only Larry's suitcase going around and around. He grabbed it and pulled it along despite the dodgy wheel. He walked through the glass doors that separated the people inside from those outside. He looked around distractedly. There was euphoria, tears, laughter, and hugs. Touts offered him a taxi service, a bus ride into Medellín, hotels, but nobody offered him a hug. Without a doubt, Charlie wasn't there. Maybe she never had been. He said goodbye: see you never, sweetheart.

He didn't see Fernanda, Julio, or his grandparents either. His only option was to wait, since he didn't have an address to take a taxi. Suddenly he heard a yell, a familiar voice: "You gonna start crying now, man?"

He turned around and saw him. There he was with the same shiftless smile, a little fatter and balder, his old friend, Pedro the Dictator, who gave him a huge hug and enthusiastic slaps on the back.

"What's up, dude!" Pedro said.

"Where's Fernanda?" Larry asked.

"Hello to you too," Pedro said. "I asked her not to come because I knew you'd be happier to see me."

"Stop screwing around," Larry said, half joking, half serious, and hugged him.

"Let me help you with that," Pedro said, and grabbed the suitcase.

They walked out to the parking deck. Larry looked back one last time.

"Are you waiting for someone?" Pedro asked.

"No," Larry said. "Let's go."

64

To confirm whether the voice on the recording was Libardo's, Jorge Cubides explained they'd need to compare it with another recording of him speaking.

"It can be a video where he says something."

"A video?" Fernanda asked.

"Or a tape recording, anything where we can hear him," the prosecutor added.

"I don't know if we have anything like that," Fernanda said, looking at Julio and me.

I recalled that when we were kids, Libardo had a video camera and had recorded us lots of times, but I'd never seen those tapes again.

"Ma, remember those home videos Dad used to make when we were little?"

"I do," Fernanda said, "but I have no idea where they are."

"Look for them," the prosecutor said, "and we can settle the matter."

"Can you give us a copy of the recording?" Julio asked. "We want to hear it again so we can be more certain."

We went back home, and Fernanda ordered everybody, even the bodyguards and the maids, to search the house top to bottom for any kind of cassette.

The first things to appear were the cassette cases with the music Libardo used to listen to as well as some mix tapes he'd made. One of the boys took it upon himself to listen to all of them and separate out the ones that might contain something besides songs. And so, accompanied by fragments of tangos, boleros, and vallenatos, we hunted through every drawer, every receptacle where we thought the videos Libardo had made might have been forgotten.

A couple of days later, while we were still searching, the telephone rang. It was Eloy, who hadn't called again since the night she'd supposedly talked to Libardo.

"What did you lose now?" Eloy asked. "What are you looking for?"

Fernanda went pale as Eloy laughed loudly on the other end of the line. Pulling herself together, she ran to the window to draw the curtains. "Nothing that matters to you," Fernanda said.

"It might not matter to me, but it does matter," Eloy said. "I haven't seen you all so busy in a long time."

"You're watching us?" Fernanda asked.

"Oh, honey," Eloy said, "since when have you and I had any secrets?"

"Leave us alone," she demanded. "I'm trying to get the money together."

"Didn't you say you already had it?"

"Not yet. Call me in three days," she said.

Fernanda remained silent a few minutes, then got up and yelled furiously for the staff, asking them who was the snitch, who was the traitor, so she could cut out their tongue, chop them into pieces. I tried to intervene, asking, what happened, Ma, what did that guy say? But she kept yelling, as did Julio, who was asking, who's the bastard who sold us out, who sold out my dad? I swear, ma'am, one of them tried to say. Who's the fucking mole? You've known us for a long time, the cook tried to say. I said again, what's wrong, Ma? And she replied, still yelling, that Eloy person knows we're looking for something, one of these guys is squealing everything, and she turned to them, maybe it's not just one of them, maybe it's all of them, you can all get out right now, unless you want me to call the attorney general's office so they can pick you up as crooks, as accomplices, as motherfuckers, she said.

She was trembling, leaning against the walls while the employees, who were as shaken as she was, filed out, the two women crying and the bodyguards solemn.

"Pour me a drink, Julio," Fernanda said.

"Tell us everything, Ma," I said, and led her to the living room, where she collapsed into an armchair and said, "They know we're looking for something important."

Julio appeared with a full glass, and she didn't even ask what it was. She took two large gulps and sighed. She gave us more details about the call, the little she remembered, because the terror of knowing we were being watched had taken her breath away.

My brother went over to the sliding doors to the outside, looked at the dozens of buildings that surrounded the house, and, with a couple of tugs, closed the curtains again.

"I'm positive one of the employees is betraying us," Fernanda said.

"They've all been with us for years," I said. "They've been here since long before Dad was taken. I bet we're being spied on from outside."

"I'm with Mom, Larry," Julio said. "There's a snitch in here."

"But Eloy didn't mention the cassettes," I said. "Right?"

Fernanda drank again, grimaced, leaned her head back, and closed her eyes.

"Did he mention them, Ma?"

"I don't remember. I don't think so, but I'm not sure."

"If the information had come from here, he'd know what we're looking for."

"Anyway," Fernanda said, her eyes still closed, "we should just fire all of them. They should go. I don't trust anybody anymore."

And so the three of us were alone in that huge house. Fernanda promised to look for new staff, but in the meanwhile, we all cooked for ourselves or ordered in. The dirty laundry piled up, as did the grime and neglect. I liked living like that. For the first time, for the first time I could remember, there were no bodyguards, no strange people invading our spaces. At night I would lie down on my unmade bed, just as I'd left it that morning. We turned on only the lights that were necessary for safety purposes, and from the outside the house looked uninhabited. The curtains remained closed at all times, of course.

One morning, we were awakened by Fernanda's shouting. "Come here, boys, wake up, look what I found!" She came into each of our rooms with a shoebox full of video cassettes. She told us to come downstairs immediately, prodding us along so relentlessly that Julio and I decided to go just as we were, in our underwear, barefoot, our eyes puffy from sleeping till eleven in the morning.

"Where can we watch these?" Fernanda asked.

"What format are they?" I asked.

"What?"

"Let me see them."

They were Betamax cassettes. The machine in the living room was VHS.

"We need a Betamax," Julio said.

"There's one right here," Fernanda said.

"That one won't work."

"Of course it will," she said. "You two watched a movie just last Sunday."

"That's VHS. Those cassettes won't work there," I explained.

Fernanda cursed. She grumbled that she had no idea what we were talking about.

"I know where there's one," Julio said, and headed for the bodyguards' room. They had an old Betamax where they used to watch porn movies.

We started connecting it to the TV while Fernanda examined each cassette, hoping to find a clue, a mark, a written date. The first one we put in had footage of some horses, taken from a car. You could hear the noise of the engine, the wind, but never Libardo's voice. Julio said the horses were from the old stables at El Rosal.

On another tape, Libardo appeared playing soccer with some friends. Fernanda recognized several of them. There's Benito, look, in the red shirt. It was a younger Benito, and Libardo, too, looked rejuvenated. He was playing, shoving, laughing, joking around with his friends. Fernanda started crying, and I wanted to too, but I held it in. That guy in blue is Genaro Robles, Fernanda said, he's dead now, she added. And she mentioned others who'd already faded from my memory. All dead, all killed. Shut up, Julio told her, I can't hear a thing. But there was nothing to hear. The person who'd filmed the video was standing next to a speaker, and all we could hear was the music playing to liven up the match. Then another player, wearing soccer duds, walked onto the field and everybody clapped. We looked at one another in shock when we recognized Pablo Escobar.

The third tape showed one of Julio's birthday parties. We figured it was Libardo recording the gathering because plenty of guests were in the video but not him. There were our grandparents, Benito again, Fernanda, me, more kids, more friends, and a number of bodyguards. How old would you have been?, Fernanda said, I think eleven or twelve, she calculated while wiping away her tears. Twelve, I said as soon as the cake appeared and I swiftly counted its twelve little candles. There was noise, music playing, voices in the background, but none of them were Libardo's.

Another tape had the sea, the beach full of tourists, ships off in the distance, as if they were being recorded from the penthouse of a hotel.

"Where's that?" Fernanda wondered, and said, "I don't recognize it."

"The water's really blue," I said. "It could be San Andrés."

"Oh, right," Fernanda said. "We went a few times, even took you two, but I don't remember him filming."

"Shush," Julio said. "Dad's talking."

We listened, but he wasn't actually talking—he was laughing uproariously. The camera lowered, and we saw the railing of a balcony and some towels tossed on chairs. Then the camera swung sharply around and focused on a naked young woman who was lying on the bed and trying to cover herself up with a sheet, laughing too. She said, no, Libardo, stop being silly, don't record me like this, silly. He moved closer with the camera, and she shrieked again, looking at him mischievously. He pulled the sheet back, and there she was, naked, curled up, both of them dying of laughter.

When I turned to look at Fernanda, she was half out of the armchair, and her face had gone blotchy with red, purple, white, and green spots. She was clenching her jaw and shaking with rage.

"It's that tramp," she growled.

I leaped up to turn off the video player, but she stopped me with a roar.

"Leave it! Let me see those fucking bastards."

"What for, Ma? Why torture yourself?" I asked. "We have to focus on what we're looking for."

"That's the girl, that skank Vanesa," Fernanda said. She stood up and clenched her fists.

"I'm going to turn it off right now," Julio said, but before he could get up, Fernanda had grabbed a bronze horse off the coffee table and hurled it at the television. She pounded the screen, ignoring the sparks, the smoke, the shards of glass that sliced into her hands.

Still pounding, she said, "I hope they kill you, you bastard, you fucking cunt, I hope they take you out, I'm not going to lift a finger to get you free, and as for you, you fucking whore, you big-boobed vulture, I'll kill you with my own two hands."

She struck the TV one last time and fell to the floor in a faint.

65

S itting on the floor in the shower with the hot water falling on my head, I see a procession of images of everything I've experienced during these sleepless, stressful hours. Medellín as one big flash of light, the smell and noise of fireworks, the raucous shouting of drunks and the dull thudding of songs that say nothing and yet say everything, saying how small we are, how small we've become: a monotonous, empty reggaeton tune, misogynistic and violent, a cult of nothingness. One day, one night, one early morning linked to this next day that's nearly turned to night again. Fernanda, Pedro the Dictator, La Murciélaga, Julieth, marijuana, aguardiente, coke, Julio, Libardo's bones, my grandparents, Vanesa, Rosa Marcela, and among all those other faces, hers, Charlie sleeping, crying, drinking, her hair on my shoulder, our hands intertwined, her sad face that is becoming blurrier in my mind with every passing minute.

The water starts getting cold and my fingertips are wrinkled. The bathroom is full of steam, the mirror foggy, and the towel Fernanda's given me is the kind that doesn't really dry you off. Outside I can hear her laughing. Is she still on the phone with Julio? He called from the farm to tell us he'd decided to bury Libardo next to a lignum vitae tree on the land next to the lower ravine. I knew which one he meant because Libardo always used to stare at it in amazement when it was in bloom.

My suitcase is still on the bed with the clothes all jumbled up as if I've been here for days. Fernanda keeps laughing hard, and then I hear a man's laughter alongside hers. She and whoever the other guy is murmur something and then laugh again. I know that laugh.

I go out of the bedroom and try to find them. The muffled laughter and fragmented sentences are coming from the kitchen. I know that voice. There they are, close together and leaning on the counter, Fernanda and Pedro. As soon as they see me, they freeze, especially him. She tries to stop laughing, like a little girl who's hiding something. But they can't tamp it down. Fernanda's nose is white, and Pedro's holding a knife with a bump of cocaine on its tip that he was about to sniff when I walked in.

"You bastard," I tell him.

"Larry," Fernanda says, but besides my name she doesn't have anything else to say.

I spring at Pedro and ram him. We both fall to the floor. Fernanda screams, but instead of intervening, she tries to gather up the coke that's spilled out of the bag and scattered across the floor. Pedro and I roll around; he's stronger than I am, always has been, and he pins me down.

"Let me explain."

I hurl every insult that occurs to me. Pedro may be stronger, but I'm more pissed off. I flail and manage to lurch to one side. I attack him again, and Fernanda digs her nails into my neck and tells me to let him go. I punch him in the face and take off running. I'm trying to get away not from him but from the entire experience. And from the truth.

At the elevator, I realize I'm barefoot. I go back to the apartment and ring the bell. Pedro opens the door.

"Give me a minute to explain," he says. "It's a long story."

His nose is bleeding. I shove him and he falls down; I go into my bedroom, grab my shoes, and leave again, slamming the door. Outside, the streetlights are already on. Where the hell am I supposed to go? The world's so big, but I've only got one place I can go: my grandparents' house. I have a sister too, but do I dare? As I'm putting on my shoes, I hear someone calling my name.

"Larry! Larry!"

I turn and see her. It's Julieth, shouting to me from Pedro's SUV. She signals me over. Inga's asleep next to her, and La Murciélaga is crying.

"Where are you going?" Julieth asks. Seeing how upset I am, she asks, "What happened, Larry?"

"What are you doing here?"

"We're waiting for you and Pedro," she says. "He went up to get you."

"Don't talk to me about that asshole," I say.

"What's wrong?" Julieth asks, surprised.

The three of them are still wearing the same clothes they were in yesterday. They stink of alcohol. They've lost their charm. Inga's drooling, La Murciélaga's eyes are swollen, and Julieth looks glazed over.

"What's up with her?" I ask, gesturing to La Murciélaga.

"She's sad."

"Why?"

"Everything."

"Are the keys in the ignition?" I ask.

"Yeah," Julieth says. "Pedro will be right down."

I get into the driver's seat and start the engine. I haven't driven for years, but it's one of those things you don't forget.

"What are you doing?" Julieth asks.

I don't answer and hit the gas.

"Where are you going? What about Pedro?" Julieth says.

Any street will do as an escape route; instinctively, I head up into the hills. A bottle rolls around under my feet and gets trapped between the pedals. Instead of braking, I accelerate. The women scream.

"What are you doing, Larry?"

I manage to drag the bottle free with one foot. La Murciélaga starts crying again, and Julieth begs her to stop thinking about that. The bottle's still got some aguardiente in it; I squeeze it between my thighs, uncap it, and take a long swig.

"There's the booze!" Julieth exclaims. "We'd lost it." She snatches it from me and takes a slug, then passes it to La Murciélaga and says, "Drink this and stop blubbering, please."

I turn on the radio and La Murciélaga yells, "No!" She slams the radio off and, freaking out, says, "I don't want music, I don't want liquor, I don't want anything, I don't want to live."

Without realizing it, I run a red light and another car screeches to a stop just short of my door. Julieth screams and La Murciélaga doesn't even notice. Inga moans, still asleep. They yell at me from the other car; back in the day, I would have gotten shot. Julieth leans forward and, feigning a dignity that doesn't match her level of sobriety, tells me, "Don't be childish, Larry. Stop being such a dick. Tell me where we're going already."

I prise the bottle from La Murciélaga and take two more swigs. My body is trembling like a dog that's just woken up.

"Answer me, Larry!" Julieth shrieks in my ear.

"To fucking hell," I say, and slam the gas pedal all the way to the floor.

66

After finding the video of Libardo with his mistress, Fernanda spent the next few days shut up in her bedroom. She came out only to make herself coffee in the morning and, at midday, to pour herself a drink. She didn't even come to the phone when Cubides called. And she didn't want to talk to Eloy either. You can go ahead and kill him, she told us to tell him, though we changed it to, she's busy right now, please call back later.

The house was a shambles. Though we opened the windows, it reeked of old food, cigarettes, confinement, and even of scorched plastic ever since Fernanda had destroyed the TV. I don't know how many weeks it had been since we'd changed our sheets. Desperate, I called Gran to ask for help.

"We need someone to come in and clean, Gran."

"What you need is someone to look after you," she said. "Come over here. I can take both of you in."

She was right. We'd be better off at her house, but we couldn't leave Fernanda alone right now.

"Thanks, Gran, but we just need somebody to help out with the cooking and cleaning."

"Where did everybody go?"

"Mom fired them. There was a situation, and she didn't trust anybody."

"Well, I don't trust her either," she said. "You'll be safe here and have everything you need. Eladio and Marcos are still with us—they can take care of you."

"Maybe later," I tell her. "For now, I'd appreciate it if you know of anyone looking for domestic work."

Meanwhile, Julio and I kept watching the remaining videos. We were certain that one of them would contain Libardo's voice. But what we found were side notes from his eventful life. Meetings with prominent politicians and businessmen that he'd probably held on to as evidence. A group of men unloading boxes from an eighteen-wheeler and then loading them onto a plane. Men shackled in a basement, their limbs being amputated by a chainsaw. Libardo and Pablo clinking beer bottles at a barbecue. Things like that, some of them awful, others insignificant. And one that was particularly moving: a trio of musicians accompanying Libardo singing. He was drunk. With one hand on his heart and his eyes welling up, gazing into the camera, he sang, *the fear of living is the lord and master of many other fears, insatiable and trifling.* The musicians were trying to follow him, but Libardo was so immersed in the song that he seemed to have forgotten that there were guitars and people around him. *It is yours and it is so mine, the fear of living that bleeds in our heartbeats like a challenge,* Libardo sang, stricken.

We finished watching all the tapes; none of them contained Libardo's voice. The song was useless for the comparison. And so we were left right where we'd started, or even further behind, since Fernanda's new attitude meant that the recovery efforts were on hold. Cubides even suggested that Julio and I take up the negotiations with the kidnappers ourselves. He was eager to show results. I refused for the same reason I always gave—I wasn't sure the voice on the call had been Libardo's—and Fernanda forbade Julio to get involved. She had a long conversation with the prosecutor, but they were unable to come to an agreement.

With life on hold, I went back to inviting Pedro and his friends over to the house for drinking, partying, sleeping with

Julieth. I no longer cared whether it was the weekend. We'd whoop it up any day they wanted. And I didn't care whether Julio and Fernanda were home. Julio kept going off to his girlfriend's house by cab, though sometimes he'd hang out with us. Fernanda didn't give a crap about my parties; she stayed shut up in her room, drinking alone.

One of those nights, Fernanda came out of her bedroom in her pajamas on her way to the kitchen, and when she passed through the living room, Pedro called her over. He invited her to join the group, offered to make her a drink, another one, since she'd already been drinking, and she accepted. She looked happy, which she certainly hadn't been that afternoon. After everybody introduced themselves, Fernanda asked loudly, "And which one's Larry's girlfriend?"

Julieth looked at me in horror and lowered her head.

"Ma," I said.

"Hey now, who's the lucky girl?" Fernanda insisted.

"Her," Pedro said, pointing at Julieth. "But he's the lucky one."

Fernanda smiled at Julieth, and she smiled shyly back. From then on, Fernanda kept watching her with discomfiting curiosity. Sometimes she'd smile when she met Julieth's gaze, but I knew there was nothing friendly about it.

Eventually, Fernanda had lost the little composure she had left. The uppermost two buttons of her pajama top were undone, she was having trouble hitting the ashtray with her cigarette ash, and she stumbled when she went to the bathroom.

"Larry, sweetie," she said, "bring the TV from your dad's study."

I thought she was looking to fill the space where the smashed TV had been.

"I'll set it up tomorrow, Ma."

"Bring it," she commanded.

"Ma."

"I said bring it, Larry. I want them to see something."

"I'll help," Pedro said, but I started suspecting what Fernanda was aiming at.

"No," I said. "We're not going to watch anything right now."

"I'll bring it for you, Fer," Pedro said, and signaled to another guy to go with him.

"You're not going to bring anything," I told Pedro.

"Why not?" Fernanda challenged me. "I want everybody's opinion, your girlfriend's too," she added mockingly. She got to her feet and said, "I'm going to show them Libardo's bitch and I want them to tell me who's better-looking, her or me."

She tried to strike a pose, but she lost her balance and wobbled sideways.

"I'm warning you," she said. "That tramp's a lot younger than me, though she doesn't even come up to my thighs. I'd like to see her when she's my age."

"Ma, stop, enough."

"Let them compare." She looked at Pedro and told him, "Bring that TV." And again she addressed the room at large: "At the age that slut is now, I'd already been crowned Miss Medellín."

She looked at Julieth and said, "Now you know where Larry gets his good looks from."

"Shut up or I'm leaving," I warned her.

"Well, leave then," she said.

They grabbed me to keep me from going. Julieth murmured to me, don't listen to her, she's drunk, but I insisted on shutting myself in my room. I called Julio to make him come back and help me, but he didn't answer his cell phone. I sprawled out on the bed and turned the TV all the way up. Julieth appeared and lay down next to me.

"What are you watching?" she asked.

"I don't know. Whatever," I said. "Did she show you the video?"

"She couldn't find it," Julieth said. "She's still looking for it."

"Please excuse her. And excuse me too."

"Why you?"

"Because I didn't say anything when she asked who my girl-friend was."

"But we're not boyfriend and girlfriend."

"I know, but I acted like an asshole."

Julieth kissed me on the mouth and said, relax. I'm not ready to be in a relationship right now, I said. Relax, she said again, and gave me another kiss. We touched each other and took off our clothes. More than aroused, I was grateful to Julieth.

67

I f you see a sign like that, one that says the best thing about a place is its people, you can be sure you've arrived in hell itself," Pedro told Larry as they drove along in the 4x4.

"So, nothing's changed, then?" Larry asked.

"Everything and nothing," Pedro replied. He studied him for a moment and said, "The look on your face . . ."

Very near the apartment, the food stands began. They were no longer the shoddily built stalls of Larry's youth. Though the basic concept remained the same, they were now solid, attractive structures, picturesque purveyors of typical local gastronomy. They stopped at one of them, settled at a table, and Pedro ordered two double shots of aguardiente to start.

"Well, you're here now," Pedro said. "You can get back all the time you've lost. If you put your mind to it, it won't be long before you're the same old Larry you used to be."

He raised his glass toward Larry in a toast, but he didn't say anything, just downed the drink, holding his gaze triumphantly. The aguardiente gave Larry goosebumps. He shuddered and choked back a cough.

"I'd forgotten the taste."

"You never forget how to drink liquor. It's like riding a bike. Did you not drink over there?"

"I learned to drink whiskey," Larry said. "Cheap whiskey."

"Well then, you're screwed. Whiskey's expensive here," Pedro said. "Want another?"

Larry said no, but Pedro ordered two more aguardientes.

"Last one," he told Larry.

Pedro grasped the nape of Larry's neck with his broad, horny hand and said, "It's not every day a guy like you comes back to this crap-ass country. We've got to celebrate it, receive you the way Libardo would have liked."

"I'm the one who's going to be receiving Libardo. He came back from the beyond so we could bury him," Larry said.

"Yeah, I know," Pedro said. "Your mom told me. All those years not knowing. It's fucked up, huh?"

Larry picked up the newly filled glass and, holding it near his mouth, said, "I never pictured him resting in peace under a tombstone or a cross. I pictured him at the bottom of a lake or being pulled along by a river, dumped in the middle of nowhere or in a mass grave."

He took a sip and pondered for a moment. All those people who left and never came back, who were heedlessly kidnapped in retaliation, who found themselves on the business end of a vengefully pointing finger that decided, this guy yes, this one no, that guy yes, and that one, and that one too.

"How long has it been since you've gotten laid?" Pedro asked.

In response, Larry tsked him. Pedro laughed and gave him a powerful slap on the thigh. Larry protested and took another sip of aguardiente. Pedro clapped him again, and Larry punched him in the shoulder. They both laughed.

"You didn't answer me, you rascal," Pedro said, "but you look like a man in love."

Larry held his gaze for a minute.

"What are you looking at, dude?" Pedro asked.

Larry watched him a while longer, in silence, and finally said, "I have to tell you something that happened to me on the plane."

68

We keep driving aimlessly. Inga wakes up and says she's hungry. Julieth suggests she shouldn't eat because she might vomit again. The food here's really strong, Inga says, and Julieth says, no, honey, what's strong is all the shit you've been drinking. The aguardiente has calmed me down a little, though I still can't get the image of Fernanda and Pedro snorting coke out of my head. How long have they been doing that? Did Pedro get her into it? I head east, toward Las Palmas again. That's where the airport is; I can't leave, but I'd really like to.

La Murciélaga isn't crying anymore, but she hasn't spoken since she said she wanted to die. She stares straight ahead as if hypnotized by the headlights. Where's Pedro?, Inga asks. He's still at Larry's house, Julieth says. That's not my house, I say. Why isn't he here?, Inga asks. I think there's a problem, Julieth says, and points at me. So where are we going?, Inga asks. Well, according to him, we're going to fucking hell, Julieth replies. Oh, Inga says.

They tell me their plan with Pedro the Dictator had been to go to a party organized by a friend of theirs named Lázaro. We were going to pick you up and then head there, Julieth tells me. Isn't it pretty early still?, Inga asked. No, she replies, the party started yesterday. They're really violent parties, she adds. In what sense?, I ask. Every sense, she says. On second thought, I say, but then I fall silent and don't say anything else.

After a while, I remark, "I think I'd rather go rest."

"You spent the whole day resting," Julieth says.

"If you only knew," I say.

"Then we have to go get Pedro," Inga says.

"I'm not going back there."

"What happened?" Inga said. "Did you have a fight with your mom? I didn't realize. I was asleep."

She's used the masculine form of the adjective, so Julieth corrects her. "You're a woman, Inga."

"Do any of you know where my grandmother lives?" I ask, and the three of them stare at me in surprise.

When Julio and I went to my grandparents' place, I hadn't paid attention; I'd had my eyes shut pretty much the whole way there. I was just thinking about the bag we were carrying in the backseat and how my grandparents were going to react. I hadn't figured I'd need to go back so soon and under such circumstances.

"Why are you looking for your grandmother?" Inga asks.

"So I can stay there."

"Stop being such a drama queen, Larry," Julieth tells me.

"She lives in one of those white houses that are really close together."

Even La Murciélaga breaks her silence and joins the others in cracking up.

"Oh, sure," Julieth says. "That's easy. Keep straight, I know exactly where that is."

La Murciélaga utters a delighted screech and then looks at me pityingly.

"Oh, Larry, you're a complete tool," she says.

"Take us to Lázaro's place instead," Julieth says.

"Pass the booze," La Murciélaga says, and asks, "Did they send the address?"

"Yeah," Julieth says, "but I don't think Larry knows how to get there."

"I'm hungry," Inga says.

La Murciélaga takes a swig, shudders, and coughs.

"I'm feeling a lot better, guys," she says. "You don't even know how awful I was feeling."

"Love you, Murci," Julieth says. "Love you so much."

"Take us to Lázaro's place and you can go wherever you want after that," La Murciélaga tells me.

"I know," I say. "Let's go back to my mom's house, and one of you can go up and get my wallet and my grandma's address."

"Larry, are you driving without your license?" Julieth asks.

I left my head back at the apartment, along with my self-control and judgment. Or maybe I left it all in London when I got the stupid idea to come back here. Or left it back in that time when Libardo didn't exist, alive or dead.

I'll be starting another story with different people, because nobody's the same now—not Julio, not Fernanda, not Pedro. Nobody.

"I stormed out and left everything upstairs," I tell them.

"I need to eat something first," Inga says, making the adverb feminine.

When Julieth corrects her, Inga protests. "But you just said I'm a woman."

Julieth sighs. Grabbing the aguardiente, she says, "Well, when it comes to eating you're like a man, Inga." She peers at the bottle. "This is running out."

I try to retrace my route, but it's all one-way, and there aren't always corresponding streets running the opposite direction. They curve; those that go up don't necessarily come down; they fork; they narrow and then widen again.

"Help me find my way back," I say. "Why doesn't one of you drive?"

"I'm drunk," La Murciélaga says.

"I don't know the way," Inga says.

"Look for the freeway," Julieth says.

"Is that how to get there?" I ask.

"It's how to get to Lázaro's party."

La Murciélaga switches on the radio, and it's the same thing as always. A noise, a droning, the endless repetition of a syllable, a voice constructed in a studio to make us believe that somebody's singing. A convincing argument occurs to me.

"Let's go back and get Pedro."

Everybody agrees. I have no intention of speaking to him, just grabbing my wallet and phone. Then I'll catch a cab and these people can go to hell.

One of them tells me to take this turn, another to take the next one, to turn around, to keep going straight, there are places I recognize, there are fireworks bursting in the sky, left over from yesterday or purchased for today. La Murciélaga searches frantically in her bag for her cell phone. Hello, she says, and immediately looks at me. It must be him, must be Pedro, but I can't hear him over their instructions, turn at the next one, this is the wrong way, go straight and then turn around. We go up, we go down, we drive along avenues and streets. This isn't the city I used to know—we were a large town bereft of God or law.

"Stop," La Murciélaga tells me.

"We're almost there," Julieth says.

"No, stop, Larry, nobody's there," La Murciélaga says. "Pedro isn't there anymore."

I pull over and ask, "What about Fernanda?"

"She's not there either. They went out together."

"Where to?"

"Pedro's heading to Lázaro's party."

"With Fernanda?"

"I don't know."

"What did he tell you?" I ask.

"What I just said."

"That's it?"

"And for us to bring some booze and stuff."

"What stuff?"

"Just stuff."

Tonight can't be like last night. I turn down the radio so I can think. I rest my forehead on the steering wheel. I don't have Julio, I don't have Fernanda, I don't have Gran or Rosa Marcela. Or Charlie. And I don't have papers or money or a phone or anything else. Just three women who might as well have escaped from a loony bin.

"Give me the car, Larry," La Murciélaga says.

"I have to go get my things," I say.

"And who's going to let you in? Do you have keys?"

I don't have keys. I don't have anything.

"No," I say.

"So?" La Murciélaga asks.

"Larry, give her the car," Julieth says. "You don't have your license, and besides, you're drunk."

"So's she," I say.

"Yeah, but she's got a license," Julieth points out.

"Let me drive, Larry," La Murciélaga insists.

I need to think, to come up with some options for getting out of here. I haven't slept, I've been drinking and smoking pot, I have jet lag, I don't know what to do. La Murciélaga opens the door and climbs out. We switch places.

"No speeding, Murci, you're fried," Julieth says.

La Murciélaga responds with a loud laugh and takes off.

"Tell me where I'm going," she says.

"To the party," Inga says. "They'll have food there."

What could happen if we get stopped by the cops? Will it be enough for me to identify myself as Libardo's son, the way it used to be?

"Open your mouth," Julieth tells me.

"What?"

"Open your mouth, doofus."

Julieth places a pill on my tongue and passes me the bottle so I can wash it down.

"What was that?" I ask after I swallow.

Julieth kisses me on the mouth and says, "Don't ask silly questions, earthling."

One morning I woke up late and found a woman sweeping the house. She greeted me with a friendly smile. She said her name was Lucila and that Doña Carmenza, my grandmother, had sent her. How did you get in?, I asked, and she told me the door was open. That she'd rung the bell anyway because she didn't dare come in, but when nobody appeared, she started picking up. I couldn't find any cleanser for the bathrooms, she said, and I used the little dishwashing liquid that was left to wash all the dishes. I peeked out and the kitchen was sparkling; it smelled clean. The living and dining room windows were open. Air was flowing through, and the sun was shining into the corners. Did you talk to my mom?, I asked. You're the first person I've seen, she said, there's not much I can offer you for breakfast, do you want something to drink? Is there any Coke?, I asked, and she said she'd go look. Before she left, I called to her.

"Lucila, are you going to stay?"

She hugged the broom and shrugged, looking around as if gauging the size of the house.

"Well, that depends on the boss," she said.

I don't know if she meant Gran or Fernanda. I didn't ask. She'd have come here knowing what to expect. She would have known who we were, what was happening with Libardo. We needed her help so badly that I'd better stop pestering her with questions and let her get back to work.

When Fernanda woke up, Lucila was already making

lunch. Predictably, she threw a fit. Over my dead body, Fernanda said, and added:

"Carmenza sent you so you can report back what's going on over here."

"I was the one who told Gran we needed somebody to help us," I said.

"That woman never helps, Larry. All she does is make things more complicated."

I asked her to take a look around, to go into the kitchen; lots of laundry was already done, I said, and for the first time in many days, we were going to eat a homemade meal.

"And she opened the curtains," Fernanda remarked. "That's just great."

She drew them again and asked me, what do you want? For people to keep snooping around? For not just Carmenza but everybody else to find out what's happening here? And she said again, over my dead body, Larry.

After a lot of arguing, the two of us reached an agreement. Lucila would stay until Fernanda found a replacement. In any event, she warned Lucila, "And no bringing gossip to that woman. What happens here stays here, understood?"

Lucila murmured, yes, ma'am, as if she'd already committed some violation.

Other warnings were: don't ever answer the phone, this is a complicated situation, all calls are recorded; don't go into my husband's study; don't open the door to anybody without asking us; don't ask where I'm going or where I'm coming from, Fernanda told her, oh, and we're going to put you on probation for a few days. Lucila agreed again, baffled by Fernanda's accusatory tone.

At least we could now sleep between clean sheets in neatly made beds, eat good food, and breathe fresh air, though Lucila barely had enough time to keep such a large house in order. In some fashion we started going back to normal, though when a person had been disappeared from a life, it could never be normal.

Julio tried to encourage Fernanda to keep pursuing the plan she'd laid out with Cubides, the prosecutor. We started arguing about the recording of Libardo's voice again, unable to come to a consensus. Fernanda insisted she wasn't going to lift a finger to help him.

"Why don't you talk to that hussy?" she told Julio. "She can take over the plan. I don't want to see him again."

Julio couldn't wrap his head around the idea that Fernanda, out of jealousy, would let Libardo be killed. I argued that they, the people who were calling, didn't have him, but at times I was gnawed by doubt. What if I was wrong? What if this was our opportunity to get him freed? Even though Fernanda had forbidden us to talk to our callers, once when Julio answered, he told Eloy we were holding firm, that Fernanda was sick but as soon as she got better, we'd be ready to resolve the situation.

Though he made it up, he was right: Fernanda was sick with jealousy, so much so that several days later she called us together and told us, "I'm going to move forward, but only so I can make him sign divorce papers."

I didn't say anything, didn't object; I wasn't willing to carry that guilt in case they were right. I was also hoping that if they were correct, when Fernanda saw Libardo, she'd be moved to change her mind. The fact that she was jealous meant she still loved him.

The person who was most enthusiastic to see the plan in motion again was Cubides. Fernanda met with him again, but not at the house anymore, almost always at the casino.

"It's no secret I go there a lot," she told us. "We won't arouse anyone's suspicions."

Another day she packed up Libardo's clothes in suitcases and boxes. She gathered the documents scattered around the study, tidied them as best she could, and stored them in boxes that she marked "Libardo Papers." When it was all together, she told us, "I hope I don't see him. Lucky for me he's going straight to prison. When you meet up with him, give him the folder we're preparing and have him sign in the places we've indicated."

She was going out every night. She'd leave in a taxi and the prosecutor almost always brought her back home. One night I heard her laughing wildly with Eloy, as if they were close friends.

"What were you laughing about with that guy?" I asked accusingly.

"He told me a joke. Want to hear it?"

"You let those bastards tell you jokes?"

Fernanda tried to stifle the remnants of a laugh. Failing in that, she said, "So this drunk walks into a whorehouse . . ."

"No!" I shouted. "What's wrong with you?"

"What's wrong with you, Larry?"

Then her manner changed, became remorseful, and she signaled for me to sit down next to her on the bed.

"I've got a calculus midterm tomorrow," I said.

"Oh, that's what's going on."

"No, that's not what's going on."

"Are you O.K.?" she asked.

For a long time now, I hadn't cared about school. I wasn't doing badly, but I just wasn't interested. The teachers were fed up with coming to the house too; they didn't say it, but I could tell. They gave their lessons out of obligation and feigned enthusiasm when Fernanda paid them.

"Pour me a drink?" she asked.

"You're drinking a lot, Ma."

"So are you," she said defiantly. "You spend all your time partying with your friends. You even shut yourself in your bedroom with that girl. You think I don't notice?"

"Well, if it bothers you, I'll leave it open next time," I said.

She straightened up, her claws out again. She lifted her chin and said, "All of this ends Saturday."

That disarmed me. Hearing that date, the precise day of Libardo's supposed return, plucked me out of my incredulity, flung me into the past, back to those times when Libardo used to go off on trips and I'd ask her insistently, when's Dad coming back?, always afraid it would be never. Fernanda would simply reply, tomorrow, the day after tomorrow, the Monday after next.

"This Saturday I'll be a single woman again," she said, as if she were talking about an appointment at the hairdresser's or with her masseuse, as if on Saturday she'd be going to a party.

70

"Tell me the truth, Pedro. Why didn't Fernanda come get me at the airport?" Larry asked.

A few drops of water started falling on the windshield, distorting what lay ahead. They were fat, scattered drops tumbling down from a lone cloud on one of those afternoons when Medellín occasionally outdid itself.

"I'm going to tell you what's going on," Pedro said. "Fernanda's called me more than twenty times today. She's really anxious. Every single time, she asked when you were arriving and told me she didn't know how to welcome you home."

"What do you mean?"

"Well, she didn't know what you like to eat, how you sleep . . ."

"What do you mean, how I sleep?" Larry broke in.

"I'm just telling you what she said to me. Are you going to let me finish?" Larry nodded, chastised. "What you're really not going to understand," Pedro went on, "is what she asked me to do as soon as I told her you'd landed."

He looked at Larry to see if he showed any objection, any gesture, but Larry remained silent, waiting for Pedro to continue.

"She asked me, practically begging, not to take you to the apartment, at least not as soon as you arrived," Pedro said.

"Did she say why?"

"No, she just said you couldn't come now, that we should call her back later."

"And what did she say about me?"

Pedro threw him a sideways glance and said, "You're acting like you're her boyfriend, not her son."

"Did she say that?"

"No, I say that," Pedro said, and turned up the volume on the radio.

An out-of-tune guy was singing a reggaeton ditty that went, *I go real high and I don't tell lies even if I'm bled dry.* Pedro sang along, *look at me, mami, look me in the eye, and look out, look out, look out with that, mami . . .*

On the highway was a sign announcing the exit to Cola del Zorro. Larry turned down the radio and said to Pedro, "That's where they started searching for my dad. Every time we heard a rumor that another dead body had been found dumped in Cola del Zorro, somebody would go out to see if it was him. They even got there way before the forensics people because Fernanda used to say she wasn't going to let anybody manhandle my dad's body or cut him open or stick him in a fridge."

Pedro looked at Larry, who swallowed hard, and then stuck his head out the window, peered up at the sky, and said, "If it starts raining, everything's fucked."

"What's everything?" Larry asked.

"Don't you know what today is?" Pedro asked.

"November 30."

"Not just that, man. Today's La Alborada."

"What's that?"

"The worst damn day of the year. Nobody sleeps, not even the people who go to bed and try," Pedro said, and smiled his roguish smile, the same one he'd used to become top dog.

He turned up the radio again. The reggaeton guy was still chanting, *if you're looking fly I'll get real high, but this guy ain't gonna cry, mami.* Pedro sang his own version, *if it's a rainy sky, I'm gonna cry, Larry, buddy, Larry, Larry.* And he kept repeating, Larry, Larry, and finally collapsed in laughter.

The tires squealed on every curve, and the SUV wove among the other vehicles. Larry stared at the buildings down below; they were much taller than the ones he remembered, closer together, untidily embedded in the mountain. He was distracted by a sign next to a store that said, "MINUTES FOR 200 PESOS."

"So where are we going?" Larry asked.

"To pick up La Murciélaga."

"Who's that?"

"Sarita Martínez. Don't you remember her from school? She hooked up with Fernández at the prom, remember him? She gave him hickies on his neck so hard she drew blood. That's why they started calling her the Bat."

"No way."

"I swear man, I saw it myself, he was bleeding. Dude was terrified too 'cause he had a girlfriend. Well, they broke up the next day, you can imagine."

"And she's who we're picking up?" Larry asked.

"Uh-huh," Pedro replied, "but no worries, she's changed a lot too. Plus we've got a surprise for you."

"I hate surprises," Larry said.

Up ahead was another sign similar to the last one: "MINUTES FOR 200 PESOS, TO LANDLINES AND ALL PHONE COMPANIES."

"I thought they were real minutes," Larry said.

"Huh?"

"What those signs are advertising," he said, and closed his eyes to ponder the possibility of buying minutes made of time, of past and future, minutes to hang on to as souvenirs or to throw in the garbage and forget entirely. Minutes to have on hand in case of need, to use in an emergency, Larry thought, for when our last minute is almost up.

71

In a whiny voice, La Murciélaga asks me, why do you never know where you are, Larry? You've puked three times, you reek, nobody's going near you, and since they saw us come in together, nobody's coming near me either, she tells me, her head resting on my shoulder as we lounge on a sofa, people chatting, jumping, and dancing around us. Please, Murci, for the last time, tell me where we are. I hate you, you bastard, she says. Where am I, Murci?, whose house is this?, whose party is this? That jagoff's, she says, and points to a muscular guy who's laughing hard. But it's not his house, she says, he just organizes these underground parties. By the way, Larry, she says, you didn't pay, you're a gatecrasher. Pay for what?, I ask. To be here, she says, or do you think this is free?, this costs Lázaro a pretty penny. I don't have any money, I say, just British pounds. That works too, La Murciélaga tells me, where are they? At home, in my wallet. Then I remember what I was feeling just before Julieth told me, open your mouth, Larry. But it isn't my home, I say to La Murciélaga, I'll just go get my things and then stay with my grandparents, want to come with me?, I suggest. No way, she says, I'm not going anywhere till Pedro gets here. Pedro's coming here? Of course, she says, he's one of the organizers. Pedro's an asshole, I tell her, and she moves away from me. She warns me, say that again and I'll cut your balls off. Do you know about him and my mom?, I ask. Of course, she says, everybody knows. Everybody knows they do coke together?, I ask. Oh, no, I didn't know that, she says,

I just know he's fucking her, but I don't know anything about the drug stuff. Pedro the Dictator's sleeping with my mom?, I ask. You didn't know?, she asks, and says, but he's your best friend. That's exactly why I didn't know, I say, because he is . . . was my best friend.

I go to the bathroom to puke. According to La Murciélaga's tally, it's the fourth time, though nothing is coming up anymore, just groans and retches. The urge to barf doesn't abate—it actually increases thanks to the filthy bathroom, the piss and streaks of shit in the toilet, the condoms on the floor, the foul smell, the truth, and the evidence. Pedro is fucking Fernanda, they're doing drugs and who knows what else, the bastards. There's nothing left of me in the mirror. The pallid image of Libardo's son, the bloodshot eyes that failed to see the best friend's betrayal, the ears that didn't hear Fernanda's moans of pleasure, the mouth that kissed the mother, the face of an orphan begging to be saved.

Somebody else needs the bathroom, somebody who must share my eagerness to expel everything and is frantically pounding on the door. I open it, and a woman says, hiccupping, you can stay if you want, I'm just going to pee. Smiling widely and shimmying, she lowers her underwear. I leave and shut the door, as I should.

La Murciélaga is no longer on the sofa. Or in the crowd either. I don't see Julieth or a single familiar face. Lázaro's over there wandering around, burly and exultant, so sure of himself that you don't know whether to envy him or feel sorry for him. A guy comes up to me and says, you look lost, buddy. I'm looking for a couple of girls, I tell him. I brought a few, he said. No, no, they came with me. Haha, he laughs, mine are better, women on the verge of ecstasy, he laughs again, the best ones here, Estrella, Tulipa, and Dolfi, he says, you choose, brother, I've also got the hottie everybody's after, Smiley, zero drama, zero blues. I'm looking for La Murciélaga, I say, have you seen her? Couldn't miss her, he says, she went up there. He points to a staircase crowded with people going up and down. Upstairs, Lázaro is throwing two men out of a room. You've got the wrong party, faggots, he yells, and shoves them, they're ashen, confused, Lázaro keeps kicking them in the legs, fucking cock jockeys, get the hell out of here, snarling an inch from their faces.

Finally I spot somebody I know. Inga. I'd forgotten she'd come with us. I've forgotten when I arrived here. Inga, Inga, have you seen La Murciélaga? Yeah, she says, she went into the prisoners' room, last one at the end. She gets really close to my ear and says something I don't understand, maybe she's speaking Swedish. I didn't catch that, Inga. Her breath stinks, like mine. Inga repeats the same thing. I still don't understand. She plants a kiss on me and leaves. She turns around and asks, is it true Pedro's coming? I don't know, I say, I hope not. And have you seen Julieth? I haven't seen her, Inga, there are too many people. She finally leaves.

So which one of these is the prisoners' room? And who are they? A rock band? That must be the place, where all those people are going in and out. There it is, yes indeed. Oh, a performance. On top of everything else, it seems the party has its more sophisticated element too. The performers are sitting on the floor, gagged and with their hands and feet bound. In front of them, a group of people are watching in silence, La Murciélaga among them. The women actors are crying. One is playing a mother, the other appears to be the daughter, and the third is the maid. I slip between the guests until I reach La Murciélaga. Murci, I say, and she shushes me. Don't say my name, dummy, she hisses. The actors moan beneath their gags. Beside the one playing the mother, a little girl is bawling her eyes out; her crying sounds muffled and her eyes are full of terror. It's a compelling scene—no wonder the audience is so rapt.

Hang on. What's that little girl doing in a performance piece?

What's going on, who are these people?, I ask La Murciélaga quietly. She says, they're the owners of the house. They're actors? She shakes her head and says, it's real, that's what makes it so powerful. One guest, a dude with a ponytail, goes up to the family and spits on the forehead of the older man, the one who's playing the father, or who's not playing but in fact is him. He shakes with rage, roars, gets red in the face, the spit sliding down his forehead. The audience cheers.

It's not a show?, I ask La Murciélaga. It's real, like I told you, she replies, annoyed, but even though she's repeated it, I don't understand. Six people tied up, abused, dumped on the floor. The little girl looks at me as if she can tell I don't have a clue. Her puffy, tear-filled eyes fill me with the fear they express. Let's go, Murci, I say. She shushes me again. What are they seeking with a nonexistent silence? When the music is making every wall of the house throb? Please, Murci, I say, and other people join her in shushing me.

"Let's go, let's go now, damn it!" I shout.

The family writhe on the floor like earthworms, they moan in chorus, they howl, and though I can't understand them, it's clear what they're pleading for. A woman berates me, you're making them nervous, beat it. That's exactly what I want to do, but I can't move. Get me out of here, Murci, I tell her. Supremely irritated, she shoves me toward the door and, stumbling, I manage to escape the room.

Still pushing me, she guides me out of the house and unleashes a diatribe that's as muddled as what I just saw, as what I feel. They're part of the consumer society, she says, the materialistic powers-that-be, and they have to pay for that, we observe them so they'll feel guilty, we force them to look at us looking at them, we spit in their greedy faces for their arrogance. Stop, I say, I don't want to listen to this. Lázaro's a prophet, she says, if it weren't for these parties, those people would go unpunished. Enough, shut up. You shut up and listen, she says. I can move more easily now. Where are you going, Larry? Where's the car?, I ask, I have to go, where did you park, Murci? Earth to Larry, she says, you have no idea what's happening on this planet.

I walk into a vast backyard where night swallows the treetops and it smells like those flowers that release their fragrance only when it's dark. And those people's materialistic violence, La Murciélaga is still saying. This is what the yard at my house was like, I tell her, it smells exactly the same. You're not listening to me, Larry. Come on, I say, let's go farther in. You just want to fuck me, she says, you're just like those materialistic pigs, you see me as an object. So stay here, then. No, wait up, Larry, don't leave me here by myself. We trip over a huge root and fall on the ground. We start laughing. This is what it was like, I say. This is what what was like?, she asks, and I reply: my world.

The stars glimmer through the trees. We stretch out on the grass. La Murciélaga clambers on top of me, pushes her face close, and kisses me on the lips. We start laughing again. With another kiss, she passes me something with her tongue, another pill. No more, I tell her, I'm topped out. Swallow, she says, and pushes my tongue with her tongue. The pill rolls down my throat. She kisses my throat, sucks on it, but I can't seem to get turned on. I don't know what's wrong with me, Murci. She bites me, takes off her shirt with a swift motion, and puts my hands on her tits. She rubs against my pelvis, my unresponsive cock. She moans, sighs, whines, giggles, spreads her arms wide and flaps them. This isn't going to work, I murmur, I'm beat. She moans loudly, wriggles around on me, and sucks my neck again, bites me. No, Murci, that hurts. She grabs my skin with her teeth. That's enough, Murci. I wrap my arms around her to restrain her. Her skin feels weird. What's up with you, Murci? What's on your arms? She stops and says, wings. She lets out an orgasmic moan, straightens up, and bares her teeth to the night, and when she opens her arms two dark, furry wings unfold. She flaps them wildly and leaps into flight, disappearing into the darkness.

72

Everything was chaos that Saturday, chaos and fear and shame. Starting very early, Fernanda was already on a rampage through the house. She spoke on the phone, and then I heard her talking to Julio. They were arguing about whether she should carry a weapon. Julio was saying yes, and she was claiming that was the first thing they'd warned her about, and plus, she told him, I'm going with Jorge. Every time I heard her call the regional prosecutor Jorge, my guts twisted. Julio was insisting she shouldn't even go, that's what the CTI agents were for. If they don't see me, there's no handoff, Fernanda declared, plus I'm just going with Jorge, he'll be there in a personal capacity. Then she said she was going to take a shower and get ready to leave.

In the kitchen I found Julio fondling the pistol Fernanda refused to take with her. Lucila was watching him out of the corner of her eye while beating some eggs.

"Mom doesn't want to take it," Julio complained.

"What good would it do her?" I asked.

"Self-defense."

"She's got other weapons," I said. "She knows how to use them."

"This is only one that's any use," he said, and pointed the gun at the window. Lucila eyed him with terror.

"Don't worry, she's not interested in rescuing Dad," he said. "She's playing for the other side."

"Stop talking bullshit."

"She's only going because she wants revenge. She doesn't care that he's missing, or kidnapped or whatever. Everything she's doing, she's doing it out of jealousy."

Lucila served us breakfast and asked us if we wanted anything else. She left us alone. Nobody can relax when somebody's waving a pistol around. Then Fernanda came in, with her hair wet and a drink in her hand at seven-thirty in the morning.

"Put that back where it was," she told Julio.

"What if they come here?" he asked. "What if shit hits the fan and they decide to come after us?"

"Stop being so dramatic. It's not the first time I've delivered money to these people."

"But it is the last," Julio said.

"What are you drinking, Ma?" I asked.

She looked at the glass and placed it on the table.

"I'm nervous," she said.

"Really?" Julio said. "Didn't you supposedly have everything under control?"

"Not about them," she said, "about Libardo."

I shot Julio a look that said *I told you so*. For the rest of us it could be the end of a problem, but for her it was just an episode in her marriage. The doorbell rang.

"That must be Jorge," she said.

Lucila appeared and asked if she should answer.

"Yes, go answer. If it's the prosecutor, tell him I'll be right there," Fernanda told her. She looked at Julio and said, "Take that gun to your dad's study." She looked at me. "You help me carry the suitcase."

"Aren't you going to have any breakfast?" I asked.

She picked up the glass again, grabbed the pitcher of orange juice, and poured a little into her drink. She took a swig and asked, "Happy?"

The phone rang. I rushed to answer in case it was them, but it was my grandmother.

"What's going on over there, sweetie?" she asked.

"Hi, Gran."

Fernanda was already talking to the prosecutor. I didn't feel comfortable saying anything.

"What's going on, Larry?" she said again.

"Can I call you back in five minutes?"

"So something is happening," she said.

Fernanda came over and asked, who is it? Gran, I said, and she waved her hand dismissively. I met Lucila's gaze, and she lowered her head and went off toward the bedrooms, alarmed.

"Answer me, Larry," Gran said.

"I'll call you back in five minutes," I said, and hung up.

The prosecutor had taken charge of the suitcase. He was smiling like he was heading off on his honeymoon, not a dangerous operation. Fernanda had been more agitated ever since he'd arrived. She said she was going to the bathroom one last time. Julio and I were left alone with the prosecutor.

"Is that a Jericho?" he asked Julio.

"What?"

"The pistol."

"Oh, I don't know. It's my dad's."

"Let me see," the prosecutor said.

Julio, hesitating, handed it over.

"Yes," Cubides said, examining the pistol and stroking it. "It's a 941. Not very common around here."

Fernanda came back and said to the prosecutor, "All right, let's go."

He gave the gun to Julio and said, "Don't take it out of the house."

And Fernanda said, "See you later, boys. I'll get in touch if there's any news."

I stood waiting for a kiss, a hug, even a tear from Fernanda. Maybe she was cold on purpose; any of those gestures I was hoping for would have seemed too dramatic, too final. The prosecutor went out, pulling the suitcase, like a pilot ambling toward his plane. He didn't even turn to look at us before closing the front door.

"I thought he was going to keep the gun," Julio said.

"I thought he was going to point it at us and run off with the suitcase," I said.

The phone started ringing again. Lucila peeked in the doorway and said, "Larry, your grandmother's asking for you."

"What do I tell Gran?" I asked Julio.

He shrugged, thought for a moment, and said, "Best tell her the truth."

"But there is no truth yet," I said.

"Then don't tell her anything."

73

Pedro pulled up in front of an apartment building. Is this where you're living now?, Larry asked him, and he said, no, this is La Murciélaga's place, she'll be right down. I love partying with her. Is she your girlfriend?, Larry asked. No, she's crazy. You never brought her to those parties at my house, Larry said. Oh, she was a good girl back then, Pedro said, and added, Julieth's going to come with her. Julieth? Uh-huh. Julieth Julieth? The one who . . . Larry didn't finish his sentence, and Pedro nodded wickedly. Larry asked again, Julieth? Yeah, dumbass, Julieth, Pedro said, or is there some other Julieth I don't know about? There was no doubt. Larry saw her come out of the building with La Murciélaga. Honestly, Larry said, I don't recognize either one.

The last time I saw Julieth, we were both seventeen . . .

Pedro got out and gave them each a kiss on the cheek and a hug. They chatted excitedly for a moment. Larry couldn't make out what they were saying. Pedro waved him over.

"The queens of the night," he said by way of introduction.

"Do you remember me?" La Murciélaga asked Larry. Seeing him hesitate, she said, "Sarita, from high school."

"Yes," Larry said, "Pedro told me, but I . . ."

"I know," she said. "It's the same with everybody."

She sidled up and kissed him on the cheek. Larry looked at the other woman, who was smiling like somebody leafing through a memory album. He'd slept with her, they'd seen each other completely naked, they'd had their hands and mouths all over each other, but apart from that Larry never knew anything about her. They hadn't talked for more than half an hour all told.

I don't even remember her voice, I don't know how she talked . . .

"Hi, Larry," Julieth said. She stepped forward and gave him a kiss in greeting. He was embarrassed by his unwashed smell, his bad breath, the hours he'd been wearing the same clothing. Julieth asked, "What's up? How have you been?"

It was the same Julieth, but to Larry it felt like she was somebody else, just like him, just like everything around him.

"All right, let's go," Pedro the Dictator commanded.

La Murciélaga climbed in front and Julieth in back, next to Larry.

This smells like an ambush, Pedro's an expert at those . . .

If he was refusing to take Larry to Fernanda's place and had brought along Julieth to stir up the past, it was because he had some devious plan in motion.

"What are you doing in Medellín, Larry?" La Murciélaga asked.

"They found his dad," Pedro butted in.

"How exciting! Finally!" Julieth exclaimed.

"Dead," Larry clarified.

La Murciélaga punched Pedro and said, "Why didn't you warn us, jackass?"

"No worries," Larry said. "It's really complicated."

"What a shame," Julieth said.

"All right, that's it, new topic," Pedro said. "We're on the party train."

"But . . . I don't understand," Julieth said.

Music filled the SUV again, rattling the windows and their brains.

"We're going to stop at Kevins first and get something to drink," Pedro said.

"Remember, I . . ." Larry tried to say, but Pedro cut him off.

"Yes, yes, I know. Don't be a drag."

"And how long are you staying?" Julieth asked.

"Did you hear that?" Pedro asked.

"What?"

"The fireworks have started."

"Just ten days," Larry told Julieth.

"Hear that, hear that?" Pedro asked again.

"How can we hear anything with the radio so loud?" Larry said.

"It was a really big boom," Pedro said, and added, "Besides, it's not a radio, it's a component."

"I need a drink already," La Murciélaga said. "Fireworks make me a little nervous."

If I'd known I was going to arrive today, I wouldn't have come, not on La Alborada . . .

Returning to Medellín was like never having left, as if the years he'd spent abroad had been a dream and, when he woke, the city had swallowed time.

Pedro reaffirmed it: "In my dictatorship, anyone who comes back will stay forever."

Nothing new to Larry. He'd always felt shunned in his own city. Ever since he was a kid, being Libardo's son had condemned him to living in exile in his own country.

"Did you all hear about that baby that predicts the future?" La Murciélaga asked.

"You and your spook stuff," Pedro said.

"But this was on the news," she said.

"I heard it," Julieth said. "He's two months old."

"And he's already talking?" Pedro said mockingly.

"He not only talks, he predicts what's going to happen," La Murciélaga explained. "Supposedly a relative came to visit him and made fun of him because he was really ugly, and supposedly the baby told him, you're going to die tomorrow, asshole. And boom, the guy gets run over by a truck the next day."

Pedro let out a loud laugh; he also let go of the wheel and they almost crashed into a pole. Julieth and La Murciélaga screamed in unison.

An accident right now could be my salvation . . .

"That's what you get for making fun," La Murciélaga scolded Pedro.

"Oh, so I'm going to die too?" he asked.

"Of course you're going to die," Larry said. "Someday."

"In the meantime, let's get drunk," Pedro said.

They pulled into the Kevins parking lot. Though it was still quite early, the bar was packed.

"This place is so decrepit," La Murciélaga said. "It's all old men and cartel guys."

"There aren't any cartel guys in Medellín anymore," Pedro said.

"Oh, sure," she said, and got out of the car, a look of resignation on her face.

Pedro exchanged hellos with the guard, the doorman, and several waiters as he walked in. Larry noticed that the entrance sign had two letters burned out, the *K* and the *V*. While they were waiting for a table, Julieth asked, "Are you still living in the same house?"

"I live in London," Larry said.

"I mean your house here."

"No. I don't live there anymore."

"The music isn't so bad," La Murciélaga said.

"I'm going to look for the bathroom," Larry said.

He walked through the crowd, everybody gesticulating as they talked. A waiter pointed him to the bathroom, and on the way he walked past a door made of dark glass guarded by a beefy guy with an earpiece. He couldn't see inside. Different music was playing from what was on the restaurant speakers. The hulk frowned when he saw Larry trying to snoop.

"This room isn't open to the public," the guard said.

Somebody behind Larry spoke: "Excuse me."

"Don Nelson," the hulk said.

Larry turned around and bumped into an older man who was bald and red in the face. He stepped aside so he could get by, but the guy stared at him.

"What's your name?" he asked.

"I was just leaving," Larry said. "I was looking for the bathroom."

"It's that door over there," the hulk said.

"You must be one of Libardo's kids," the man, Nelson, said. "You look just like him."

Larry didn't know how to react. Libardo had left so many enemies in his wake that he wasn't sure how to respond to Nelson.

What if one of those enemies has been waiting to settle a score for twelve years? What if waiting has only intensified his hate? I could say, no sir, I don't know any Libardo, but I've never denied my father in my life; I'm certainly not going to do it now that he's dead.

"Yes, sir," Larry said.

"Which one?" Nelson asked. "There are three of you, right?"

"No, sir, just two."

"Huh, that's weird, I thought there were more."

Larry still didn't feel safe; he didn't know which side Nelson was on.

If he were one of Libardo's enemies, he'd have already slammed me up against the glass door . . .

"I knew your father well," Nelson said.

Larry, still on pins and needles, only smiled.

"We used to do business together. You probably don't remember because you were really little." Nelson put a hand on Larry's shoulder and added, "There are more friends of your father's inside."

Larry didn't know what friends Nelson was talking about. He'd spent those years abroad thinking that Libardo had been surrounded only by hatred and vengeance, that nobody had loved him besides his family.

"I heard he'd been found," Nelson said. "Are you going to put on some kind of funeral?"

"I haven't discussed that with my mom yet," Larry said. "I just arrived from London."

"Oh, so you're the one who went away. Harry?"

"Larry."

Nelson slapped him on the back a couple of times and said, "Come on, join me. The boys are going to love seeing you."

They entered a world that was unfamiliar to Larry, full of a smoke that got into his throat and made his eyes burn. It wasn't a large group, all men, all older, like Nelson. One of them, microphone in hand, was singing in front of a karaoke screen. He warbled out of tune as the song lyrics scrolled past. The others watched in silence. They waved to Nelson, but nobody dared to interrupt the man who was singing. On the tables were bottles of whiskey and rum, lit cigars and cigarettes.

What's that smell? . . .

Another guy gestured to Nelson to sit down, and the two of them settled into a couple of armchairs at one end of the room. The singer closed his eyes and raised his hand to his chest. A waiter came up to Nelson and spoke in his ear. What'll you have, Larry?, Nelson whispered. Nothing, thanks, I can't stay long, my friends are waiting. Just one little drink, son, with us, your dad's buddies. The waiter was still standing there, waiting.

This smell reminds me of something . . .

If you live in London, you probably like whiskey, Nelson said. Yes sir, Larry replied. A whiskey, then, Nelson said, and gestured to the waiter. The singer still had his eyes closed. The words on the screen no longer matched what he was singing. Larry looked at the men, who were listening with something approaching admiration. Cell phones and guns lay on the tables. He willed the whiskey to come soon. Nelson was bobbing his head along to the music.

I know what it smells like . . .

Finally the whiskey came. Finally the song ended. The men applauded wildly. Without anyone asking him, Larry said out loud in wonder, as if he'd discovered something huge, "It smells like Libardo."

74

H is is the one voice I don't want to hear, but if a person is lost and hears his name being called, he has to follow that voice, even if it belongs to the devil himself.

"Larry, Larry, what are you doing here?" Pedro the Dictator calls from the car.

He's appeared out of nowhere on this dark road; I didn't hear the engine or see the lights of his SUV. He's following me, as he's done ever since we were kids; he's hounding me; he hasn't let me rest since I arrived, and plus, he's sleeping with Fernanda.

"Get lost, asshole," I tell him, and keep walking. I'm not heading anyplace; I'm just going wherever the road takes me. In the SUV, he's matching my pace.

"Get in," he says.

"Leave me alone."

"Larry," says Julieth, who's in the passenger seat, "it's dangerous around here, get in."

"I'll take you home," Pedro says.

"I don't have a home," I say.

"Don't be such a crybaby," he says. "There's a rough neighborhood up ahead. You're going to get yourself mugged."

Pedro speeds up a little and swerves the SUV to block my path. He climbs out, and before I can take off in another direction, he gets in my face.

"Get in the car right now, you hear me?"

"What are you going to do to me next?" I challenge him.

"I haven't done anything to you," he says.

"What about the thing with my mom?"

"That's with her, not with you."

"But she's my mom."

"She's a very lonely woman, and you split for London and haven't bothered coming back till now. And your brother is holed up on that damn farm all the time. She doesn't have the two of you, Larry—you haven't given her any attention."

Julieth sticks her head out the window and says, "Guys, get in the car, this isn't the place to work your stuff out."

"You've got her doing drugs," I say to Pedro.

"Would you look at that," he says, and rolls his eyes at Julieth. "The son of a narco claims to be all upset because his mom does coke."

I leap at Pedro, but I trip over my own feet and crash to the ground. Julieth shrieks.

"That's enough," she tells us. "Cut the bullshit, and let's get out of here."

Pedro grabs me by the shirt and helps me up. I can barely stand. He opens the back door and pushes me in.

"I don't have her doing anything," he says. "She has herself doing everything; I just join in."

"You're sleeping with her!" I shout.

"So what's the problem?" he asks.

"She's my mom, asshole."

"So?"

"And you're my best friend."

"I don't get it," he says. "Are you jealous over her or over me?"

It was my feet that got tangled up before, but now it's my words. Unable to speak, I cry instead. Pedro angrily slams the door. He starts the engine and, a few yards on, makes a U-turn and heads back.

Nobody says anything, there's no music; the only sound is the rumble of the engine. We don't pass any other cars, and there are no houses or buildings along the road, just shrub-land, dumping grounds for garbage and dead bodies.

"Stop making a fuss, Larry," Julieth says.

"Where are we going?" I ask, sniffling.

"To your house," Pedro says. "We're going to drop you off."

"My mom's place?"

"Yeah, your house."

"Drop me off at my grandparents' instead," I say.

He doesn't say anything; he's concentrating on the road. There's not a light to be seen, not a single human being, nothing, as if Medellín didn't exist.

"At that party," I say, or try to say, because my tongue is too thick, "at that house the people were captives."

Neither one says anything, as if I weren't in the car. Julieth turns on the radio. Britney Spears is on. I can't complain; it could be worse. Julieth sings along, pretending to sing in English, but it's not English or Spanish or anything else. It's cute.

"La Murciélaga flew away," I say.

They exchange glances again and laugh. Pedro joins in on Julieth's singing; he sings every word of the song in English.

Finally, in the distance, the lights of Medellín glitter. Or maybe, in my exhaustion, I've started hallucinating.

75

The moment Fernanda and the prosecutor walked out of our house, our story took a sinister turn. Or maybe recklessness simply hastened the course of the inevitable: us fleeing, leaving the country with whatever fit into a couple of suitcases; Fernanda, Julio, and I hiding like sewer rats. Or maybe it was earlier, in the instant when the regional prosecutor, Jorge Cubides, first crossed paths with Fernanda and she, once again, let herself be guided by the wrong man.

Clearly, that day was going to be unlike any other. There were pieces that didn't fit, reactions that made no sense, unconvincing explanations, yet we allowed the possibility of having Libardo back with us to gain strength. Who wouldn't be fueled by the return of a missing father, by the anticipation of seeing someone who'd been given up for dead? What person wouldn't give hope one last chance when it seemed there was little to lose and so much to gain? So that day we gambled against our fears and doubts and gave in to the dream they sold us.

Even still, as soon as Fernanda and the prosecutor left with a suitcase full of cash, the atmosphere grew strained, and when I lied to Gran and told her nothing was going on, everything was fine, I was aware of the opposite: nothing was fine, and things could definitely get worse.

It's always easier to connect the dots of the past than those of the present, and it's easy now to see the signs we missed back then, even the most banal ones, like the way the morning, which had started out sunny, covered over with a blanket of storm clouds as soon as Fernanda and the prosecutor left. Or the way my grandmother, at the end of our call, told me that my grandfather had come down from outer space and in five seconds of lucidity had told her he wanted to say goodbye to his grandchildren. Gran thought he was still confused or that he'd sensed he was going to die, but afterward, when everything went down, we linked his comment to our hasty departure from the country. And other similar warnings. Scattered dots, lost in the present, that we are able to connect only with the passage of time. Not entirely, because not everything became clear. There were lingering questions that Fernanda never answered, because she didn't want to or wasn't able, because she never accepted the responsibility for her failure. Julio and I hovered by the phone from the moment they left, even though we knew we wouldn't have any news for at least a couple of hours. Their supposed appointment with Eloy was set for southern Medellín, at a restaurant just inside the city limit with La Estrella.

At around noon, the meeting would have been over for a while, and they should have been back already. Unable to eat lunch, we stayed next to the phone. At three, Fernanda still hadn't called. Julio and I could only stare at each other in silence. There was no way we could tell Gran.

At about five, though, I told Julio, "This is really weird. I'm going to call her."

"Maybe they didn't show," he said.

"All the more reason for them to have been back a while ago."

"Don't call yet. Let's wait a little longer."

A number of scenarios flitted through my head, from the simple to the brutally gory and lethal. Anything was possible. Julio was probably going through the same thing, but he'd be afraid to mention what he was imagining too. It would make all the possibilities too real. He called his girlfriend several times, but they spoke only briefly—we had to keep the phone line open. He talked to her about trivial things to keep his mind off the wait.

Sometime after seven, the phone rang. Julio answered, but nobody said anything. But he told me he thought he'd heard Fernanda laughing in the distance.

"Laughing or crying?" I asked.

"I think laughing," he said.

The worst part was that it was possible. Often when she'd gone out at night, she'd call to let us know she'd be late or to give us some kind of instruction, and sometimes she'd go into a fit of laughter so intense that she couldn't speak, so she'd wait or call back after a couple of minutes.

"Maybe it wasn't anybody," Julio said. "I mean, maybe it wasn't the call we're waiting for."

Much later, Eloy called. He was really upset. He asked for Fernanda, and Julio told him she wasn't back yet. Eloy got angry and said he was going to make us pay for not taking things seriously; he called us liars and, before hanging up, warned us to get ready to receive Libardo's corpse. In a rage, Julio kicked the shit out of a door. I wept silently. Then I called Gran. Julio didn't stop me.

"Gran," I said, "we've got a big problem."

I caught her up on what was going on, she was quiet for a moment, and then she said, "You can't stay there. I'll send Eladio to pick you up."

We waited, sitting on the stairs, where we'd always sat ever since we were kids when we were left alone, staring at the front door. Fernanda and Libardo used to find us there on those steps when they came home late from their parties. While we waited for Gran's bodyguard to arrive, I told Julio, "Usually it's kids who fight against their parents and not the other way around, like it is with us."

All he said was "hmm" in a way that encompasses all of life's ironies. Then he said, "Speaking of fighting . . ."

He went to Libardo's study and came back with the pistol he'd been fooling with that morning. He sat down next to me. There we remained on that step, no longer the children waiting expectantly in their pajamas for their parents to come home, but two armed young men who had stopped expecting anything from them.

76

"W asn't my house around here?" I ask Pedro.

"Which one? Fernanda's?"

"Mine, the one we lived in with Libardo, the house from before."

"Yes," Julieth says animatedly, "it's around here, I remember."

"Can we go see it?" I ask.

"Make up your mind," Pedro says. "First you want to go to your grandma's house, then to the old house—why don't you go to Fernanda's place and stop running around in circles?"

"First to the house and then to my grandma's place," I say. Maybe returning to the house will reconnect me to this land. Returning to the good memories, to my boyhood days, days of backyard and swimming pool.

"What if somebody's living there?" Julieth asks.

"No," Pedro says. "It's empty. The government confiscated it."

"See that?" I say to Julieth. "That's somebody who knows more about my family than I do."

"Are you done yet?" Pedro asks me.

Two more blocks, and there's the bunker. The rush of memories clamps my heart. The time I lived in that house as well as my years of absence. The happy years, the uneventful ones, the lazy afternoons, the tumultuous mornings, the anxious nights, the tenderness and violence. Everything squeezes me, pains me, and frees me. The headlights illuminate the façade, which is painted with clumsy graffiti and fractured by the roots and branches that have seized possession of the house.

"I want to go in," I say.

"How?" Julieth asks.

"Through the door, obviously."

"Do you think there's any booze left inside?" Pedro asks.

I get out and walk toward the booth that always used to have a heavily armed guard. I try to open the gate, but it's locked. So I do what anyone would do when arriving at a house: I knock. I hear footsteps on the other side of the wall and the soft singing of a song that seems familiar. *The fear of living is the lord and master of many other fears*, sings a voice that's familiar too.

"Who is it?" somebody asks from the other side.

"Me," I reply.

The voice keeps singing, *insatiable and trifling, in a dull anguish that rises unbidden*. I hear a key fighting with the rusty lock. The door opens, and he appears, smiling, his face aglow, the way everybody must look when they've been resurrected.

"Pa," I say.

"Give me a hug, son."

I hug him with the strength I've been storing up for this moment for twelve years. He smells the same as always: a little bit like liquor, a little like cigarettes, like his cologne, like fireworks, a little like horses, like soil, like money—all in all, he smells like Libardo.

"Come in," he says.

"It's dark, I can barely see."

"Don't worry. I'll take you."

He takes me by the hand and leads me through the front yard, which is overgrown.

"Can you believe they're trying to sell the house?" he says. "They've been trying to do it for years, and they're going to waste another thousand years at it because this house will never be sold, not as long as I'm looking after it."

"How long have you been here?"

"I never left, son. They haven't been able to get rid of me, even dead." His laugh echoes through the empty rooms. A bit of light from the other buildings finds its way in. I start shaking—I don't know whether it's out of excitement or fear. "What's wrong?" he asks.

"I don't understand," I say. "Just this morning we went to get you, to get your . . ."

"Remains," he says, since I can't. "Reason doesn't need remains, Larry. The heart doesn't need proof, and that's why you and I are here." He squeezes my cold hands and says, "Wait for me. I'll be right back."

I go over to the glass door that leads out to the backyard and see that it's getting lighter. A new day is dawning, yet another day where I haven't slept. The living room fills with a glow; it's him, returning with a lit candle. He's singing the song he greeted me with, *the fear of living is an act of bravery, trying to take on each new day.*

"You always were afraid of the dark," he says, and places the candle in the middle of the living room.

Outside I can hear Pedro and Julieth laughing loudly; they've gone into the backyard and are horsing around like little kids.

The candle reveals more clearly the man I've seen only in my memory for twelve years, the man who's been fading day by day and whose photos I started studying to keep him from disappearing altogether. He seems tired, but he's still smiling at me. He looks out at the backyard and says, "That Pedro. He's still running around, just like when he was a kid. He's a good friend."

"No," I say. "Pedro betrayed me."

"Don't judge him," he says, "especially not for that."

"You knew?"

He makes a gesture that says, *that's life*.

Pedro calls for me to join them. He's shirtless, and Julieth is doubled over with laughter on the grass. Pedro starts removing his pants and yells, "Larry, come here, let's go swimming."

He tries to take off Julieth's shirt, and she stops him despite her laughing fit.

"No," Libardo says. "Tell him not to do it."

"What?"

Pedro calls to me again: "Like we used to, Larry. Last one in's a rotten egg!"

"No," Libardo says.

Pedro, in his underwear, runs toward the pool, shouting wildly like when he used to compete with me to see who'd be first to leap into the cold water. Julieth shrieks excitedly but is too chicken to follow him.

"Tell him to stop," Libardo says.

"Why, Pa?"

Pedro keeps yelling all the way to the edge of the pool; it's a shout of triumph, of winning the race. He leaps, momentum carrying him forward, but instead of the splash of him hitting the water I hear a dull thud against the cement floor.

The wind blows out the candle. Libardo vanishes with a sigh. Julieth keeps laughing until the silence compels her to call to Pedro, Pedro, Pedro, who doesn't answer. The only sound is the occasional firework in the distance. I go out into the backyard and tell Julieth to come with me. She wraps her arms around herself, trembling with fear or foreboding. We look over the edge and see Pedro in the bottom of the empty pool, swimming in the gush of blood that's spilling from his head.

77

Fernanda came back two days after she left with the prosecutor. Those days had been a living hell, more uncertain than when Libardo had disappeared. Not only were we reliving that history, but we might end up without Fernanda too. In addition, Gran was upset with us because we hadn't told her earlier. She hammered home that Libardo was her son and she had the right to know what Fernanda and the prosecutor were planning. To top things off, Fernanda didn't come looking for us when she returned. Lucila found her sleeping in her bedroom and called us at our grandparents' house.

"What about my dad?" I asked Lucila.

"She's alone, or that's what it seems like. She hasn't woken up yet," she replied.

"Wake her up and ask about him."

Meanwhile, Julio and Gran were arguing by the front door. Julio wanted to go see Fernanda right away, and Gran was forbidding it with the same old arguments: that woman's crazy, she's a danger to you boys, she's irresponsible, a gambling addict, and other claims that she'd repeated many times over the course of our lives. Lucila came back to the phone and told me, "She's locked in her room and isn't answering."

I hung up and joined in Julio's argument with Gran. We had even more reason now to go back home.

"But what kind of mother doesn't even call after putting you through this agony?" Gran said.

Julio threatened to go out and flag down a cab. Seeing that we were determined, Gran relented on the condition that Eladio stayed with us.

"Don't let them out of your sight," she ordered the bodyguard, "and call if there's any news about my son."

On the drive there, which was mostly silent, we talked about the slim possibility that we'd find Libardo at the house. He would have been the first to let us know he'd been released. And Eloy's accusations confirmed that the plan had failed.

Lucila was waiting for us outside. The look on her face made it clear the news wasn't good.

"She's alone in the backyard," she told us.

We raced inside and from the living room saw her lying on a chaise longue, still in her pajamas and smoking. She was staring at the sky and slowly blowing smoke into the air. When we slid open the glass door, the noise made her turn toward us. Julio stepped forward first, his aggravation on the tip of his tongue.

"What happened, Ma?"

Fernanda turned back to stare upward and took a long drag. She was pale, with a reddened nose and puffy eyes, perhaps from sleeping, crying, or drinking. She didn't respond to Julio. She coughed as if she'd choked on a bit of smoke.

He said again, "What happened? Where were you? Why didn't you get in touch?"

Fernanda stuck out her tongue a little, as if she were spitting out a flake of tobacco. Her eyes welled up.

"Nothing happened, that's why I didn't get in touch," she said.

"What do you mean, nothing? Did you meet up with them? Did you give them the money?"

"I told you, nothing happened. I didn't meet up with them. I didn't give them the money."

"Why?"

"They don't have him."

"How do you know?" I asked.

"I found out."

"How?"

"I found it out. They don't have him. So we're right back where we started. And I've had a rough few days; I need to be left alone."

"What about the money?" Julio asked.

"That's what you're worried about?" Fernanda said.

"Of course I'm worried—it wasn't ours."

"It should be the other way around," she said.

"If you knew they didn't have him, why did you take so long to come back?" I asked.

She turned her back on us and said again, "I need to be alone, please. Go away."

I left ahead of Julio. I shut myself in my room and wept with rage. Not only had we reached a dead end but, worse still, she'd put us in a situation that would be impossible to escape unscathed.

Gran pleaded with us to return to her house. Julio insisted on staying to see if he could get Fernanda to tell him anything, but she barely talked to us. She was trying to go on with her life, avoided us when we confronted her, didn't even join us for meals, ate very little, and drank a lot. Then the calls started again, not just from Eloy but also from Libardo's friends who'd put up money for the rescue. Fernanda responded to all of them lethargically, as she did to us. Until events spoke for her and we learned, from a news program, that the regional prosecutor Jorge Cubides had turned up dead, murdered.

Julio and I flipped out. Gran told us she was going to get us out of that house, even if it meant getting the police to do it. Libardo's friends started calling more frequently. Investigators from the attorney general's office came by several times to talk to Fernanda. We begged her to explain what had happened, but she told us firmly that the attorney general's office had already questioned her and she was done talking.

But the news made public what she had kept quiet. They showed Cubides in a video from the Palace Casino, sitting at a gaming table next to a woman. In another video, released a few days later, Cubides was driving up to a motel with the same woman, at four twenty-three in the morning. Seven hours later they left together, and the prosecutor opened the door for her to get into the car. The woman, of course, was Fernanda, and because of that image, the last one anybody had of Jorge Cubides, we were forced to flee the country without really knowing what had happened.

78

W hat room will he be in?" Fernanda asks me, clutching my arm.

Written beside the door of each room at the funeral home is a name. Everybody must shudder when they see the name of the person they're there to see. Will the room we're going to say "Pedro the Dictator"? Sole potentate, through violent means, of the republic that he alone inhabited and whose constitution was drafted in accordance with strictly sexist, classist, misogynistic, racist, and otherwise bigoted parameters? Dictator of the only country in the world that has no poor or ugly people? Or will it say, "Pedro, lover and drug dealer of Miss Medellín 1973?" A hand grabs my free arm. It's Julieth.

"I'm all fucked up," she says.

"Where is he?"

"In Room 2."

"That sucks," I say. "He would have wanted Room 1."

I introduce her to Fernanda. I remember you, ma'am, Julieth says. Fernanda smiles faintly. I was at your house a few times, Julieth says, and Fernanda replies, oh, yes. At this moment she doesn't care about remembering who Julieth is. Plus, Julieth hasn't slept either and has been partying for three days straight. She's unrecognizable, like me.

"You're all dressed up," she tells me.

I look at the jacket I'm wearing. It's too big.

"It's the suit my dad got married in," I say.

"You should keep it unbuttoned," Fernanda suggests.

"Are you coming or going?" I ask Julieth.

"What do you mean?"

"Are you on your way out, or did you just arrive?"

"I went to the bathroom," she says.

"Come see him with me," I say.

We walk past Room 4, Room 3, and in Room 2 we find my friend, in a casket he wouldn't have liked either. It's too somber, completely incongruous with his lifestyle. Again I say to myself, this can't be happening. I should go up, knock on the casket, and tell him, open up right this minute, Pedro, stop the bullshit and get out of there, we've paid you our respects, you fucking dictator, we've mourned you, quit joking around, dickhead. Julieth sits down on a sofa between two elderly women and leans her head against the back.

Fernanda tells me, "Come on, let's go say hi to Óscar and Luz María. Poor things."

"People are looking at us," I say.

"What's the problem?"

The problem is that even after all this time, I'm still Libardo's son, and she's still his widow. People still survey us from their immaculate bubble. The only one who never watched me with those inquisitor's eyes is laid out in that casket there, mocking us. Fernanda doesn't care how people look at her; she goes up to Pedro's parents and hugs them. I only hang my head. I feel guilty. I took Pedro to my old house, Libardo told me not to let him jump, I saw Pedro get undressed, saw him run toward the pool, and I didn't do anything. I never do anything, not even right this moment when instead I'm standing very still and staring at my feet, aware of how solitary I've walked in this world.

"Pedro told us you were back," the father tells me.

"I just arrived the day before yesterday," I say.

I take a few steps backward and glance again at the casket,

hoping for Pedro to get up. I'm the one who should leave. The scent of the flowers is making me feel sick.

Outside the room, I lean against a wall and manage to pull myself together. The only thing I need is sleep; maybe when I wake up, none of this will have happened.

In Room 1, a litany begins. Startled, I recognize it. A powerful voice recites, "Do not go gentle into that good night. Good men, the last wave by, crying how bright their frail deeds might have danced in a green bay." It sounds like Professor Leeson's deep voice declaiming at the end of class.

I don't know the name written on the door. I don't know who Antonio Rivero Conde is, but why are they reciting the Dylan Thomas poem? I try to look in, but the room is packed. The dead man must be very important. Is this coincidence yet another joke? I try to make my way inside. Excuse me, excuse me. People's perfumes mingle with the cloying smell of the flowers. Why are they looking at me like that? Because I'm the son of Libardo, who's finally at rest under a leafy lignum vitae?

"Do not go gentle into that good night," a doleful man is reciting as I reach the middle of the room. "And you, my father, there on the sad height." There is the father in the casket he deserves. Without tacky fripperies, with the simplicity of true elegance. And sitting next to her family is a downcast daughter, Charlie, the woman I gave up for lost because I didn't go after her when I should have.

Life returns to my body. The certainty of believing that this is in fact happening.

"Charlie," I call to her out loud.

Everybody looks at me, and the man who's reciting goes quiet. She lifts her head and opens her eyes wide, as if reproaching me for not having arrived earlier. The poem fills the room again: "Do not go gentle into that good night." Charlie gets up and walks resolutely toward me.

ABOUT THE AUTHOR

Jorge Franco was born in Medellín, Colombia. He studied filmmaking and directing at the London Film School and Literature at the Pontificia Universidad Javeriana. His first short story collection *Maldito Amor* and first novel *Mala Noche* were both awarded numerous prestigious literary prizes.